The Washashores

The Washashores

Provincetown Stories

R. D. Skillings

The Washashores
Copyright © 2018 by R. D. Skillings

Published by HomePort Press
PO Box 1508
Provincetown, MA 02657
www.HomePortPress.com

ISBN   978-0-9992451-3-2
eISBN   978-0-9992451-0-1

Cover Design by Grant King

To my beloved wife, Heidi Jon Schmidt
and to our dauntless daughter,
Marisa Rose Skillings

Foreword

A generation or so ago
Washashores were émigrés, non-native devotees of
Provincetown,
seldom in easy circumstances,
often in flight from past mishaps or confining conformities.
They made for a great society,
Exuberant, rambunctious and original
Until heedless raw wealth evicted them,
Bought-up summer houses
Now no longer for rent in the off season,
Meager-ing Everything.

Acknowledgments

Dossier—Mira Washes Ashore

Transatlantic Review—Waders of the Sea

Tri-Quarterly– Good Samaritans

Provincetown Arts– Last Days & The Freedom of Shadows

Notre Dame Review– Wits' End & All They Wanted,

The Weather, The Dude, & Books and the Phantom Zero

Table of Contents

MIRA WASHES ASHORE

Providencetown?" Miranda Nichols wondered. "Where's that?"

"P-town," David said. "Tip-end of Cape Cod. Little hook of sand, bunch of shops and honky-tonk, a zillion bars, beaches, fishing, drugs. Whatever you want. Zoo in the summer, snooze in winter. Summer's always a scene, actually several scenes– art scene, street scene, gay scene, bar scene, beach scene, boat scene, pot scene, scene scene, always a lot going on. Thoreau said, 'A man can stand there and put all America behind him.' And *I* say, 'So can we.' So let's go."

Why not? Mira thought. Why the hell not! It might do for the moment. She'd met him at the Blue Parrot the week before and flirted with him because he was likeable and responsive, and she, late of her former life, was miserable, in dire need of distraction, to say the least. She had a right– didn't she?– as to how she chose to combat her numb shock at no longer having an apartment she could afford, nor a husband she still cared for, nor any friends, all her friends being his, nor the slightest idea of what to do next.

They'd run across each other again on the street and had spent the sultry forenoon of June 1st, 1963 hanging around Harvard Square, nipping whiskey from his tarnished flask. He seemed about her age, twenty-six, maybe a year or two older, a graduate student with a newly finished novel in manuscript, "A work of the exaggeration," he called it, "a lousy book destined for greatness as a film."

He was a bit worn-looking, a bit glib, not elusive exactly, just digressive perhaps. Still, he seemed nice enough on this second go-round, his sudden grins continuing to appear unpredictably.

"We'll find a place to stay," he said. "We'll just sit on the meat-rack till somebody comes along..."

"The meat-rack?" Mira wondered. "The benches in front of Town Hall. If worse comes to worst we can spend the night there. We won't be the onlys."

Mira hoped he wasn't a rapist. He certainly didn't look the type—though what type was that? He was lanky and languid with long, well-washed, blond hair, frayed jeans, beads and hippie verities—kinship of all living things, music the medium of spirit, absolute the rights of love, self-fulfillment, freedom.

All men are rapists at heart, her soon-to-be ex-husband Phillip would have decreed. Though certainly *he* would never have stooped to rape, nor would any of his supremely cool friends around whom women dallied with acquisitive eye.

He wasn't, Phillip assured her, leaving her for anyone in particular. He had been extremely nice about the divorce, pleasant in a way that was quite unlike him, having virtually ignored her for the latter half of their three years together. He was brilliant and handsome, the center of his circle, everywhere in demand; they were all brilliant, destined for brilliant lives, the women cutting or snide; only she was dull, doubtful, drab, anxious to do the right thing, if only she knew what it was, agonizingly aware of people's feelings, always getting her own hurt without quite realizing it till afterwards, when sharp retorts occurred to her, which in any case she would never have uttered.

And so, in a moment, it was arranged. She told the restaurant where she waitressed that her uncle had died, threw some things in a knapsack and sat on her steps till David came in his cluttered van, and they were off, off, leaving Cambridge, now such an alien, painful place.

Could she get the gas? He was a little short. She could, yes, she would, gladly. And then, windows wide open, they were really off, rattling down the Southeast Expressway, radio booming Beatles and Stones, too loud for more than brief exchanges, soon forgone.

In din and buffeting wind, Mira fell back to brooding about Phillip's affairs. She knew he slept around, coming in late at night, or not at all, sometimes not even troubling to explain that he'd stayed over at some friend's house, and she assumed he knew she knew. Why had she never brought it up? She had grown used to the situation, which once begun had progressed imperceptibly, somehow at the same time both slow and fast, and finally she had resorted to taking pride in Phillip's conquests– the word made her squirm now. But why should *she* be ashamed?

From the first she had been in awe of him, remained, she had to admit, still in his thrall, but liked him less every time she thought of him. Certainly there was little love left between them, and that saddened her. She couldn't be sure he even believed in love. Anyway, he didn't believe in truth: truth, he always said, was individual and evanescent, what you made of it, and when, etc.

She had to respect him for one thing though: none of his friends ever made a pass at her, unless, in hindsight, that merely marked her as his exclusive domain. Nor had he ever shown a trace of jealousy when she flirted at parties, playfully to be sure, always remote at evening's end. No, she had grown accustomed to condescension, having concluded that male nature was incorrigible– such were her expectations, though it hardly made her think well of herself, and yet, at rock bottom, she had trusted him. Somehow, she would never have dreamt that he would simply desert her, move out when their lease was up, and institute divorce proceedings as casually as he might have sent back a dish he didn't like.

Well, if he wanted out, what use to object? She didn't want to impede him, had always tried to be helpful, keep a calm demeanor, no complaints, all casual, no mention made of alimony– they were above that sort of thing– and she had some savings from her various jobs, not much. In a moment of lamentable pathos she had asked him what she now couldn't quite bear to recall, and he had answered, with uncharacteristic curtness, perhaps a rare flinch of remorse, "You've got your father."

Dad, in Manhattan– another brilliant man– editor of *Practical Psychology*, who chortled at all human foibles and illusions, who had once confessed to wishing she were a boy he could go whoring with, though afterwards he vehemently denied it, a reformed alcoholic, eyes a-gleam as he poured Phillip huge holiday cocktails, an impeccable dresser, on the street prone to comment on passing women's anatomies and chuckling pinch Mira's bottom in punctuation while regaling her friends with amorous escapades of his drinking days, always turned, to give Dad his due, doleful and comic in their hapless denouements.

"My good god, she was beautiful!" he would breathe, his face alight with boyish mischief.

Her mother, a delicate, withdrawn spirit, had died when Mira was nineteen, almost willingly it seemed. To Mira's horrid amazement, Dad had mourned long and hard, then never spoke of her again. In the last year or so, sensing the true state of Mira's marriage, he had taken to writing her witty, charming letters, as if to an ex-mistress. She could not go there, to his tiny apartment with its roll-out, extra bed, not till she felt less demoralized.

How disconcerting life was– hers at least– with nothing to sustain her, and no one to depend on. And so it had always been, now she thought back on it. She was simply used to discomfiture– her ill-paid teacher's job at an elite girls school, the hateful, mannish suits, nylons and girdle she'd had to wear, always conscious of the Headmistress' disapproval, and her students' overt sense of superiority; her dreary series of waitress jobs, worst of all her present one with Colonial uniforms that had to be ironed daily, for the cold-eyed inspections of the lecherous manager.

Well, she was a dope of a dupe or vice versa, had no one to blame but herself, and badly needed to be somebody else– that at least she understood. Meanwhile, she would mourn no more, at least not during this little respite before starting to look for a new place to live, new job, new everything. It almost began to feel exhilarating. She looked forward to a deeper acquaintance with David, perhaps even some light-hearted, non-kinky sex.

In just three hours they were rattling past glassy Pilgrim Lake, the dunes rising steeply from water's edge, their clear, upside down reflection dark as a shadow. David said, "I told you this was a boss place," and Mira felt an inkling– of what she didn't quite know.

They drove the narrow length of Commercial Street, stopped briefly to gaze at the green marsh and Long Point's tongue of sand low in the swollen tide, then rode back, parked, made their way to the meat-rack and sat down among old women sedately chatting, people taking the sun or having a smoke or reading or writing post-cards, mostly just watching the passing scene. One guy had a parrot, one dozed, another was searching his pockets, muttering like a maniac. A circle of girls laughed together with raucous derision.

Bare feet, ragged jeans, backpacks, beards and guitars, a ceaseless stream of young people flowed both ways, on the sidewalk and in the street, or stopped to talk. Or bum cigarettes. Harvard Square had grown a bit motley, but nothing compared to this.

No one David knew came by, so they walked out on the wharf and looked at the fishing boats– the smell of brine thrilled her– then came back and shared some fried clams on the street. Then they sat on the meat-rack again, till David got antsy and went to make a phone call, came back, said, "I'm going to score some dope, I'll be right back," and left her sitting there, totally engrossed, thinking she could do this forever and never care for another, bitching thing– Phillip's favorite curse-word, she noted with renewed chagrin.

The day started down. It grew cooler. Fortunately she had a light jacket with her. Suddenly she felt ravenous– David had eaten most of the clams– and went to the car to get her wallet, which was in her knapsack, but the car was gone.

There was nothing to do but go back to the meat-rack, and wait, so she waited, making little forays up and down the street, not going far enough to miss him, but he kept not appearing. Twilight came, then night. The smells of garlic and fried food sharpened her hunger. Where *was* he? Perhaps he'd been busted? At eight o'clock she took courage, went down the steps to the Police Station under Town Hall, and asked if they had found her lost David.

Silent head-shakes, taking her in, none met her eye, chit-chat resumed as if she were no longer standing there. Feeling foolish she went back to waiting. A ragged boy came by, seeking spare change. She had in fact not a nickel. It seemed an endless night, segmented by people going by, stopping to ask for a smoke, also did she know some place they could crash?

She drowsed, awoke dank at dawn, and went for a walk on the beach, pretty sure David was no early-riser, then sat up against a bare log, startled by the gargantuan red sun obliterating the whole horizon across the bay. Dropping her eyes she spied amid some picnic debris a tightly-rolled dollar bill, sniffed it with a sense of turned luck, hurried back to the meat-rack, half-expecting to find David.

No, but at least Poyant's Bakery was open, and she bought a large, black coffee– starved or not, caffeine came first.

As she was walking back to the meat-rack she took an impatient gulp, got scalded, spewed it out, spilled another bitching splash on her bare toes, dropped the cup in a grand splatter, and shrieked with rage.

A young woman walking briskly by eyed her with interest, smiled, showing a plenty of teeth.

"Don't mind me," Mira said.

"Rest assured," said the smiler, un-slowed.

Mira sat down again, mortified. A voice called, "That's right, darlin, nothing like a good scream," which gave surprising solace.

About nine a skinny guy with a ponytail and her knapsack over one shoulder came meandering, scanning the benches. She stood up.

"It's me," she said, "Mira."

"David had to split," explained Pony-tail. He said to tell you he was sorry, but he'll make it up to you some day. I'm Bill."

"And why, "she asked, "did he have to split?"

"Don't know," Bill said. "Didn't say. Just said to tell you..."

"He had to split," she said

"Yeah," Bill said. "That's right. He had to split."

Mira stood there uncertainly, glancing about. He too still stood there. "Well, thanks," she said.

"Sure," he said. "Anytime. Hey. Wanna go for a walk, smoke a joint?"

"Oh, no thank you," she said.

"Maybe see you around," he said, half resentful, half forlorn. She watched him amble back the way he'd come. Forty dollars were gone from her wallet, leaving her thirty.

Deciding she should be thankful to be rid of David so cheaply, and lucky that ponytail hadn't stolen the rest, she had just begun to dread going back to Cambridge, when the briskly walking woman returned, and grinned pleasantly, "Feeling better, dear?"

Absent her usual shyness, Mira said decisively, "As a matter of fact I am."

"Bravo!" The woman showed her teeth again boldly, sweetly.

Mira found herself sketching her plight. The woman listened attentively, shaking her head with disgust. No one had listened to Mira in years, and she ran on with a velocity and bitter wit that first surprised, then impressed her.

"A plague on all men," said the woman cheerily.

They sat down on a bench and made friends. Edie Baruch's MFA mentors at Columbia had insisted that she work, as they did, in the Abstract Expressionist mode. In exasperation she had quit being a student, now bicycled two miles into town every morning at 7:30 to a studio she shared with three others. She was on her way back there now, but– as another matter of fact– she had a room for the whole summer in a house out at Mayflower Heights with two beds in it, cots really, for $300. If Mira had $150 she could have the other one.

Why not? Mira thought. "That sounds perfect," she said.

The house, across from the beach, stood halfway up the southern lee of a forested dune out on 6A, the old road into town. Grey-shingled and ramshackle, it had a screen porch that ran the length of the living-dining room, with a large, round oak table at one end. There were two shabby couches and some armchairs, four small bedrooms on the second floor and two more, smaller yet, in the attic, one of which was Edie's, the other would be Mira's. There was a bumpy brick patio out back with a grill on cinder-blocks, and a supply of firewood, courtesy of the owner, who had made no trouble about anything, including departure date– as long as they wanted to stay was all right with her. It could get nippy by October. All she had said was, "Be nice to it. Try not to flush too often. My husband and I had many happy years here."

To Mira's relief the household welcomed her without ado. Howard and Rachel– and their baby Cassiopeia– had gathered a group of Brandeis and New York friends, unsettled types, vaguely in sync with academe. The downstairs was always busy. Jake Rosen sat reading, glad of distractions. "I'd rather read than write," he said, "unfortunately," but he preferred talk to either, and while he indulged his social bent, it made him ironical. He never left the house without his knapsack of books, notebook, pens, pipes and tobacco.

Howard manned the grill, did yoga, meditated, read eastern philosophy, tracked the stock market, plotted a new play. He kept on his feet, spent hours a day in the dunes with only a pair of shorts and a flute. Mr. Discipline he was, a bit distant despite his avuncular cordiality.

Others came and went with the weather. They waded far out on the tepid flats at low tide, and stood chest-deep like Easter Island statues watching the slow dumb-show of cumulus formations above Wellfleet across the bay. Or swam at high tide, bobbing in the mild waves if the wind blew, or lay with a book in the hot sand and got tan. Pot was plentiful, the ashtrays seldom lacked a sizable snipe for anyone wanting a toke without having to roll a new joint. There was a pile of fine LPs, but early on the turntable arm got stuck and a favorite Otis Redding album kept repeating the same side till someone flipped it over, the great, soulful voice hymning half a hundred times a day, *That's how strong my love is, That's how strong my love is.*

Mornings Mira drank coffee on the screen porch, trying to think things through. In a single day she bussed up to Cambridge and disposed of her possessions, all but a few of her favorite books— Emily Dickinson and Elizabeth Bishop, Jane Austin, Virginia Woolf and Colette— some clothes, not many, and a bank account, small but adequate to her $5 weekly food assessment. Howard, having a taste for wines, supplied the dinner table, fostering Mira's new yen for stimulated states.

Who or what was she? In deepening consternation she went over her every hurt and humiliation, all the more awful because she could think of no possible revenge she could wreak on her husband— worse yet, saw no way, had no will even, to wish him harm.

She had been an appendage, half-alive, for longer than she could remember.

Never, she had never been happy with herself, uncertainties and slights her familiar lot, a pervasive sense of nobody-ness, of insignificance, nor had she ever tried to feel otherwise, out of respect for truth. Now she surveyed her nondescript person— face faintly freckled, slightly crooked nose, dazzling blue eyes of ever-vacillating rue and delight, fine legs, round fanny, pretty little tits now that she'd dispensed with bras— how shyly exultant she had been those first few days she'd let her nipples show— wiry, a fleet runner, good dancer, lithe of tongue once properly primed, but long-content to wait on the fringes with veiled eye till asked to do something for somebody, quick then to respond— yes, it was self-interest she chiefly lacked and needed.

Edie was an ideal roommate, self-possessed, matter-of-fact, brusque, every minute she wasn't painting busy reading Thomas Mann, writing in her diary, washing the dishes, doing the shopping, singing in the shower, "Oh, the navy gets the gravy but the army gets the beans-beans-beans-beans." She did not ever simply do nothing, or smoke anything, or drink more than a single glass of wine mixed with water, though she did take LSD after dinner one night, just to see what it was like, then went to bed at eight o'clock, next day explaining that she'd begun to experience unpleasant sensations and had gone to sleep to get rid of them.

Mira and Edie had nothing in common, except both were only children. Edie approved of Mira's laissez-faire Dad, having suffered a domineering mother, whom she was determined not to let rule her life, and a diplomat father, patrician and remote, who treated her like a grown man, not a son exactly, more an exasperating nephew, uneducable and uncouth, *vide* their recent visit when Edie had insisted on wearing a magic marker mustache and goatee and a bowler hat the whole while, "Red banner to bulls," she allowed to Mira's rolling eye, nor had it shortened their stay by so much as one minute. Edie's parents didn't think lesbianism was wrong, just un-likely to beget a happy life. Well, how long was one going to live, anyway? And who knew what happiness was?

She had followed her college-days lover, Rachel to Province-town. Rachel and Howard had decamped from Somerville with no future in view beyond a summer's adjustment to their developing situation— whether divergent or merely increasing the scope of their marriage, fall would tell.

And what would Edie do? No idea. She did enjoy Cassi, but sex with Rachel had become a contest for psychic supremacy— a kind of wrestling— anger, resentment, tears for Edie, who always lost, being the least savage of the two, but discontenting to Rachel, be-cause Edie didn't fight back hard enough.

Rachel wanted a roughhouse friend, Edie a lover. Edie had— she still— dated men, sometimes liked them— depending on their intel-lects— but had never met one she wanted to sleep with. Plus they were sometimes hard to get rid of, which made her wary. She envied Mira her untrammeled heart, Mira admired Edie's cheerful work habits and powers of concentration.

By the second week of June, the house was a kaleidoscope of comings and goings. Howard's civil-rights-worker sister, Sybil, came up from Mississippi with a seventeen-year-old Negro boy out on bail for stealing a pig.

"What did you want a pig for?" Rachel asked.

"Just did," Lee Berry said, nonchalant.

"You were going to eat it?"

"Kill a nice little pig like that? Naw."

"It'll turn into a hog," Rachel said.

"*Then* I'll eat it," Lee Berry grinned.

Mira didn't know who was the more pitiful– blowzy, tousle-haired Sybil, already twice divorced, who lounged about the house in nothing but Howard's short red bathrobe, her vagina visible half the time, or Lee Berry who reacted to her compulsive caresses as if he were made of wood, though he was seldom out of reach. One afternoon coming into the empty house Mira heard them at their pleasures, and they certainly sounded happy. The next day they left for a commune in Vermont.

"The Above-ground Railway," Jake said.

Long sunk in her own nightmare, the news was suddenly news to Mira. Freedom Riders, fire hoses, police dogs; murder and arson had merged into one inferno of strange names– Montgomery, McComb, Greenwood, Greensboro, Shady Grove, Selma, Danville– and some young Negro preacher named for Martin Luther.

Wars, elections, public issues, all such things belonged to men. Mira had ignored their arguments, the one-upmanship and the passionate abstractions: Vote Nixon her father had said, so Nixon she secretly picked, if only to spite Phillip, but now she liked Kennedy, his looks and charm, his Massachusetts accent with its hint of urgency, his grinning answer for everything– nobody ever got the better of *him*. Still, what was going to happen? The South couldn't secede again, could it? Well, no, Jake said without a trace of sarcasm, it couldn't.

One night when there were a dozen or so people sitting around the living room– there were rumors of mass demonstrations to come– Edie observed in her acidic way, "There's certainly a lot of Jews here." Count taken, Mira proved to be the only Gentile, more news to her, and to everyone else apparently. That odd interlude ended with Jim Miller saying he was a Jew only when he met an anti-Semite. Mira went to bed strangely reassured and gratified.

All the same, each morning she awoke desolate. Then the day lurched between wretched remorse and somber exhaustion. Where was she going? All unsuspecting, she had jotted half a page of diatribe against her husband's supercilious circle. Pleased by her harmless release, with dawning excitement and equal trepidation, she glimpsed the path she had stumbled on, led mainly by misery. Though suddenly she didn't feel so miserable any more, at least not all the time, not all the time, not any more.

Her house-mates were absorbed in their purposes, but she had none. In present circumstances she didn't need a job, at least not until she had to leave Mayflower Heights. Meanwhile she sat on the meat-rack with a book and notebook and thought about writing, always her blue eyes quick to take things in.

Among others, Smoking Man, as she called him, also spent his days on the benches, getting up to toddle east for a few minutes, then come toddling back, sit down again, then pull himself upright and toddle west, soon to toddle back again, the whole time chain-smoking Pall Malls, red pack in one hand, Bic lighter in the other, moving with invalid deliberation, halting to chain-up, suck a cheek-collapsing puff or two, then drop the butt, step on it, set off again with the other foot.

Strolling in thought one day, Mira saw his trail blazed on the sidewalk ahead, his pants pockets spilling packs of Pall Malls.

She picked up three, caught the fourth as it fell. "You seem to be leaking," she said.

He turned slowly to her voice, not startled, his facial muscles immobilized it seemed with some unremitting dolor, his black eyes haunted. He took the packs of cigarettes from her hands without a word— stuffed them in his pockets— and started on again, then stopped and said in a hoarse whisper, "You new in town?"

Mira nodded. He turned and went on, slowly, like an old man with a young man's crew-cut thick and stiff as a shoe-brush, his grey, acne-scarred complexion pitted with grime or blackheads, his clothes stained, his fingers nicotine-yellow. She fought to quell her revulsion.

But she'd made a friend. His name was George. He lived with his mother. He would come and sit beside Mira, till she could no longer stand his pungency.

"Going to walk?" he'd say. He spoke only to ask questions: Where did she come from? Where did she work? Did she think it was going to rain? Who was this or that weird-looking bird passing by? His expression never changed. Sometimes he coughed and the phlegm burbled in his throat. He would ruminate and hawk, then bend and let drop between his knees a yellow-grey, clotted splot.

Once she ventured to say, "Don't you think it might be better if you didn't smoke so much?"

His eyes met hers. "I tried to quit one time, but it made me too nervous. I'm a very nervous person. I'm on disability, my doctor said it was probably better I smoked than I didn't."

One evening, as she was skimming a Times she'd plucked from a trash barrel, he sat down and said, "How're you doing tonight?"

"Hello, George," she said, trying to sound cordial, then resumed reading, while he watched her every eye-flicker with his strange devotion.

"How're you tonight?" he said.

"I'm fine, but I want to read this," she said, feeling defensive.

"What's it say?" he said. "I can't read."

Touched by his lack of constraint, she read him the first paragraph about President Kennedy's speech, announcing unilateral suspension of nuclear testing.

"D'you think they're going to do it?" he asked, his hollow, black eyes fixed on hers.

His tone surprised her. "Well, he *says* so," she said, and read aloud, " 'No government or social system is so evil that its people must be considered as lacking in virtue.' "

"I think so, too," he said, leaving his mouth more ajar than usual.

"So do I," she said, doubtful of his comprehension. "Khrushchev said it was the best speech by a President since Roosevelt."

"You really think they're going to do it?" he said.

"What?" she said, perplexed.

"Have a war. Drop the bombs."

"You mean in the long run?"

"Yes," he said. "Pretty soon."

"I don't know," she had to admit." Nobody knows."

"I think they're going to do it."

"Who?"

"The Russians," he said. "D'you really think they'll do it?"

"No," she said, "I don't. Please don't worry about it."

"I think they're going to do it. Don't you?"

"Well, whatever happens won't happen here. We're too small to bother with."

"I think they're going to do it," he said.

"No," she said, standing up, feeling guilty, "no, no, no, they're not going to do it, no one's going to do anything. Just don't worry. And stop smoking."

"I have to smoke," he said. "The doctor said I should."

"I'm sorry, I have to go," she said unhappily, and hurried down the street to the Unitarian Church for a poetry reading.

She arrived just as it was getting started in a meeting room under the chancel with a little stage and a hallway off to one side. People were grouped around in folding chairs. A woman in a flowered gown was thanking the pastor for his hospitality, and reminding readers of their solemn promise that there would be no profane or obscene language, and no inappropriate subject matter. The elderly pastor stood in the door of the hallway wearing a hesitant half-smile.

A grizzled man took the lectern and read a rollicking poem about cocks and cunts.

The woman pled loudly against this betrayal, but the relentless bass and audience hilarity over-rode her. The pastor aghast with chagrin stepped from sight.

"Please, please, please, please," the woman kept pleading.

Order restored, the featured novelist drew an idyllic scene of surf-casting by moonlight. An immense mound of stripers and blues was the measure of the man's Herculean week. When he stopped to contemplate the carnage he stroked his stubbled chin.

A Land Rover pulled up beside his jeep. Two women got out, holding hands over their noses and berated his criminal stupidity. He tried to explain the elements to them, but they shouted that he should be castrated. He kept calm, trying to enlighten them about significance and purity, respect, eternity, and immutable, ever-triumphant nature, the deep peace of the sea.

They burst out laughing, mocking him to one another. The world whirled with his outrage and he brought his spade down on both heads, never a peep from either, neatly done, he had to admit, but they had spoiled his mood. As he drove away he glanced back at the two bodies flopping hopelessly in the surf, and smiled to think of the way things were.

Amid applause Mira slipped out and joined the blizzard of faces on the street. At the To Be Coffeehouse another poetry reading was underway– there seemed to be as many poets as portrait artists and leather shops– and she found a seat on the floor. Here macrobiotics and teas reigned, transcendental meditation, I Ching coin-flippers, astrological sages, gurus of the several levels of enlightenment, chess.

One hirsute poet ended to soft applause, another, known to all as The Valentine Man– his shop sold valentine pins and accessories, his logo, *Every Day A Valentine*– began to read a poem to his wife sitting in the window. It was a poem of adoration spoken directly to her, but his voice broke, he choked up, resumed, kept breaking down, face contorted, tears streaming. His wife smiled serenely, while his audience beamed, some touched to tears of their own.

Mira escaped to the Fo'c's'le just down the street. Iris, an older friend of Edie's, beckoned from the inmost end of the bar, and began bewailing the husband who'd left her after twenty years, saying he'd never been happy. Not even for one day.

"He can't really mean that," Mira protested.

"Oh, he means it, he even thinks it's true."

"And for you?" Mira wondered.

"Comme ci, comme ça," Iris said. "That's life, but he doesn't know it."

"Yet," Mira supplied.

"Oh, he'll be happy, I know him. There's nothing about this that I can stand. My life's a mess. I'm completely paralyzed, I can't even get myself to hunt for a new shrink, the one I have now's completely useless, I hate alcohol, I thought this might help, I've never been alone in a bar in my life."

She wiped a tear from each cheek with one finger. "It's all a bad joke. I fell in love lots of times, but I never did anything. I fought not even to consider it."

Mira started to tell her own tale, but Iris interrupted:

"Sooner or later, they always fuck you over, every man you ever let into you."

"Every one?" Mira wondered.

"Always," Iris said. Then abruptly, "Thanks for listening, it was good to have a fresh ear, I've worn out all my friends. Here, you drink this, I can't stomach it."

Mira watched her out the door, then on impulse sloshed her straight Scotch down with beer, instantly buoying her spirits. It was an interesting world, after all, if one didn't feel too sorry for anyone, especially oneself.

While she was mulling what sorts of things she might write, a man sat down two stools away. She glanced curiously at him. Pallid, balding, slim, he sat perfectly motionless, except when he poured an inch or two of his beer, which he drank in little swallows like medicine, then put the glass down and let it stand empty as if forgotten.

His aura of distant rumination struck her as preposterous, ditto his faded, too-large tan suit, with old-fashioned, wide lapels and a rather grayed-with-wear white shirt, perhaps the plainest man she'd ever seen. She ordered another Scotch, felt free to inspect him, since he looked nowhere but straight ahead.

When she let her gaze linger, he seemed to draw breath, as if taking courage, turned his head halfway, said, "Shall I join you?"

For some reason she felt no trepidation at all, said, "I'll move," picked up her glass, and slid over.

He looked a stark fifty or more, and had an exacting accent. "Romanian," he said. "I emigrated in 1945 after the Americans liberated us."

As he seemed disinclined to go on, she said, "You were in the Second World War?"

"In a manner of speaking," he said. "And you are a college girl."

"I graduated in '59."

"Americans are eternally youthful." He had yet to meet her eyes.

"Are you married?" she said.

"I was," he said.

"Was?"

"She's dead," he said shortly. "She was probably younger than you are now."

"I'm sorry," she said.

"Everybody dies, don't they." he said in his matter-of-fact, precise diction.

She could only nod, and wait, but he spoke no more. So far as she could tell he never glanced at her; certainly he didn't deign to turn his head a second time.

Thinking he might be some sort of refined bully, aware the warmth of Scotch was making him seem intriguing, she said, "Sooo..." puzzling for some way to lighten the mood, "are you going to get married again?"

He shook his head very slightly, ghost of a shudder.

"How can you be so sure?" she said, pushing her glass toward the bartender. "You may meet someone."

His forehead wrinkled, a faint smile seemed to touch his lips as her shot glass filled to the brim.

"May I buy you...?" She'd never bought a man a drink before, nor woman either.

He seemed half to shrug. "Shall I keep you company? But no more beer, please."

Some company, she thought, then realized she liked him tremendously, but had no idea why. "Why?" she said.

"Why what?" he said.

"Why anything," she said. "The world is mysterious."

He poured his last inch, swirled it, seemed to contemplate the bubbles.

"Don't you want children?" she tried. "Even one?"

Came the same, automated head-shake.

"Would you and your wife...?"

"Of course," he said.

"Oh, "I'm so sorry," she said. Then, "You must be tired of people saying that."

"They can't help it, can they," he said, not a question.

She felt suddenly absolved, strangely happy. She was having a good time, wanted to make him happy, too. But he wouldn't cooperate. He didn't seem interested in her, or in anything at all, it was quite aggravating, he was too civilized perhaps, or world-weary. His one smile– that *had* been a smile, hadn't it?– seemed to have been uncaused. It *was* friendly, wasn't it? Shouldn't he have got over his wife's death by now? Maybe he was morose by nature, never spoke first, always answered in that same matter-of-fact, flat tone. Wanting to say, Who are you?

Mira said, "You don't look much like a vacationer."

A barely perceptible hunch made minimal concession.

"I'm here by accident," she said, loath to explain herself.

"I, too," he said.

This is deadly, she thought, wanting to reach out and touch one of those exquisite, alabaster hands that lay on the bar as if they belonged to someone else. With hectic zest she began describing the poetry readings, from church to coffeehouse, faltered briefly at the image she was about to mouth, then invested all the ingenuousness she could in Valentine Man's tears and his wife's sublime complacence.

He made no comment. She wasn't sure he'd listened. They sat on in silence like planets whose orbits approached hailing distance only every other millennium. Mira tried to think of something that might get a response from him. Personal questions apparently would be unwelcome.

"Say something in Romanian," she said finally.

He paused with lowered eyelids, then uttered a few phrases unintelligible, grave and formal, like a little speech, bowed, fell silent again.

"It's most unfair of you not to tell me what you said." Mira felt quite giddy, verging on flirtatious. Scotch certainly did wonders for a body.

Rising, he said, "I am very pleased to have met you, but now it is time for me to go."

"Well, me too," she said, her own glass conveniently empty.

She stumbled following him to the door. "But you said more than that. What else did you say?"

He turned as one cornered. "I implored the gods to grant you all good things in life."

"That's very sweet of you," she said.

"There are no gods," he said, some kind of guttural racket in the words.

"It's still very sweet," she demurred.

He closed his eyes at the word. They walked along slowly, him with hands linked behind his back, her she felt with a child's dragging feet. Too soon he pointed up a narrow street at a guesthouse with tattered awnings.

"I'll walk you," she said, amazed at herself.

They went on half a block in silence, halted at a rickety, picket gate, the fence on both sides buried beneath a huge profusion of wild white roses, their lush canes arching, drooping over the grass-grown, brick walk, dispensing a heavy fragrance.

"I do believe I'm going to swoon" Mira said. "Isn't that the word?"

"Swoon, yes," he said. "Shall I ask you to come up?"

"I will," she said, "for just a minute." She thought, I shouldn't be doing this, then, Why not? Still, she had no idea what might ensue— this her first brush with outright promiscuity.

They had to duck to enter. The front door was not locked. He led her up some stairs to a hallway with doors, stopped at #4, said, "The bathroom's that way," she nodded, and he let her in and closed the door quietly behind them.

And then nothing, just nothing. With a kind of fascination she noted the room's features in the dim light from the one window— everything old and shabby, an indeterminate smell of human usage, faded, peeling wallpaper, a white, paint-chipped iron bedstead with visibly sagging mattress, a bureau with a mirror and two unmatched water glasses on a cork tray with a dead fly on its back, a single armchair, comforting anonymity.

She did not quite dare to look at him, nor speak, nor could she expect many words from him, social scene or not. It was awkward standing there. She would have liked to sit down, but he was standing in front of the armchair, the only chair, and she didn't feel quite easy about sitting on the bed, a bit whorish that might seem, perhaps, too obviously willing, or even inviting, also too late for change of mind. From which to which? Why had he even asked her up? There was certainly little here to occupy them.

She ventured a glance, and saw that he had taken off his shoes and socks, was now taking off his shirt and undershirt, the old kind commonly called "wife-beaters", which broke her heart. He saw her gape, pulled his pants halfway back up, hobbled to the window, dropped the shade.

In a panic of indecorum she shed her clothes like liquid lightning, and got into bed, moved deeper into the sag to make room for him, and he got in– and there they lay, on their sides, tilting toward each other, nearly nose to nose, neither doing anything but breathing in and out, in and out, which began, as time went on, to seem, all in all, a perfect sufficiency. She had given up trying to think of things to say. He certainly had nothing to say, why should she?

He began touching her face with almost imperceptible finger-tips as if he were blind, just barely feeling the available side of her face, her temple, her ear, her cheek, nose and lips, began in time soft caresses of her hair and throat, like an afterthought commenced slowly kissing her face all over with little more than breaths. Sliding closer she began kissing him back, he avoided her mouth at first, but she, in a sudden fit of tenderness madly kissed his face all over, a laugh escaped him, a surprised child's giggle, she took his face in her hands, held it in place and kissed till he submitted to tongues.

She felt like a rare vessel being checked for cracks in the dark. Well, if he wanted, she had. His penis remained unengaged., though they were little by little warmly, if deferentially, embracing. He was not a young man, after all, his wife had died how long ago, since then he had done what, and with whom? While she was cogitating, somehow their breaths caught together and quickened his hand's slide down her thigh to her bottom. She abandoned herself to its caressive explorations, her glutinous muscles contracting. An awkward, inadequate entanglement ensued, he seemed to quake, and she slipped herself beneath him, a feat she hardly felt, because he so quickly levitated, then lowered himself upon her with that same strange delicacy, as if she were a bubble that might burst. She locked her legs behind his knees, pulled him to her, and yes, he was, he *was* hard, as hard as he could be.

"May I come in?" he said with the faintest mockery.

"Oh, please," she breathed with a shudder of relief, as he went at once up to his groin in her, held firmly there, took her face in his hands, still barely touching, and began tongue-tip licking her lips and tongue, while she tried to swallow him and suppress her whimpers and trills.

They enjoyed each other greatly, it appeared to Mira, who at one point wept and wept for no reason. Behind the tides of Eros she sensed some mystery reigned in him— not tenderness, not lust, not curiosity, not courtesy, desire to please, pity, friendliness, though it was certainly friendly, not even love of a sort, nor flight into oblivion nor dream.

At last he lifted himself from her, still as if she were fragility itself, and lay on his back. "Sleep now," he said, but she snuggled closer, reached over, pulled his outside arm around her, hauled him altogether on his side, pushed her bottom into his soft prick, held tightly to his arm, slept in the sag.

She awoke only as he was getting dressed, glimpsed on his inner, left forearm a blurred black number beginning with A, the rest impossible to read as it disappeared beneath the worn white shirt, then was gone beyond recall under the tan jacket.

"It is time now for you to go," he said, went to the bed where she lay speechless, bent, kissed her forehead, said, "Such a beautiful woman should not be so sad."

It was a gorgeous, glittering day. "Be so sad, be so sad, should not, should not, be so sad," Mira sang to herself all the way to Mayflower Heights. The house was empty. She couldn't think what to do, she should sit down and write something, but she was too overwrought, and anyway, write what? Well, at least she could read the newspaper.

Kennedy had made an unscheduled speech on Civil Rights– right while she was in the Fo'c's'le. "We are confronted ," said the President, "primarily with a moral question, as old as the Scriptures, and as clear as the American Constitution."

That this needed to be said seemed surprising to Mira, but what did *she* know? Or rather, what *did* she know? Except that she couldn't be still, couldn't read beyond that first page, kept jumping up to look out the windows or sidelong in the mirror– was she really beautiful? Finally looked full-on at her staring self, conceded at least that she really might not be *un*-beautiful, looked quite blooming in fact, felt so exhilarated she began to yearn for a drink of something commensurate, but all there was in the house was wine, and wine was too slow, too crepuscular, and here was a flood of sun. She found no calm in a shower, stayed under the lukewarm drops only long enough to decide to don her faded-est jeans, a fresh blouse, and her favorite earrings the eerie blue of her eyes. She set off in- stantly with Otis Redding hymning at her back, stunned to under- stand now beyond doubt that the number on his arm was a Nazi tattoo.

She began to hurry. He was the one who was sad. Hardly the word. Mira fled horrid imaginings for memory of his half-laugh at her flurry of kisses. She would rescue him from his woe, devote herself wholly to him, whither he went she would follow. She would cook him lovely dinners, and grow flowers and vegetables for his table– vows, she was aware, exactly opposed to those she had sworn only a month ago. But never, she had never met anyone so, so...

dear. She remembered thinking as she fell asleep with his arm clutched around her, This is all I ever really wanted.

Her empty future suddenly brimmed as she stepped through the guest house door, climbed the stairs, went down the hall and found the door to #4 wide open with sheets bundled on the floor.

Quaking a bit, she went back down and knocked at the office. The owner opened with a smile.

She said, "Could you give me the name and address of the man who was in # 4 last night, also his phone, if you have it?"

"Of course not," he said. "I can't do that."

As she went down the walk the cloak-like, cloying rose-smell almost choked her. Why had she let him get away like that? With no names exchanged. Too floozled she'd been. That word, too, her husband had pinned on her, when she lost her cool, or got over-enthused. When would she ever learn self-control?

Heartsick, she hiked back to Mayflower Heights, found a cara-van of people, some known to her from Museum School painting classes, which she had not kept up, wretchedly inept, feast of cha-grins, never to touch paintbrush again, especially now that she was (theoretically) a writer. Still, for no reason, she had complete confi-dence– if only she could get sat down to it, but there was no hurry really, she was just getting acclimated, shedding her marriage like a chrysalis.

Therefore this bustle was welcome, a changing into bathing suits, bumpings in doorways, a heading for the beach, a coming back for something, a heading off again. One guy was rolling joints at the dining room table, another was tuning a guitar, others were sitting around talking or looking out at the water from the screen porch. Several pretty, young– chicks, Phillip would have called them– came downstairs in bikinis. On the patio two wifely-looking women in long, loose dresses stood by themselves, blowing smoke skyward, nodding vehemently, then Terence Reed and Don Palmer appeared, people she actually knew, Terrence as always charming, exuding vitality, his gaze ever-flattering, Don, sweet, shy, earnest– teaching an ordeal for him– glad to see her, almost tongue-tied, good painters both, Terence the better known, admired for his bold portraits, Don a landscapist of delicate complexities.

"Phillip here?" Terrence inquired, smiling around.

Mira had never seen him not genial and electric, his slightly pock-marked cheeks always making him seem somehow less black or at least less manifest among whites, his dark face attentive to every woman in sight, no matter whom he was talking to.

"We're getting a divorce," she said. "*And* I'm leaving Cambridge."

"We'll miss you," Terrence said, sheer gallantry, as they seldom saw each other, and then only at openings, when he was mobbed by entourage. He had a wan, white wife, a little older than him, perhaps forty, with a ten-year-old daughter from an earlier marriage, and lots of girlfriends, or so Mira had heard. Well, Bikinis, watch out!

Fastidious Edie in her one-piece, black bathing suit, stepped with stone visage around strewn belongings, went upstairs, came down in no time flat, said, "I won't be back tonight. Somebody can have my bed."

Howard came in with provisions, Rachel took Cassie to the beach, Mira sat at the dining room table, one moment sure the Tattooed Man– as she now thought of him– would come looking for her some day, the next knowing she would never see him again.

By evening, lulled by wine, she ate some salad and a piece of crisp chicken, felt remote, restive, bored, watching Terence sample the women like a regal bee amid salaaming blooms, none superlatively tempting, all the while accepting Mira's steady regard as his due. She couldn't help it, she wanted him to choose her. And bed? Different question, that. Well, it *was* nice to be without a husband, especially hers– nice, too, not to be in a funk. She'd got quite giddy with the Tattooed Man. With Terence she'd be implacably cool, languid and lewd– she'd drive him mad, and call it entertainment.

Don Palmer was manning the hi-fi, ordering the LP's, pinpointing the needle on one cut at a time on one disc at a time– but she wasn't listening, watching Terrence's suave banter evoke flashing eyes, display of charms.

Passing by, he squatted near her thigh, like a cowboy at a campfire he seemed, looking into the dark. "Pensive?" he said.

"A bit," she said. "Not to bridle."

She saw the skin around his eyelids pleat, his torso jerk and slacken with a faint guffaw. "Don't ride?" he said.

"I don't know," she said with unexpected gravity. "I'd want to sleep on that."

"I've always liked ponies," he said, giving her a dazzling grin, rose to his feet with a soft grunt. "Not getting younger," he observed.

Brief elation. The blithe Bikinis were dewily adorable, she couldn't compete with them, of course, unless it was maturity he wanted, but that wasn't her either. Why was she always so timid? She stared blindly at her empty glass– her third... fourth?– trying to conjure her Tattooed Man's still face, which evanesced at the sudden stir of departures, a van-load headed for the Rumpus Room, "a little sweatbox of a dance-place with a local band called the Barbarians," Jake told her, opening Cassirer. Who was *he?*

And yes, there sadly went Terence with both Bikinis aglow. It *would* be fun to dance with him– or anyone– but no one had asked her to come. She felt a hollow pang, as if life were passing her by minute by irretrievable minute, as it always did.

Rachel was upstairs telling bedtimes to Cassiopeia, Howard was meditating in the lotus position on his prayer rug, Jake was writing in the margins of *The Myth of the State*, only Mira was brooding, stymied, alone.

Don Palmer came back in, approached deferentially, with soft eyes said, "I decided not to go."

"Oh," she said, "do you want to?"

"No," he said definitely. "I don't. I'm just glad to see you. Did you like the music I played? I played it for you, you know."

"Oh, she said, wilting a bit.

"I could feel I was getting through. It was pretty complex, but basic. All I can't say."

"You can paint," she said hopefully. "I love your...

He drew breath. "I never knew you had a husband. Who...?"

"The Blond God," she said.

He looked puzzled. "I never saw anyone like that."

"Eye of the beholder," she said. "And he was never around. Shall we have a little wine?"

"I don't drink," he said.

She emptied the bottle into her glass. "I find it inspires me."

"I'm always inspired," he said earnestly. "I can never afford enough paint."

"Don't you have girlfriends?" Mira asked.

"Once," he said. "I could never get over it..."

"My goodness," Mira said.

"We only met once. Nothing like that ever happened to me before, or since. We were perfect together. Next day she went back to Long Island. I was supposed to call her but I never did. I was living in my studio with a hotplate. I didn't have a phone. She was too far away. She was the kind who'd want children, I could tell. I couldn't split my life. Lucy Lumens..." he murmured.

"She could've helped support you."

"I couldn't do that," he said to the floor. "Four or five years later I was in New York, taking my portfolio around. I called her. Some friend answered. She said Lucy was getting married in a month, and it would be better if she didn't mention my call."

"I guess she liked you, too," Mira said.

"Oh, she loved me," Don said. "She said she did. And it's been years now, if I meet someone, which hardly ever happens, I start to dream about her all over again, and that ruins it. I've never told anyone this before. I think she would let me... I mean my psyche would... I mean if you..."

"I still feel married to my husband," Mira said. Her glass was empty, the bottle, too, all the bottles. "Come on," she said. "Let's go see what the Rumpus Room's like. Maybe you'll meet someone."

"I don't want to meet anyone," Don said. "You go if you want to."

Mira seized the moment, assuaged her abandonment by offering him Edie's bed. As she went out, he took his sleeping bag up the stairs with slow tread, head down, like climbing a mountain.

She hiked into town, excruciated by Don's sensitivities, mad to dance with Terence, but first she went into the Fo'c's'le to fortify herself with Scotch.

The place was packed. She got into a crazy badinage with three young guys about nothing apparently but her flying wit, but they all seemed, defensive and slow. In trying to goad them into levity she trespassed on their solidarities. They began to condescend and sneer, and then, for all further notice they took of her, she might as well have gone the way of the bubbles in their beer.

She whirled off into orbit around more men, who guffawed at each other while shying her on to the next, unwilling to break ranks or admit clemency. Time swallowed in Scotch, she never got to the Rumpus Room, ended up eating pizza on the street and going home at two o'clock with a handsome townie, who– not to disturb the bed– humped her over the arm of a couch as if she were an exercise machine in a gym, while she wished he would come and be done, whence he hurried her out, saying, "I don't want you here when my girlfriend gets off her shift."

Don was lying awake on top of his sleeping bag. He said, "I couldn't get to sleep, I can't even keep my eyes shut. Can I come in bed with you?"

After such a day it seemed petty to refuse. "All right," she said. "But I should tell you I was with someone tonight."

"With?"

"In bed."

As he went down the narrow stairs, his sleeping bag buckles tick-ticking the banister rungs, he choked off a sob, and Mira realized with chagrin that he had not been asking for sex, only comfort.

In the morning, loath to wake up, she heard Edie come and go, amid phantasmagoric dream fragments heard breakfast voices and screen doors, then needful oblivion coddled her till noon.

The guests were gone like a mirage, house swept clean and empty. The day seemed both hot and chill, the bay a twinkling frolic. She sipped cold coffee, head pounding, guts churning, heard from the low-tuned, never turned-off kitchen radio, that a Negro Civil Rights leader, Medgar Evers, had been killed by an unknown gunman in Jackson, Mississippi just after midnight. After a moment's incomprehension, hand to her mouth, she lurched up in time to puke in the sink.

Thereafter news from the South pervaded each day, ignored only by Edie, who said, "It's all shit, North, South, East and West, the society, the government, the whole country."

Brooding on what people thought, Mira varied her meat-rack sitting with spells in the Fo'c's'le windows, where she could nurse a 35-cent schooner of beer, doodle lines in her notebook, and listen to people talk.

"A-tripping we will go," sang a purveyor of acid tabs. A turned-on culture would have no truck with cruelty and war. People were quitting school in droves and going to India, or setting up communes beyond reach of the law. Timothy O'Leary had invited Swami Vishnudevananda to Harvard; he'd stood on his head in a loincloth and freaked out the squares.

Mira wasn't trying any acid. Mescaline once was enough, hyena-hilarious, pack-marauding in the street, mocking suits and dresses, till she thought, This is not me, and veered off in shame.

There did seem to be scads of writers around, none published, except an always unshaven one, who reeled off a string of magazines with bizarre names. She asked what they paid. He laughed. How did one go about copy-writing something? He answered in sarcasm, "One writes something, Dear, why do you ask?" his tone swarming toward indulgence, tutelage, bed.

Another said he'd begun a novel, but switched to poetry, a breeze compared to prose, adding, "Four lines'll get you into history, in proof quoted Pound,

> What thou lovest well remains,
>   the rest is dross
> What thou lov'st well shall not be reft from thee
> What thou lov'st well is thy true heritage[1]

For which he seemed less of a dolt. But what did *she* love, and who was Pound? Next day in the bookstore she found nearly half a shelf of him, bought the *ABC of Reading*, her education exploding.

She went around in faded shorts and halter, book in hand, found a true love, an abandoned man's bike, old but sweet, by day explored the bike paths, from a knoll near Herring Cove saw whales blow, breach gleaming black, one rainy dawn was charmed out of mind by a sea-serpent of seals perusing the empty beach in procession, two shrewd eyes in each loop.

People said, 'How do you get so tan?' You work on a boat? Half the time she realized she was having a grand romp, half the time

---

[1] Canto LXXXI – Ezra Pound

she feared she was becoming a pitiful sister who would never write a word; still she felt occasional, reassuring urges, if not surges, in her pretend pen– her spinning compass, her sole hope, if truth be told, her whole future.

On June 26, the household, minus Edie, went up to Boston for the Medgar Evers memorial service. Somehow separated from her friends, uneasy amid the huge gathering around the Parkman Bandstand on Boston Common, Mira covertly studied the mostly-aged, graven, black faces– intelligent, intent, stark, solemn, mature, decent, stalwart, she thought, fine, better than us by far, of course, of course, with uncomfortably crossed arms linked with black hands on either side, sang "We Shall Overcome" on a wave of high feeling that this day could not fail to bring an end of prejudice and bad faith, at least in Boston.

Towering over all with his high-held placard, *Let Us Be Free In '63*, Bill Russell moved along Mira's row with a number ten can filling with bills, handfuls of coins whispering, clinking to the bottom. Mira folded a ten, recalled the five-dollar mad-money kept in her wallet, glanced the other way, saw a beautiful young black woman about her own age. Their eyes met and held for a long moment of aching hope and belief, recognition and understanding, their eyes glassy with sprung tears. Mira looked down, trying to loosen the bill stuck in its plastic sheath, looked up– gone, she was gone.

Mira twisted to look about, not sure what the woman was wearing, something black with red trim. Too shy to push through the jumbling rows now randomly, somberly talking, Mira knew she should have moved at once to embrace her like a long-lost friend, or clasped her hands, said something, anything, anything at all, felt instant by instant more deeply and painfully the shame that through hesitance she'd missed some precious chance to join the world.

At a party in Cambridge that night, Mira combated her sorrow with Scotch.

A mischievous mother asked, "Don't you think women who become active in women's... activities... tend to lose their... femininity?"

"Good riddance," said one all in brown to the cuffs of her stylish slacks, with a stiff, little face, which might have been pretty, above a very starched collar, who was writing a thesis on archetypical females in fairytales.

The mother glanced her up and down, smiled invincible pity.

A bald man spoke sotto voce into his beard to three colleagues about an FBI check of someone in their department.

"Is he giving away our secrets?" Mira asked, thinking, how stupid!

Startled, the beard said, "He's been acting strangely. We have to be careful, he's dealing in codes."

"But why the snoopery?" Mira wondered. The beard looked uncomfortable, the others downcast, like children aligning their toes.

Mira withdrew from averted eyes, mulling their description of the agent as "a baby-faced young man in a drip-dry suit with a brutal haircut."

Mishearing the Green Bay Packers as Packards, she broke in amid a confab of men to insist that it would be nicer if all teams were named for cars, like Jasper Jeeps, Dayton Dodges, Fearsome Fords and so on.

Her whimsy having expired for lack of a smile, she sailed off like dandelion fluff and settled in the corner of a violently blue couch, woke some while later from a dream of a couple she'd liked earlier in the evening.

The party had shrunk to its terminus, her new friend Lillian's voice like a French horn announcing that she wanted to leave Hinckley, who stared at her, while the remnants sidled away, smoking like fiends.

"But why?" Hinckley said.

"Why, why, why?" Lillian mocked. "Because I can't stand you, isn't that enough."

"But why?" Hinckley said, stolid as a tombstone, but somehow soft.

"I'm moving out."

"We should discuss this at another time and place."

"Why?" Lillian mocked.

Aside he murmured to Mira, "I hope you won't get a wrong ideas of us. She gets mad at me. She can't help it, I can't help making her madder, unless I say nothing, which makes it worse."

Lillian said with rising stridence, "Hinckley, why don't you fuck Mira. I'm not the only woman in the world."

Hinckley sat back. "You're the only one I'm married to."

"So you say, but I'm leaving. You have my permission," she said to Mira, as if both knew no one in her right mind would want him.

"Where are you going?"

"Where do you think I'm going? I'm going to Hale Brackett's."

"Who's he?"

"He's the man I've been sleeping with."

"Oh, now, I take that very ill. That's a vile slander of yourself. What are you talking about?"

"Fucking. Resting from fucking," she said, and set out for the door.

"He's the one you said was Platonic?" Hinckley said.

"Was," Lillian said. "I'm sick of philosophy." And let the screen door close without a sound.

Hinckley blinked and sat on. In the darkened house, he talked about how impossible love was, married or not, and Mira quoted Phoebe, "To fall in love is an act of complete despair."

"Some people," he said, "can slip in and out of each other like two loops of a square knot and never come loose. I'm not sure we have the knack."

She thought him very dear. By the time he left she was drunk and said, "If I were Lillian I'd love you," which seemed to cheer him up– her one good moment of the whole, god-awful day. But, boy, was she ever drunk.

She woke in a blinding blaze of sun in a white room in a white bed, her head sunk in a white bolster the size of a snow-bank beneath a white canopy. She came dizzily down the stairs to find Jake with his pipe and the Times. He'd gone to bed early, Howard et al were at some other friend's house. They didn't care much for parties, "not after the first hour," Rachel had said.

The hostess fed Mira a bagel with cream cheese and lox, with finely-sliced onion rings and a sprinkle of capers, then about noon took her in tow to a florist to help pick up a strange South American succulent without leaves or trunk like a green sponge.

The place was full of people, crowded like a subway, Mira thought. She smelled whiskey and looked up, and up, and up, into a black profile, then down again and saw a black hand extend two pincer-like fingers and take the exposed bills from a woman's coat pocket.

Mira felt first fear, then revulsion, then anger. Tall as he was he was shorter than his companion. He was half-turned from her, she tapped him on the shoulder and said right into his eyes, "Put it back."

"What?" he murmured as if waked from reverie.

She thought, Here comes the knife either from him into my front, or from his friend into my back, and all these people pressed around us not knowing.

She said, "Give her money back," then grabbed the non-compos woman by the wrist, saying, "He stole money right out of your pocket."

"What money?" she said– exasperating dolt– felt from pocket to pocket, said "I don't know how much money I had."

By then everybody was staring at everybody but the blacks, then began advising each other to check their pockets, Mira shaking because she was unstuck and still alive. By then there was a quizzical, quiet, little furor spreading, and the tall guy said, as though someone had offended him mightily, "Let's get out of here, caw-mon, man."

And they sauntered out, one turning left, the other right, a cheery young man appeared with the succulent– strange plant indeed, and lugged it to the car by himself.

Mira didn't mention her brush with death. Bizarre to have thought she might get knifed. They were thieves, after all, not murderers, and anyhow it might have been mere opportunism, those nitwit bills visibly begging to be snitched, but then with what alacrity they turned left and right!

Who really knew anything about anybody? Certainly no one knew her, including, she had to confess, herself.

All the way back down Cape she dozed in discomposure, half-waking it seemed every ten minutes to hear President Kennedy's drawn-out, thrilling call:

"Ich bin ein Berliner." Bareleenah! Bareleenah! Bareleenah!

July brought crowds of carousing day-trippers. Mid-town Front Street was an erotic bath of strollers. The house was all comings and goings, acerbic Edie seldom seen. Howard imperturbably grilled simple dinners, was otherwise a glowing-eyed, silent listener. Indifferent to everything, Rachel played with bubbling Cassiopeia. Gesticulating with his unlit pipe, Jake talked with one and all, while typing pages of a fast-fattening journal, the aura of cannabis unnoticed except briefly upon entering the house, Otis Redding hymning away.

Edie in vexation confessed that she had met an older woman even more domineering than her mother, who'd wanted a nude portrait of herself, then one of Edie as Odalisque, while she directed Edie exactly how to paint it. Edie didn't mind painting in her bedroom– with breaks for tantalizing kisses– not a bit. Neither did she mind being bossed in bed. There she was glad to be enslaved. But it was humiliating to be led like a child through her 114 set propensities and opinions about life, and have them all dismissed by this woman's irrefutable sophistication. She was becoming the arbiter of Edie's soul, if she had one, which she did not, which made it all the worse.

Mourning her Tattooed Man, Mira asked, "And Rachel?"

"I tell her about everything but the sex, which I refuse to do, and then she gets really piqued and wants to wrestle, but we're getting back to our original state of simple friendship, better for us both."

Mira had hoped never to run into Handsome Townie again, but suddenly he was everywhere, walking beside her on the street, pushing in among the people she was sitting with in the Fo'c's'le, spouting moronisms, while she pretended hardly to know him– which was true enough– though he kept going to the bar one afternoon, keeping a fresh schooner before her, when she just wanted to drink and daydream.

Thanking him– she knew it was unwise– her mind toying with a way to get rid of him: every time he turned up, drink at his expense, then disappear, till he gave up on her.

All men but Mira, the table got raucous, telling dirty jokes, competing for the worst, the last she heard, What sits on a wall and bleeds?

Humpty Cunt.

Which got the loudest whoops of mirth yet.

"What's so fucking funny about that?" Handsome demanded. "That's just disgusting."

Amid redoubled hilarity Mira set out casually for the loo, veered around the chimney into the storage room and out the back door, walked down the beach to the Surf Club, regained Front Street, had just passed the meat-rack, bound for the Old Reliable Fish House and a dollop of Scotch to top things off– so far not a cent spent of her own– felt her arm painfully gripped, looked up into Hand-some's scornful leer.

"Going somewhere?" He half-dragged, then with open palms slammed her ahead of him like a common culprit, barging through the gladsome mob, a man of outraged rectitude. She looked desper-ately about for some escape, a responsive face, but she was invisible, a cry for help caught in her throat. Who among these tame sybarites would dream of intervening? Passing eyes flicked over her, brushed by, brushed by. If she screamed she'd just be making a scene.

Casual and aloof, Handsome hauled her, mute with chagrin, up the brick steps and into the Crown & Anchor, dim with black decor, nearly empty at this hour on a beach day. He hustled her stumbling through the cocktail lounge and into the back bar– dimmer yet, a few track-lights the size of golf balls trained here and there in the stale cigarette and antiseptic gloom. He swooped her up onto a stool light as a doll. "Now," he said, "we'll really drink."

Which gave hope of respite, till he added, not quite to her par-ticularly – she recalled later– but straight ahead, like some sort of declaration, "I'd like to punch you in the neck, kick you in the ribs, fuck you in the face…"

Heedless with outrage, she backed off her stool– the bartender staring concern, cute little guy, no help there– and made unsteadily for a red EXIT sign, but Handsome caught her in two strides, gripped her arm with steel fingers. She cried out, legs buckling. He let her fall back on her elbows, stood over her, grated, "Shut up. Shut up and Get up."

"Shut up yourself," said a quiet voice.

"And git out," said another, equally soft.

"Sez who?" said Handsome, turning about.

Unnoticed, two men were seated at a table against the wall. Handsome was big, but these guys were beyond big– belonged to some club no doubt, club of two– so big she couldn't see the chairs under them.

One was black and skull-shaven in a white t-shirt, the other in a black t-shirt was white with a flock of blond curls. Their t-shirts looked painted on, their biceps the size of Handsome's thighs. He pulled Mira up almost solicitously, muttered, "Let's get arta here."

The black eased to his feet, mammoth as he rose, bulging pants tight as his t-shirt. He popped his knuckles in staccato, then flexed his digits at each other like irate tarantulas, said, "Git and leave the gel to us."

Handsome started for the door, pulling Mira, who might have held back had she seen a tic of smile or glint of humor in these guys' eyes, but they looked locked beyond appeal in their grim dominion.

"You ever seen Dub fix an arm?" the white one said. "Take him but two seconds, make it go round like a clock, tell time all day long, whatever you want, forward or back..."

Handsome dropped Mira's hand. Dub made an idle feint, and Handsome bolted headlong crash into the door, reeled back, dazedly heaved himself again against the latch-bar, which gave, spilling him into the sunlight on hands and knees. The heavy door swung shut on one shank, wedging the foot within, while he squalled, corkscrewing to get free, stripping ankle skin.

The two guys would have had more interest in a panicky cricket.

"Well," said Dub, "what we got here?" swept Mira up with one arm, dandled her on his lap, hands molding her everywhere. "Nice tits," he commented. "For a ten year old. No ass though."

Mira struggled weakly, entombed in cologne, begging, "Please, let me go. Please. I haven't done anything to you."

"We just done you a favor," Dub said. "Now you owe us. One apiece. You'll love it."

Mira began to cry, hateful, hateful, halfway to hysterics, her tears fervent to melt them. She should scream for help, but feared they'd rather kill than rape.

"Yeah, little gelly," Dub said. "What's the biggest shit you ever took?"

Mira was so terrorized she hardly knew what was happening, heard the white one say, "Okay. That's enough. Let her go."

"Hey, I ain't even begun," Dub said.

"Let her go," the white said. "She's nothing to us."

"We just got her," Dub said.

The white one stared down the long hallway toward the rest-rooms, revolved his head as if he had a crick in his neck, met, held Mira's eyes for a slow moment, jotted his chin at her.

In the pause she felt static between them, waited, half in terror, half fascinated. The white one was looking away now, remote as the moon.

"Aww right, Bud, your call," Dub said, pushed her off his lap, quick-brushing his thighs as if she'd left some residue.

She didn't know whether to thank them or what.

"Go, go, go," Dub said. "No hard feelings."

Bud snorted.

She shook in the sun all the way back to the Fo'c's'le. Her bike was gone– she never locked it. By the time she got home she felt demented with horrors she could never tell, and bereft of her best friend.

For two weeks Mira hardly left the house, reading *The Feminine Mystique*, which uncannily, like déjà vu, kept spelling out things she'd just that moment realized herself. Finally, sick with fear of never writing anything of her own, she ventured into town, found her bicycle where she'd left it.

Still, she felt her old, hopeless self again— till her first Scotch took hold and she was able to look around and meet people's eyes. It was several days before Handsome appeared. By then her dread was all contempt, and he acted as if he didn't know her.

And Mira fell in love— first time *that* had happened to her since childhood— an instant consummation, Sorrel seeming to treasure her equally, openly to prefer her company to that of all others. The first thing she'd said was, "I borrowed your bike one day, I hope you didn't mind."

"Any time," Mira said.

"Mine's back on the road," Sorrel said.

Hoarse, loud, voluptuous, she was always the center of regalement. Like a goddess, she cared for nothing and nobody, came straight from clamming or shucking scallops or fishing or banging nails, her shabby shirts and jeans muddy or bloody or flecked with sawdust, her streaked hair a golden tangle, her face just hinting at signs of wear, a missing eyetooth the only obvious token of her drastic life. She'd fled a Cleveland orphanage at fifteen, raised herself in California, Louisiana and the Carolinas, fetched up in Key West, working on boats of all kinds, for now called Provincetown home.

One day a grizzled fisherman, one of her exes, brought a photo album to show her his month-old niece. Toward the front were

nude pictures of Sorrel only a few years younger– shockingly beautiful, the most ravishing woman Mira had ever seen in the flesh–
astride a motorcycle, perched on the hood of a trailer tractor, fig-
urehead to a beached dory, lounging in lewd poses, or simply laughing at the camera, all outdoors, none without cigarette or bottle in
hand, often with men in the background.

In no time at all she and Mira became inseparable. Mira felt
protective of her, though in practical fact Sorrel was the protective
one, lightning rod and shield against unwanted attentions. She took
her pick of the men, kept none for long. Her tale of the brawl that
cost a tooth caused Mira to relate her own mishap with Handsome.
Sorrel shrieked with glee at the stuck foot, but Dub 'n Bud damped
her jubilance. "Two make each other worse," she said. "I never try
to cry, I'm always too mad, but I'd've been scared of those creeps,
too."

They traded sexual histories– minus the Tattooed Man– with
infinite interest, but little nostalgia, neither enmity nor respect on
Sorrel's part for any of her innumerable name-forgotten men.
Once, years ago, she'd tried to count them up, till she realized she
was missing more than she remembered.

"You've never been married?" Mira asked.

"That's the one mistake I never made."

"You don't plan on having children?"

"Nah. A kid would be better off with no mother than me. I
used to wonder what mine was like, till finally I figured out I already
knew. Are you? Going to?"

"I can't even imagine it," Mira said. "Not for a long time anyway."

"Then we'll be sisters," Sorrel said, and gave her a hard hug, which Mira returned with sad sincerity. It was so sweet and simple, her eyes welled. Mira had never felt such loyalty from any human being. Sorrel believed in her absolutely, had no doubt that Mira would become a famous writer, never mind that she had yet to write a word– well, notes, lots and lots of notes.

After Labor Day Sorrel would help her find a cheap rental and a job or jobs to get by on, preferably outdoors, only one nix: waitressing. Meanwhile opulent August swelled the trees, parched the cemetery grass to straw, brought troops of visitors to the house. Suddenly all the college kids were gone. Wanted signs appeared in restaurant windows for dishwashers, cooks, waiters. The crowds of last chance commingled on the cannabis– and patchouli– redolent street. Toward month's end the sense of departures freighted the air, delicious and sad, for Mira wasn't going anywhere.

On the 23rd Jake drove Edie back to the city. Howard left by bus the next day for Boston to buy a car and go he had not yet decided where, to write his play. And the day after that Rachel and Cassi set off in the van for a women's farm in California.

Mira lost all track of time. Passing the Fo'c's'le one afternoon she stepped in to see who was there– no one she knew. At the furthest end of the bar people stood gathered, staring up at the TV. Others had turned on their benches to watch.

Mira moved closer to see. "What's going on?" she asked but no one answered. The screen showed vivid black faces, agitated placards. A baritone swelled, "I have a dream..." Now she could see the man at the podium, crowded round by dignitaries. He had a little mustache.

A hard voice close by shouted, "Martin Luther Coon. Shut that fucking nigger off."

Mira gaped shock at the stocky man, clean white shirt, sleeves neatly rolled just past his elbows, who stared back at her with implacable contempt. His buddies, glaring demand at one and all to stand with them, ranted murder like patriots of outraged hate. The Dream refrain swelled again, then again.

The man beside her with upward jerk of chin spat at her— just a gesture, like jetting grit off the tip of his tongue, a fine spray that damped her eyelids and lips. The resounding baritone Dream pulsed yet again, with settled, soaring triumph, the maddened table convulsed, and she fled into the street.

When Mira told Sorrel about it that night, Sorrel said only, "There's lots of people like that." She was having a few for the road. At midnight she was catching a ride on the fish truck, the daily ten-wheeler that would hit New York by dawn. She loved to ride high up in the cab above the little cars below. She was going to see some friends, and paint the town red; she'd be back in a week or two.

"I miss you already," Mira said as the truck rolled off the wharf, stopped at the corner and idled while they hugged.

Mira started back to the Fo'c's'le for last call, then shrugged and biked on home to the heart-hollowing, sweetly deserted house.

Labor Day came and went. The town emptied overnight. The portrait artists vanished like gypsies. A few elderly tourists still strolled. Day by day shops were boarded up. Town people stopped in the street to swap summer postmortems. Mira seldom went out, except for beach walks or bike rides, avoided the bars, hardly spoke to a soul beyond the Post Office, library and A&P.

Alone in the silent house, she dreamed her hours away with coffee in a cozy corner by the best window, staring into her blank page, glancing out at the bay that glittered all the way to the horizon. Birdcall or cricket din now and then broke her concentration. Then she went back to conferring with her pen. In the evenings she read *Letty Fox: Her Luck,* till she fell asleep.

Late in the afternoon of September 14th, a sultry day with distant whispers of thunder, Mira meandered far, far out on the flats– skirting slimy, green patches that glowed in the sun– and sat down on a slight rise of dry white sand, to watch the tide come in. There was no one else on the beach, as if the world were hers. The moment felt almost unbearably poignant.

What a summer it had been! Like a spasm. Thank god it was over. Men! Well, yes, men. At least she no longer envied them. And Jews. Jews, Jews and Jews. She'd made a lot of friends. The world was full of good people, her heart brimmed over to understand. She remembered a scrawny woman rasping, "My husbands were no good, neither one of them, my brother was no good, my father wasn't much good, and my uncle, he was just plain bad."

It was true, Mira had to face it, men were a problem, maybe *the* problem. You had to have one, but you'd better take care. She wished Sorrel would come back. One night, after a spell of horny men lacking all appeal, Mira had walked her home and danced lonesome blues with her in her backyard in the moonlight. What a thing it was to have a friend!

And her Tattooed Man, he too would be with her always. She hugged her knees, watching the water slip toward her on minuscule ripples overridden before they could recede.

She noticed now off to one side another sand island with three seagulls standing still as windless weathervanes, envied their choice— to float or fly.

She felt a drop, then another, then a sprinkle. The sun was shining and it was raining, lightly, lightly. She could see splashes on the smooth, gathering water, felt them on her skin, gentle as caresses, blessings, benedictions, this moment, she knew, like none other in her life, perhaps like none to come.

If it came down to that though there *was* one man she *did* like— that President Kennedy. Any man that had Robert Frost read a poem at his inauguration was a hero to her. She could see the Life Magazine photo of their breaths billowing in the cold dazzle of sun— the blinded old man with white hair speaking from memory, the impossibly young man listening, so graceful, so grave and clear.

If she couldn't have her Tattooed Man she'd like to have one like him, even if she had to go live in the White House.

Oh, now she wanted everything to happen at once. She could wait no more for anything. First she would write, as best she could, an elegy for her mother. Then she would invite Dad to come for a visit. He would be so pleased. The rain fell lightly, mixing with her tears. A shaft of sun still shone upon her. The gulls and their island were gone. The tide came sliding in, as if with tacit intent. Closer and closer it came, shrinking her circle of sand. The rain increased as the first lip of water touched her dug-in heels. She reached to wet her fingertips.

She might not know yet who she was, but at least she knew who she wasn't.

For a moment, gazing out across the sun-dappled bay, she heard ripples rhyme to the rain's applause, then stood up, briskly brushed her bottom, promised her new life aloud, "Tomorrow we'll begin."

WADERS IN THE SEA

When Arthur Bartlett leaves the motel it is seven o'clock in the evening and the beach looks deserted. He carries a transistor radio and a bathroom glass brim-full of warm gin, not to lose volume to ice. His wife is still deep in the before dinner nap from which he has just silently arisen with the idea of wading out in the dead low tide, and there getting the news from Walter Cronkite. Normally he watches it on TV in his study with a cold martini while Louise makes dinner, but this is a vacation, with its predictable mix of diversion and inconvenience.

He wears only a pair of plaid Bermuda shorts, uncomfortably conscious of his belly which slumps over the matching plaid belt. The plaid embarrasses him, the flab too— he played football once, and baseball and tennis. In recent years he has resolved to start playing squash at the Y, a promise he now supposes he'll never keep. Faced with the bother, the simple effort required to keep even minimally fit, he doesn't really care, or care enough, and this, added to his sense of multiplying uncertainties, depresses him, given this vacant moment to dwell on the future. He is growing fat, feeble, clumsy, prematurely old, the fate, so far as he can tell, of those who spend their lives in offices, at desk, conference and phone.

Well, he has money— money enough— and will retire in just two years. No, no, not likely, nowhere near enough. Three, four years, maybe. Never enough. The one stupid truth all can agree on. He blinks down the beach. His eyes ache with sun. He steps into the inch-deep, tepid water. The shallows go out and out before him, an archipelago of little sand islets stretching away, draining toward the low horizon. The coiled typography is disorienting. Why should the sun be on his right, and why so huge? And orange. The whole bay has turned color. Beautiful really, if not a bit bizarre… ominous perhaps.

The possibility of nuclear war weighs on him. The Cuban Missile Crisis only– he counts on his fingers– ten months ago deranged his boss's nineteen-year-old daughter, who called home from college to warn that missiles were on their way to Cleveland, the sky above the whole country a rain of Russian rockets. Twice she had to be institutionalized, till finally, after a love affair with a perfectly nice, black taxi driver, she committed suicide. The office has yet to recover.

Head down he meanders despondently; the news murmurs at his side, unintelligible for more than a few words at a time, not that he's listening. He can't stand Goldwater, or Johnson either. He may decide not to vote at all.

At his feet tide-pools swarm with hermit crabs, snails, tickle-fish and squirming, transparent sea-life he has no name for. He walks carefully, not to step on anything vengeful, then stops to watch the crabs. They cluster, waving their claws, stirring up tiny storms of sand; he can't tell if they're mating or merely fighting– over what? A bigger shell? He stoops and separates two with a curious finger; in an instant they rush together again as if magnetized. Weary of inconsequence he treads on.

For the first thirty yards or so the water barely covers his toes. The haze makes distance indefinite. Remnants of old weirs slant like black sticks in all directions. They look close enough to wade out to, an eighth of a mile? The windows blazing in the low skyline around the bay hurt his eyes, but if he looks a few degrees to the left– east it must be– he can see no human sign whatsoever, beyond the reach of orange nothing but pale blueness. It must have looked like this when the Indians were here, better than now, more harmonious, beauty everywhere. Perfect. Mystical. He supposes this strange ache he feels is some sort of nostalgia for pre-history, which only makes things seem more disjointed and him more anxious and askew. Where are we headed? He doesn't know, hesitates to speculate.

The little boy in front of him– where did he come from?– is deeply engaged in killing crabs. He might be eight years old, burnt healthy and brown by sun, hair and eyebrows burnt white, his eerie, pale eyes shrewd with discovery. He lays a crab on a half-buried cinder-block and smashes it with a flat slab of rock, wipes the mush off into the water, plucks another crab, holds it up, watching its pincers swim in empty air, leisurely, almost formally.

"What are you doing?" Mr. Bartlett inquires.

The boy studies him. "Nothing," he mutters, and smashes the crab. Bemused revulsion blurs his face as he rinses away the bits of shell and goo.

"You shouldn't do that," Mr. Bartlett chides. "You wouldn't want it done to you," then feels awkward at his basso, office tone.

The boy pays no heed. He picks up another crab, watches it flail in slow motion.

"They want to live too, you know," Mr. Bartlett says, wondering if this child is too young for the obvious.

"Sometimes they can live," the boy says. He mocks, or seems to mock, a more elaborate inspection of the next carefully selected crab, pulls a pincer off, drops it, picks up another, instantly smashes it.

"It's wrong," Mr. Bartlett remarks gravely, "to destroy life without a reason."

The boy bends for another crab, picks up, examines and discards three, smashes the fourth. "Sometimes they can live," he says.

"That's a decision we usually reserve for God." The word sounds pompous to Mr. Bartlett's ear, on his own tongue now only an occasional oath. The last time he went to church was how many years ago?

"Dear God!" he murmurs, doubtful of himself, of his frail, stork legs, the radio, the glass of gin. This strange little creature is somebody's son, and may be staying at the same motel.

"It's wrong to destroy life," he tries again. "You'll understand when you're older."

But he feels no such certainty, and when the boy bends again Mr. Bartlett clumsily tousles the sun-bright curls, shocked by their softness, then resumes wading, behind him hears an almost, orgiastic smashing of shells. Hoping a show of adult dismissal is stronger than outrage or dismay he doesn't look back.

Now the water encloses his ankles, in another five yards rises toward the tender hollow behind his knees; it really does seem he could wade all the way out to the weirs, and suddenly lines from a college course in the Romantic Poets come to mind:

It is a beauteous evening, calm and free,
The holy time is quiet as a Nun
Breathless with adoration; the broad sun
Is sinking down in its tranquility;

The gentleness of heaven broods o'er the Sea.
Listen! The mighty being is awake
And doth with thunder make
A sound like thunder—everlastingly.[2]

Something is askew with the visitation that now somehow deserts him from that time when he cared about books beyond the practical, and he rounds on the thought that has dogged him ever since they arrived: it was wrong to come here. He can't say why exactly but he wishes they'd gone to the White Mountains, as they usually did, watched cloud shadows cross the unbroken green forests, or had rented a cabin on a lake with a canoe, listened at night to haunting loons, rodent scurries on the roof, nuthatch tappings. They might have been alone in their familiar silence, made a simple dinner for themselves, or eaten leftovers on a screen porch, while the light faded and they yawned toward a walk in the dark or early bed.

For this late August town at the tip of Cape Cod is full and overfull, its main street given to guest houses, shops and outdoor cafes, knickknacks, trinkets, leisure wear, dark glasses, souvenirs, sidewalk artists doing idealized faces in charcoal. Louise had wanted him to have his done, but he shook his head, and when asked, so did she. "I prefer the mirror," she smiled to admit as they strolled away.

New motels are going up on the four-lane highway in and out of town, guest houses, swimming pools, restaurants, putting greens,

---

[2] "It is a beauteous evening, calm and free" - William Wordsworth

cocktail lounges, burgers, fries, ice cream, seafood, hotdogs, "Worse every year," he heard someone say, without being sure what was meant, except perhaps the towering, garish signage.

He halts in the lowering sun with a sense of nadir. Everything has the wrong effect on him. His lone martini burns in his gut. He feels no despair, fears he's too fat, too tame for that. As if to feed his malaise the town is over-run with un-youthful youth of a kind he has never seen, only read about— Beatniks, what a name! The boys are bearded— at least many are— the girls have long hair, both dress shabbily, like sexless gypsies, are insolent, sullen, profane, cynical, wary, embittered and gay. Perhaps they aspire to art, more likely they want nothing at all but freedom from responsibility. By day they inhabit the benches in front of Town Hall; panhandling or fleering at the passing tourist throngs; their harsh laughter taunts him. At night they are drunk in the streets, sleep in doorways between police proddings. They have a common, mutinous look as if the world had gone wrong and they knew who to blame. He thinks he sees contempt in their eyes, concedes that they may well be right— but what is one supposed to do about it, it or anything else? Brace for the future?

He is lucky, he is blessed, he has beautiful, healthy grandchildren, happy sons, one in Saudi Arabia, not a terribly homey situation but remunerative, the other a design engineer for Boeing in Seattle. He walks on, mulling the boy with the hammer and his own loss of quietude.

Something stubborn in the boy's face takes him back to his first summer after college. Not yet married he and Louise were staying at her aunt's cottage. They had invited a poet friend to visit them, who had just been released from a hospital in Omaha. He drove without stopping to reach the haven they offered. They tried to be kind to him. He needed rest; he did not want rest. He drank beer and smoked marijuana without cease at the table they had arranged for his typewriter: it was painful to watch him, after a certain point in the day, one eye shut, aiming for one key at a time with a determined finger, heaping the huge ashtray, coughing and spitting into the wastebasket beside him, finally regaling himself with unintelligible, derisive-sounding rants.

Awakened one night they came downstairs to find him naked in the kitchen holding his palm over a candle-flame– nothing showed in his face but steadfast attention.

"Where fire goes go I," said he, his perfect enunciation triumphant over all he had drunk since breakfast, and then he smiled, so mild, so sly, so serene a smile, it seemed exalted.

They treated his hand, got him back into bed, talked him to sleep, next day took him to the hospital, worried to distraction. They feared what he might do next. His madness shadowed their comfort in each other, acted on them as reproach. His monologues grew ever more unmoored, as if addressed to some present but invisible observer. He laughed constantly at nothing they could discern, once avowed, "Oh no, I'm not telling anyone *that.*"

He seemed bent on some personal cataclysm, perhaps, consciously or not, was rehearsing worse, and as soon as he was fit to drive they told him the doctor had said he must go home, where he could get proper rest and care, back to Omaha, and stay with them no more, where he seemed on the verge of dissolution or worse– true, all true.

Mr. Bartlett still broods on this enforced departure. They heard no more of their friend, who never went home. What can have become of him? Confined or dead or eking out a meager existence in some shabby neighborhood, an eccentric, beloved English teacher, drinking in secret, faithful to his fate?

Madness? No frequenter of reunions, that much they knew. The memory of their friend smiling in his naked candle flame seems suddenly wondrous and splendid, though now somehow also tinged with rebuke.

He walks on, knowing this for unfair, yet truth is there too, for him at least, if not for their lost friend. Worse every year yes, so it is, or so it lately seems, everywhere. The first thing he has to do when he gets home is fire John Parker, a long-time sales manager, once a cracker-jack, jovial hustler, several times Best of the Year. They are not friends exactly, but he knows a lot about Parker's family situation, about his philandering and depression. It's rough, these dismissals, they take their toll on him, the hardest thing he has to do; he hates to count how many. Either you hack it, or you don't or won't or you can't— so you're out, done, kaput.

It's often cruel, sometimes somehow wrong, but that's the rule of profit or loss, of business acuity. Of life really. Of impossibilities. Thirty years ago his secretary Marilyn Timlin had to go— she went of her own accord, he couldn't have fired her, he hadn't the will, and she knew it. There had to be an end of their delirious trysts, or an end of his marriage. He still feels guilty for starting up with her, for not staying with her, for deceiving his wife, for fearing Marilyn might try to blackmail him, or more terrifying, openly fight for possession of him.

And then the years of doleful shame for indulging dreams of her, trials of heart-ache behind a bland, intrepid face, a secret, second life unlived except in some impossible, future happenstance.

And where is she now? He would like to speak to her. But what would he say? What could he?

The water reaching his loins is blood-warm; it makes him squeamish. He turns down the radio to escape a sense of reckonings, gets a deodorant ad, lowers the radio into the water; then, after a silent yard or so, without forethought simply lets it go glimmering till it's only a shadow on the bottom like something draped for concealment, then after another yard or two, simply slipped away, lost to nothingness.

He would like to be quit of the glass, too, now that it's empty. On impulse he fills it with water, gulps a mouthful, gags, spews. Drowning is said to be the easiest way to die, the dreamiest once begun. He thinks he'd choose, if he could, a good heart-wallop, never to nurse another thought, then feels shame at this new propensity for resignation, then guilt for the jettisoned radio.

After a half-hearted search he accepts the dismay of all things irreparably gone, yet still feels awkwardly encumbered, finally stuffs the glass in his hip pocket. It's not his after all, and he tries to abide by the laws, especially in minuscule matters, and rightly so, it seems, wiser than not, if only because possible. The big questions are always moot. He could build a bulwark of a case for absolute pragmatism. In college he had been unrelenting at debate, prizing the struggle among truths, the need to pick and choose, the sheer inescapability and practical necessity of it.

Thigh-deep, he forges on, a bit anxious now, his eyes fixed on the skin of water, where tendrils of sea-foliage float on the surface ahead. As the water encircles his waist, he moves into a kind of submerged meadow. Eel-grass, slimy seaweed, kelp, who knows what? Thick and thicker in all directions, weirdly wavering around him, clasping, entangling, unforeseen.

Now glimpses of white sand flicker maze-like in the depths. He picks the clearest path, and moves cautiously along it, holding his hands in the air, as if to keep them dry. Why should he? Still he holds them out before him, palms down, like one about to strike up a concerto.

At his feet a horse-shoe crab drags its barbed spine in and out of sight. Doubtless other sea-creatures are at home here, and he stops to take heed. He doesn't want to step on anything hostile. Distorted by the depths, his feet look ghostly and remote, wavering, as if no longer feet, or rather somehow feet not his.

He has to wonders if sharks venture in this far. He has seen gull-eviscerated dogfish on the beach and great black rays like crashed aircraft, rotting in the sun. Far from his Ohio heart-land of stone and steel, he feels immersed in strangeness, deplores his unease, reasonable though it may be.

The path maunders, disappears, reappears, branches, re-branches, until he finds himself no nearer the weir perhaps, but engulfed in a matting of purplish, slimy, clasping vegetation. Traces of white sand still glimmer, as if blazing their own trails. He cannot predict where they might lead, and the question of vengeful creatures recurs. He imagines some long-extinct python, still extant here, if nowhere else, malign at being the last of its kind, coiled and ready to drag down the unwary, or strike with deadly sting or bite.

Fear here is doubtless childish, if not contemptible, but in fact he knows nothing of the sea, so he is dumfounded when he turns to get his bearings, and finds he is no longer alone.

The Washashores

Twenty yards out– to *starboard*– a bit smug this inveterate land-lubber feels at hitting on the apposite lingo at first try– but what is truly weird if not wholly incomprehensible, is the human head apparently neck-less as a bowling ball afloat upon the perfect stillness of the sea maybe twenty yards further out, a completely inexplicable phenomenon, a bust it must be, motionless, aimless, blameless, just facing out to sea, somehow anchored there, floating at least, or perhaps standing on some sort of mechanism or sunken pedestal or just treading water, hoax or joke of some sort.

Who is it, or what? Not to mention Where from and why? Doing what out there all by its lonesome? A sculptor's bust? Doll or puppet's head? Lobster buoy with grimace or grin? Lame joke? Flotsam or jetsam– is there a difference? Live or dead? The never alive can never be dead, no?

Stagnant, the motionless tide feels, both moribund and somehow pregnant. The head may be just a wader, like himself, must be, or maybe just dog-paddling. Mr. Bartlett can't tell– mayhap it or perhaps whoever has been floating out there all along, or treading water, or has only just now swum or floated in or washed up from behind and passed him as he brooded, making his cautious way toward the vast, empty horizon, or perhaps this solitary head has somehow simply drifted in from some isle or estuary he knows nothing of.

Against the blazing sun and crimson bay he can make nothing of the wader's features, if any, or even if it's human. It must be neap tide, ebb's end– there's not a ripple, the whole bay is molten, lifeless it would seem, but for the slimy, clasping foliage, ghostly and invisible below.

Edging outward, first thigh deep, then waist high, nearing his nipples, then close to armpit-high, Mr. Bartlett meets with a gently rising sandbar, to which the wader– he thrills to wonder– could it be a woman?– suddenly offers cupped palms, like a pious acolyte petitioning sea and sky, so formal it feels sacrosanct, as if spawned out of time, himself drawn into its– or he hopes– *her* orbit, his astonishment instantly transformed into childish enchantment.

He finds more and more sand beneath his feet, stops still, shades his eyes, strives for a clear sight of this strange head without visage. Does it not know he's there? Should it bother to care? Or him either? But how not, after all, how not, all now seeming so uncanny and unique?

In place he turns slowly, carefully, full circle, amazed by how far he's come, or rather gone, how far out they are, way, way out, it seems, in the middle of the bay, in some psychic latitude remote from the one they had both set out from doubtless only a brief while ago, in another life entirely it now seems, the beach behind them wan, dwindled near to nothingness by sheer mystery. He or she seems rapt as well, yet must be aware of him by now. Mustn't he or she? Yes, it's a woman, surely a woman.

A hint of her inviolability touches him to awe, and for a moment he tries to see the world with her eyes, with the eyes of untrammeled sanity, call it common sense– the weir that seems no nearer than before, yet somehow now exists in some obscure dimension of its own; the bright, toy town behind them bereft of human signs; the rosy bay, the thin thread of beach beyond, now alien, strangely remote– such that he has to admit his inability, finally, to feel anything but an alien himself, an alien in paradise– there's something crass about the phrase– something dreary, if not preposterous– and he reflects that nature is always and only itself, never ugly, never inept.

The thought though is only a thought, clumsy beyond proof or disproof, useless, irrelevant, likely not even true. Things are as they are, can be no-way else, and soon he must return to the motel, wake Louise and dress for dinner. She has already picked out the restaurant, the most regal in town, where people still dress.

The head seems to float outward, almost inscrutably, and he forges after her, wishing she were older, a woman traveled and wise. At a better angle he realizes with shock how exquisitely beautiful she is, ageless, glowing, golden, gorgeous, goddess-like, profoundly female– easily the most desirable woman he has ever known or been in the personal presence of– the more he looks the more he realizes he's never seen female beauty of this order, not in dream nor fantasy. Mermaid, he murmurs, to mock his wonder, now a need to draw near, perhaps to declare or receive some unique avowal or message.

Their mutual movements seem to have acquired a tension– so it feels to him now– almost a kind of psychic gravity. She turns, and he turns with her, hoping to find clear sand ahead. Nor does she deign to glance his way, though by now she must know he's there, just twenty yards behind her, twenty or thirty to her left, to port, a kind of right triangle, the long hypotenuse between them, perhaps un-navigable by mere mortals. Such splendor needs bow to no one: he should lay flowers at her feet, dive down and bind them with garlands.

Garlands? What garlands? To be found where? What can he be dreaming of?

Now raw fire of desire inflames his psyche, swells his member, riddles his soul. He gazes at her hapless, hopeless, wanting nothing. But in dire truth, what would he not give to know this goddess, if only for a moment, had he only the courage to behold her fullness in his arms, be one with all she is, all she has ever been, all she dreams of, all she knows of love and life, all she will in future fact become. What might she say to him?

To sound their tongues now seems bound to meet immortal harmonies, ultimate truths. On the sandbar, she comes ever more into view, if somehow no closer. She turns her profile slightly, as if to take full measure of him, and he realizes it is no illusion, she really, is surpassingly beautiful, perfection beyond anything he can remember ever having met with in waking life– or dream, either– the loveliest woman in all his years of life or dream, or so it seems, possible or not, mad or not. Nor is she wearing a commonplace bathing suit, but only some sort of veil-like translucence of flowers.

"Mermaid," he murmurs.

No, but can this glimpse be true in plain, mundane, abundant fact? Dare he really more than glance at her again? He has no power to look away, were he even willing. Now has lost his will as well as mind, simply become spellbound? Well, women were all-powerful, wonder-workers, who ever doubted or would deny or want a world less perilous or fantastic? So nature hath decreed, no doubt for the best. To mate with her might be to perfect his life, instruct and im-mortalize his soul. Is this not true? Can it be?

So it may seem, yet fantasy cannot be real nor proved but only exist as human illusion. And yet, and yet, yet and yet...

Now she moves deeper into the meadow, as if to dare or draw him on. A little ripple strikes his chin. She's only the back of a head

now, moving away–doing a little dog-paddle. Where can she be going? A breeze announces the turning of the tide. Would he could
constrain or accompany her– but how? Say what? A nice day! A fine
life! What a predicament!

Then he could laugh, she would turn to him her human face
and smile sad wisdom of the ages, then they could turn back together, enough wading– well, dog-paddling, for one – day of unmet
lives, thus to part in the final shallows with adieux, intrepid and
profound.

But might they not, ought they not, at least, at very least, share
one kiss? How not and not wither of sheer wrong? Of blank refusal.
Of plain cowardice. All Nature decries denial, outrage, contempt,
fear.

The shy sun has dropped behind the town, the water is black,
the distant blue more intense. He hops now, hop-bobbing outward,
entangled below, nothing but a head himself, two heads they are,
on the surface of the sea. With marveling intake of breath he gets
water, some goes down the wrong way, he chokes, gags miserably.
Has she turned to look?

Something touches his foot, he yelps, blind to all below, mimes
a last estimate of the beach. He is in rout, and knows it, forges with
abandon through the wall of vegetation, breasting the waters, feeling her eyes on his back.

He slows, makes cautious haste. There are horseshoe crabs all
about now, moving away, fan-like, huge bottom-skimming brutes
with primeval armor and long spiny tails. He takes evasive maneu-
vers, finds himself back on the sandbar thigh-deep.

All's well after all. Weary of his game, the youth has gone home
to supper. Sheepish on dry sand, Mr. Bartlett looks back, at this

distance sees only the shape of his mother's squat teapot, un-thought-of in years, not since her burial and the horrid urn of ashes, some of which somehow got spilled, he now remembers though nothing was said of it at the time, too macabre ever to be mentioned, much less swept up amid the un-mown grass.

He broods on his momentary sense of debacle, tells himself it's just a girl dreaming of her boyfriend or someone's wife seeking solitude, but that doesn't answer– nothing will answer, he knows, nor can, never before nor ever after, much less again. Time remains the impregnable mystery, irreparable, irreducible.

He feels a weight sudden in his belly, heavy and smooth as marble, recalls the beautiful ellipsoid boulder he'd found as a child on a stone beach in Nova Scotia, too heavy to bring back to the car, beautiful, sea-hewn to perfection by the ages, the only certainty to be found within human grasp there.

He might have been ten. Mother and father had both been sorry, nor could they quell his tears. There was no way they could have gone back for it, even if they could have found it again among so many stupendous boulders the size of bathtubs, much less could have budged it even with all three straining together, and now only him alone this low tide day thirty odd years later to be recalled to its solitary promise.

Composed by imponderables, Mr. Bartlett waits. Blurred by the heavy atmosphere, the shape can no longer be seen to move, cannot even be said to have a shape, now can hardly be distinguished at all, wisp of a wisp in a void of wisps.

If or if not this were truly the most beautiful woman in the world, what can be better done than acknowledge, adore, bow and pass by? Heartsick, Mr. Bartlett trudges on up the beach, caught in thought, enters the lobby, a place of wicker and loitering help.

"You've cut your foot, Sir," one notes the blood between his toes.

"So I have," he sighs gravely, nods thanks for the concern, continues on across the carpet, walking on one heel. Bingo is played here on Tuesday nights. The dining room and cocktail lounge are just around the corner, in the new wing, where they ate last night, inedible fare for people on vacation, with nothing to do but eat. On the wall a poster says, *It's Smart to Buy Art*.

He finds their door, unlocks it, sits on the bed. He can hear himself breathe, laborious, it sounds. The blinds are drawn. Louise is in the shower behind the shut door of the bathroom. A fat paperback, by some author he's never heard of, lies flat, half-read, on the night table beside a bottle of lotion. He dabs at the cut with a corner of sheet. The blood wells un-stanched. He is surprised at the dark, plush red of it, curious that he feels no emotion.

In disgust he rubs at the cut harder, and still harder, till he finally feels a distant pang.

"Art?" Louise calls from the shower.

"I've cut my foot," he murmurs.

"Arthur?" she calls, sharp with doubt.

"It's me," he says. "I'm here. It's nothing." The effort of raising his voice exhausts him.

She says something he can't hear, then, gaily, "I'll be right out."

The shower stops. She's drying herself, he imagines, before the steamed-up mirror. He feels obscure dread and bitter remorse, knows now what he would say to Marilyn Timlin— heartbreak not to know where she is, to be able tell her at last: Thank you.

Louise emerges from the towel-strewn bathroom, shaking out her hair. After an instant he stands to take her in his arms, glad, so glad to see her, he starts to cry.

ALL THEY WANTED

There's too much calculation in modern art.
I stand for the painting of feeling.
                                        -Maurice de Vlaminck

The Post Office steps is the most dangerous place in town. I just stand there until some disaster strikes, then I go home and hide till the next time I'm seized with the need for mail. I could have it delivered, but then I'd never go out.

Just this morning, sorting through my handful of junk mail and bills, wondering who might turn up if I wait just two seconds more, I had it quite nakedly inflicted on me that whatever your state of mind at the moment– and mine never changes, thank God– there is also no such thing as past history in this town.

First comes Freida, still wearing long skirts, hair down to her waist. We smile, but what must she be thinking? Bayou and Grumm loved her, not me. She was mad for Brade, another fool of crazed ambition, who never loved anybody in his life, but who liked to treat me to grand dinners and fuck all night. Carousel.

Next comes Alibi Arby Ruzo, sozzled as usual, Freida's first husband, whom she could never completely let go nor get free of, who tried to console himself with me. We half-nod like we might have met once but can't remember where, then resume our absent faces. It's like being at the wheel of a ship in a bottle.

After that every person that appeared– I'll spare you the list– reminded me of some side of The Crime of the Time, which nobody has the whole picture of, even after all these years, least of all the perpetrators.

These were people I was intimate with for a brief period leading up to the denouement— shall we call it?— then went on living in the same town with, but hardly ever came across, for years on end, except at the P.O. Maybe that's why the past remains so vivid, there's so little to bury it between then and now!

Of course everything else has changed completely. When I first came to town you could live on nearly nothing here. Surviving it was called. I had a lot of crummy jobs and I moved around a lot. There was a lot of drinking and drugs and a lot of sort of wild affairs, not to mention how dingy it was, with people trying to commit suicide all over the place and murders in the dunes, ODs, rapes, mutilations and so on.

Too much happened all at once, even to register, much less digest. Bare feet were just being banned in the bars. Manny Zora was already a legend, and he didn't die till '79. Hofmann was still alive. Nina Simone and Ella Fitzgerald had sung at the A-House not too long before. Only the Little Bar at the A-House was gay in those days. The Ace of Spades, where the Pied Piper is now, was lesbian, but discreet, very sedate. Smoking jackets and pipes. Women could dance together anywhere, but not men. There was still plenty of fish, and the Portuguese still had their swagger.

In New York it was the start of the Be-in and what I think of as anti-art. Down here I got arrested for cohabiting with the boy I came with. We had to lie that we were married to get a rental. The judge was an old walrus with white mustaches, last of the patricians. He got most indignant. "Perchance you think this is a brothel?" he says. "Be-gone by noon tomorrow."

Outside the court room– in those days it was right in Town Hall– one of the cops who was always trying to date me says, "Don't worry about it. Nobody takes him seriously."

My boyfriend split to Mendocino, I never heard from him again.

Vietnam was driving the country berserk. The people I fell in with refused to read the papers, or even hear about it. They'd come here to get away from all that. Music and marijuana were the only keys to truth. Words were rigid, evil, lies. Mind was the enemy. Love was all. I was a child quite wide-eyed, though I know you can hardly imagine that now. I wasn't pining to get married, but I certainly wanted a man of my own– not other women's men, all in a clot, which was what I got. I think it cured me like a thrombosis.

Anyway, at that time nothing in my life seemed to fit but my name. My flutist father loved birds and every night, just at dusk in the summer, he would play me the veery's call, like a falling spiral. It haunts me still. I grew up, as you see, to be cinnamon-colored like the bird– at least in hair and clothes– and like the bird I am– or rather used to be– too easily deceived by imitation distress.

Youth loves misery that doesn't know itself. By middle age invisibility and silence are more valid, more adroit. Anyhow my social virginity ended when I met Grumm's mother.

She was like a postcard of a lace doily. She looked sweet enough to eat, with her little girl's voice and her tinkling enunciation. We drank about ten creme de menthes together one Sunday at the Colonial Inn, and then somehow we took to sitting around in the wicker furniture there at all hours of the empty afternoons. It was so dim in the bar, so far from the windows across the dining room, that on certain hazy days the bay looked moonlit.

We kept saying how beautiful everything was, but I wonder now, how much did it affect us? From her I learnt of avarice. I think she wanted a daughter. Eventually she tried to rule her son through me.

Grumm was a guru, and come to think I probably *did* first see him on the Post Office steps, just smiling his mustache up at the sun as if it were an old pal of his. He was into eastern wisdom, and he was always surrounded by pretty girls, but he was above sex. He was a marvelous wood-worker, a master craftsman, a designer and maker of furniture, but he didn't care about material things. He wanted to be a philosopher. When I disagreed with him he'd wind up saying things like, "Good God baby I'm not going to discuss this ridiculous matter with you any more, you're clearly befuddled."

It was Bayou's mind that fascinated him. They both did a year behind bars, but neither was ever quite sure how he got there. For a while afterwards they each kept trying to pry out of me what the other had said, and what Grumm's mother had said, and how exactly they came to get caught.

What Grumm really wanted was eminence, prestige. He was secretly impressed by wealth, background, culture. But he wanted it to be absolutely independent and unconventional. He was trying for a certain nonchalance, self-invention of a sort. By the end he wanted to disown the whole sham so much he moved out of town. At the time it was the thing in his life he was proudest of, maybe the first thing in his life he'd ever *been* proud of.

It was who he really thought he was, or at least whom he wanted to be, but he couldn't breathe a word, never a hint, till he let me in on the secret. That must have been the one thing in connection with the heist that Grumm ever did without asking Bayou first.

When they got out early on good behavior of course people asked embarrassing questions. Bayou made jokes about it in public. He seems to have enjoyed jail the way he enjoyed everything else. Ridicule that wilted Grumm only seemed to make Bayou more luminous— I think— because he had such a knack for people, for seeing who they were. And no prejudices. Not even preferences. He was the most truly democratic man I ever met, though one must admit that in his private polity he was definitely First Citizen.

Him I met at the old Sun Gallery. The first thing he said was, "How would you like to go to Zanzibar with me?"

"Lead on," said I, straight to his bed. He was fantastically handsome and clever, and he looked like the quintessential beach bum with his ragged straw hat, seersucker cut-offs, no shave and those teeth. He had the kind of charisma that comes of seeing everything as potentially funny, even the grossest, grimmest things.

He was a natural criminal with a taste for extravagance. He had a pedigree a mile long and all these diplomas from Princeton and the Sorbonne. He left his investment bank and his several families and did nothing but scheme. He was wry in a way and brilliant, neither brave nor afraid, and he never spoke a serious word, much less an honest one. He always smiled, and he made people laugh. From him I learned to listen, and forgive. He had a strange power over Grumm, not sexual. Grumm admired him because he was unmoved by any human being. Bayou would say things like, "Baby, you've got to stop hating me, it's no good for you."

He and another fellow quite larcenous planned to steal Columbian art, but the forgeries were getting so good he had to come back and study to tell the difference. Then he was going to smuggle cars to Peru. Then he tried to persuade me to go to Saigon with him.

He'd pimp and we'd make a fortune. I thought that one a bit much. In court he claimed Grumm was the brains. The judge just laughed.

All the while I knew nothing. While they were thinking I suppose exclusively about *it*, I was thinking about *them*. I marvel to remember. I didn't even know they were friends, much less in cahoots, until I had slept with them both. Then I kept trying to choose, though neither minded. They were most complacent, Alphonse and Gaston.

Eventually the robbery got noticed. It took forever because the museum was closed all winter and the custodians were always stoned or lost in their own affairs, poetry or whatnot, but suddenly the word hit town like Mardi Gras. The local papers were full of it. That's all anyone talked about. Overnight the thieves were famous, heroes, giants. There was a lot of respect for their brilliance and professionalism. Rip Off Artists! People were impressed, completely admiring. No guns, no blood, no harm to anyone, considering whose loss it was. There were rumors that the whole swag had gone for a fortune to a ham baron's chateau in Bastogne. They were romantic figures, whoever they were. Gods! It was terribly heady stuff. But Grumm was still only Grumm to the world, and there was no one he could tell, which was a downer.

That's how I became the art heist moll. Sometimes he would even deign to make love to me— but one night when we were just getting into bed he said, "Veery, you've got a good head on your shoulders. I need to take you into my confidence, I need you to check my perceptions."

It pleased me to think he meant some kind of exotic foreplay, but nothing followed but more talk. Little by little I began to wonder what he was saying, or not saying about the big brouhaha. I was lying there licking his shoulder, pinching his nipples and pushing my bush against his thigh. So I wasn't really paying attention until he fell asleep.

Bayou was the passionate one. It would take him suddenly, without any warning. One night we were on our way to a party, and he dragged me into the shrubbery, people going by on all sides. That sort of thing was so contrary to his cool nature, it almost had to be put on, but he seemed to enjoy it. He snorted like Poseidon. Another thing I learned from him: never wear underwear in the summer. Pardon my digression. I know you like this sort of thing. A bit more?

It never occurred to me that I was becoming an accomplice. For a while it was all quite exciting, quite flattering, too— which took the crassness off. Even at conception the theft itself was never merely a matter of money. It was ingenious how they foiled the security system. Then they waited for one of those deep February fogs when you can stand in the middle of Commercial Street and look both ways and never see anyone for days on end, plus of course it was about three o'clock in the morning. They got some small works by minor European masters. Real ones. More's the credit to them for that. The museum was full of forgeries. Already there was gossip. A whiff of scandal hung over the place. The owner was said to hold orgies there, though as a matter of fact I doubt he had the gall for that. Though at this remove why I should doubt anything is beyond me. There really was no limit to what people did in those days.

Here, finish that. We'll open another.

But the main thing, la pièce de la résistance, was a little Vlaminck. It was truly beautiful. Perfectly diffident, unobtrusive at first glance, but it was an extraordinary painting, sheer magic, and it saved my life one day– I'll tell you about that, when we get there. Enough now to say, it was just a narrow village street, cobbles, cracked walls on both sides, very somber, deft strokes, brickwork in the right corner, a sort of purplish, dark center leading away, some chimneypots, doorways and shutters, just pure genius, spontaneous joy, absolute truth, not at all nice, bleak as could be, but undeniable. It probably took half an hour to do. Of course one doesn't know it didn't take him twenty years, but it had that look of casual mastery, of something simply done in a wink. Like something done just because it *could* be done, like the point of a life well-lived.

Now spare me your long-suffering look! It was hardly the most precious painting they stole, but it was the only one they really cared about. The others they chose for dollar value– they got quite a few really, but all together they didn't fetch the price they should have got for the Vlaminck, if the world had eyes and paid fair. Which it doesn't. And the money they did get didn't last long, as money won't. They were about broke by the time I met them.

Grumm's mother's name was Katherine, by the way. She liked art– who doesn't?– but she was not sentimental about the Vlaminck, especially once Bayou had found a new fence, someone eminently respectable, with good contacts, whose discretion could be counted on, someone absolutely beyond the law. It was getting to be quite a classy caper, and safe, with a whole fantastic future coming into view!

Bayou and Grumm doted on this painting. They were proud of it, not least of how they got it, and by the time I came on the scene it was the last one they had left, which made it all the dearer, a trophy, nostalgic, you might say.

They had created a world around it, down in Grumm's mother's basement, a little replica of a drawing room with gurgling, singing pipes overhead and all this stored junk and spiders and little sand ant-hills along cracks in the cement floor like a range of volcanoes and the furnace chugging away with the Vlaminck on one grungy wall with a spotlight on it. They had installed a little antique table with lion's feet and two old oak chairs and they would have a drink and look at the painting, and talk about it. They acted like lords.

Katherine almost never came down. She was too nervous, but still she wanted her cut. When she would ask when the great transaction was due to take place, and what they expected to get, Bayou would discourse about how priceless a work of genius it was, how shameful it would be to part with such a treasure for mere money, or at least how foolish it would be to let it go before they had lived in its aura for some considerable while. He even suggested they might sneak it back into the Museum so everybody else could enjoy it, which made Katherine go quite icy. After all, he said, they could always steal it again. He was amusing himself no doubt, which was what he did best, but Grumm took him seriously, and fell in love with the painting. Or got infatuated with possession, or the high remove of secrecy itself.

Bayou was not one bit romantic, but he did love to dream up macabre scenes of French peasant life behind the doors in that painting, which he said looked like black tombstones. They were more like miniature cathedral windows at night, according to Katherine, who could match him whimsy for whimsy, if it came to that. "Not my rainbow at all," she said to his grisly imaginings. For some reason he was intrigued by animal squalor, had pigs and sheep living inside with the people.

Those were the great days of smuggling– not rum-running like Manny Zora, but cannabis from Mexico and the Caribbean. Brade was going to make his fortune. He was the chef at the Colonial Inn, where Freida was hostess, poor thing. I resented her then, I don't envy her now. She could neither have him nor get away from him. And Arby drank there every night at the bar, his mournful eyes following her around, and she always found an errand or a chore for him.

Brade invested in a few voyages. He was going to buy the Inn. A boatload was worth a bundle. You'd see people suddenly driving Porsches. The F.B.I. was all over the place about that, too. It was a bit creepy when you met somebody new. You had no idea who they might be.

"Seduce him and find out what he's up to," Bayou said to me, when some stranger started mooching around for friends. That might be the one thing he ever told me to do that I didn't.

It wasn't all a bed of roses. I saw Mick Mulligan the day he got back from a year in a Jamaican jail. He was sitting on a bench looking out at the bay. I hardly recognized him. I said, "My God, where'e've *you* been?" He was always a very cocky guy, very big. He looked as frail as a boy. Or an old man. I never saw him like himself again.

Meanwhile, consorting with all these older men– there were several other affairs I won't mention– I consumed my youth. It went by without my even noticing. I was a frazzle. Everybody drank all the time. I don't mean they were drunk. There was just always an open bottle around, or they dropped into the Fo'c's'le for a quick shot– it souped them up, like race cars. Some of them at least. Not to mention hashish and mescaline and mushrooms and acid. People would turn up in town with a suitcase of pharmaceuticals. It was going to be a new world. The millennium was about to dawn, never mind that things were going smash at the moment. Smash was what was going to save us.

I listened to a lot of talk. Men seemed to do nothing *but* talk. I didn't know what to take to heart. I was typing for Wilberforce at the time. He was writing a book named *The Autobiography of a Nobody*, which he planned to publish himself. I remember Bayou saying, "For the kidnapper the child is the great imponderable, but the just-finished manuscript of a millionaire– that's the ideal hostage. Let me know when it's done."

I was mad for Bayou. Maybe you can imagine. He was pure, in a way. He lived to scheme. He was completely charming, kindly, solicitous, and distant as a star.

I wonder now if that wasn't when he got the idea of getting a fat ransom for the Vlaminck. They discussed it, but in the end he decided there was more hope with the insurance company than the museum, since the owner was a shyster himself. He drank champagne for breakfast every morning and always wore an ascot, a blue blazer and a black beret. He was notorious for acquiring paintings from poor artists. He'd wait till the middle of winter, and then he'd say like everyone else he was a bit embarrassed for cash, but it would be good for their career to be in his collection, and he'd give them a show and a nice opening— well, he would put out some Soave and cheese– after which the painting went into storage until the artist got pricey, I mean dead, and he never had to pay them.

Grumm would have liked to play Robin-hood. That would have been a real feather in his cap. He talked about sharing some of the proceeds with the artists. They– not Katherine– spent hours trying to think up safe ways to funnel money to various of their favorite painters, but finally Bayou got bored with philanthropic fantasies and faced the obvious, that they'd never squeeze a cent out of the owner. This was a man, by the way, who preferred repute to real possession. He was not deterred by forgeries. I think he collaborated in his own deception. And who's to say what's real if you don't want to know?

Then Bayou got the idea that once they'd banked the ransom for the Vlaminck, they'd demand some fantastic sum for the return of the other paintings, which they'd threaten to burn one by one if the money wasn't forthcoming pronto. It was all preposterous, but I never asked myself where it would end. It was like I was not really there– in more ways than one– I was in all these beds though.

Grumm got to be a nervous wreck. Katherine could hardly contain her impatience. She had to contend with a lot of talk herself. All she wanted was just to live a little. Grumm would have been glad to have her gone and out of his hair. Bayou simply got more whimsical and pretended to shilly-shally. The reason– the occasion– for these wild, new schemes was that the great new fence in Boston had warned Bayou never to communicate with him; he'd call Bayou when the time came. But he never called.

So they had time on their hands, and nothing to do but sit around and dream up more and more grandiose doings for the money. Which made it necessary to imagine a bigger and bigger payoff. They lavished themselves as if it were millions, a few paltry thousand dollars apiece, nothing on today's scale. Also I think Bayou just liked juggling ideas. As soon as he said something, he'd unsay it, or refine it till only a geometer could have made all the angles fit. I think he loved impossible puzzles.

Katherine of course wanted him to stay home every moment, in case the fence called. She'd get excruciatingly jumpy while he and Grumm hung around her basement with the Vlaminck. So long as there was enough to drink and smoke they could muse all day about the good life– which according to them meant having perfect mobility and no ties to anyone or anything. Katherine's eyes would go around and around the walls as if she were trying to find her way out of a maze. She begged for one of us always to be in Bayou's apartment 24 hours a day. She offered to do a shift herself, but of course he wouldn't hear of that, and the simple fact is, he never liked to hurry. He had a languid streak, like a mental voluptuary. He was hatching more schemes, and I think he wanted to keep the Vlaminck to amuse him until he had a new jewel to sit on.

His phone did ring one time when I was there alone. Whoever it was hung up when I said hello. I wonder now if it was Bayou. He'd just stepped out for cigarettes.

If Grumm hadn't spilled the beans that night in bed I would never have been sitting around with them all that time, listening to them pontificate. Poor Grumm– what he wanted was to *be* somebody. Money was a side-issue for Bayou, too. He loved the adventure, the challenge of it.

Bayou said to Katherine, "Veery could make us give her a cut, too."

"Veery is not mercenary," Katherine said. "She has no part in this."

I don't think she thought she did either. She assumed some saintly judge would be too gallant to involve her. After all, she was just Grumm's mother, and he owed her homage. It was her way of restoring him to his class, her class. She felt he'd fallen to manual labor and low companions. She wanted him to dress better and shave off his beard. And squire her around and be polite. She cared more for appearance than substance. She wouldn't have denied it. Of course Grumm always talked in terms of spiritual levels, and claimed she couldn't understand. About that stuff she could be quite derisory in a sly way. She was not a stupid woman.

I suppose in the end Grumm was standing me against Bayou and Katherine both. Once he'd told me about the Vlaminck he never made love to me again. From then on it was all just talk. We spent a lot of time in bed too. He claimed he wanted my advice, but he always scoffed at anything I said. And there was no reason really even to open my mouth, if you'll pardon me. He just wanted a way to listen to himself. He was almost always high by then, he never came down any more if he could help it. He needed me to sooth his jitters, bolster his ego. He'd started screwing his little acolytes—against all his principles. It was pure escapism.

All the while Freida was driving him mad. She couldn't help herself. She had to exercise her charms. Bayou and Grumm might have locked horns over her if she'd given them the chance, but she never flirted with them except separately, so neither knew what she was up to. They figured her for a frigid tease.

She was just honing her skills, trying to make Brade jealous, but he cared not one jot. Every once in a while he would give her bottom a good, resounding smack, like a connoisseur. And she would blush over her shoulder, with eyelids lowered. It was embarrassing. Love is a ludicrous thing. I don't mean he wasn't nice to her. It was an appreciative whack, nothing affectionate. She used to present herself, she couldn't help it. He was nice to everybody. It made no sense to him to make enemies.

Me he treated to lavish dinners on his nights off. He liked the best– Pepe's, waiters in white uniforms, the perfect bottle of wine, the finest liqueurs, and then a walk on the beach with a tremendous joint like an after-dinner cigar. He didn't like complications, which was why he liked me. For me he was a rest, pure luxury.

Brade was a would-be power-broker. He aimed to own the whole East End. He was seething with energy and ambition, hardly what you would call cool. Odd that Freida fell under his sway. Out of the kitchen he wore tweed jackets and looked like a doctor. She was the acme of hippie gypsy, all bangles and beads, black eyes and ethereal voice. She could almost float in those scarves and dark tresses. But he was absolutely impervious to anyone that didn't advance his fortunes. He was playing the market– according to him– like a zither. Down-payments was his mantra. He had a line on various ventures, and he did a little dealing in cocaine, too. That was back before it came into vogue. Not my cup of tea fortunately. In later years coke brought lots of my friends down, including Arby in due course, who in those days was always saying, *Seek what you will find*. It was like a shield against all follies. But all it was, was an excuse. It meant absolutely nothing. What he found was Freida. Ten years before. And never another thing in his whole life. And Freida was all he was ever true to. Even today he keeps her lawn mowed, fixes her faucets, does odd jobs, no matter that she's on her third husband. Everything else he betrayed or lost interest in. Many beginnings, no ends, or at least none of his own. He wore his shoulders up in a perpetual shrug. He was pure pathos to me, weak, or, as he would have said, strong in his weakness. I suppose I just wanted to comfort him. I couldn't stand to see Freida winding Bayou around her finger. It seemed out of sync with the universe.

He was my god. I was already horribly tormented. But that was like an assault on my pride. By then at least I'd got my fill of Grumm. The faster he fell apart, the more sententious he grew. There was a doomsday atmosphere around everything anyway. Live today, die tomorrow. It's hard to imagine this is 1983, that whole world gone and forgotten, except for vestiges, like ourselves.

Ah, yes, the painting. Another little taste? So much talking dries the tongue. Katherine turned into a monster once she learned about the Vlaminck. Before that she was only Madame Crème de Menthe to me— that sticky green. I used to love it, it almost did me in, or something did. I suppose it was the mix.

She'd try to pump me about Grumm, give me bees for his bonnet about moving back to Westchester. She said I'd love it there. This had started even *before* she learned about the heist.

Grumm was living with a lot of people out on Race Road, and couldn't hide the paintings there. Bayou wouldn't let them in his house. All but the Vlaminck went out of her basement in duffel bags one or two at a time to a fence in Providence without her ever noticing. But one day when Bayou and Grumm kept coming up for ice she went down to investigate and found them like acolytes at an altar. All that was lacking were some candles. She wound up feeling cheated not to have been cut in from Day One. It was her basement after all. There was a loud, dumb song in those days, We want the WORLD, and we want it NOW.

Fortunately she could never figure out— and for a long time neither could I— where all the money from the first paintings went. Bayou had a catch-all phrase for plans gone wrong, "Gurgle-gurgle," which always made Grumm wince. I finally deduced that Bayou had talked Grumm into letting him try his luck in the futures market, and once they started losing it just disappeared. I'm glad Katherine never knew, she was already miffed enough that it was all gone, and never a penny to her.

She was relentless, she never let up on my sympathy, aging away in this sordid burg with her degenerating son. She wanted me to reform him and settle down *en famille* in some idyllic suburb— anywhere really, so long as it wasn't Provincetown— with her ensconced nearby, though what she at present most urgently needed and justly deserved after her recent life of privations was a sojourn in Paris, where she had once had the "summer of her life," as she called it, back in her salad days, before she got married and had Grumm.

Of course I would never have tried to influence Bayou— or even hint that the painting should be unloaded sooner than later. I could not have conceived of such presumption.

In this at least Grumm by now agreed with his mother, but he didn't talk to her about it. Or anything else. They were never in collusion. For this once they happened to be on the same side. He just wanted to get it over with and get the money. He had begun planning to open an ashram in the Green Mountains. A whole swindle of yurts. He certainly hadn't told her any of that.

I was experiencing memory loss, I mean blackouts, finding out days later what I'd said or done from someone else. Other people knew more about me than I did myself. They'd say, "Well, yes, Veery, you did, you actually did that, it was pretty impressive, it really was."

Crazy things were going on all around. There were continuous accidents of one kind or another. Fires especially. Contusions. Car wrecks, walking off of roofs. Everyone seemed to be wearing a cast or an eye patch. I was scared of myself, I was so volatile. I'd fly off the handle and give anyone, particularly strangers, a piece of my mind on whatever subject was being hashed, never mind whether I knew or cared one bit about it. I had all the answers to everything except my own questions. A little like you used to be, come to think. And now look at you!

Thank you. And to yours. That's all that matters now, isn't it? Life is simpler at least. Shorter. What's left of it. I have no regrets. I wouldn't want to do it again. Or I would do it differently. Who wouldn't?

Arby was cheering on the Viet Cong, ranting about The System. He wanted to see the country's face rubbed in its own filth. Up the Revolution! Down with everything! Destruction is creation!

Bayou laughed at me for being possessive and I slapped him. Then he laughed at me for calling Freida a slut.

Brade got flying one night. He talked about running the town some day, having henchmen on all the right boards. He wanted to put a boardwalk around the town like the Fontainbleau in Quebec and build a causeway with a pleasure palace on the end of it out in the middle of the bay, a huge casino with everything anyone could imagine. Kubla Khan. After which he'd be a billionaire, and ready to move on.

"Money is all that talks," he said. "You just have to know the language. And buy, buy, buy. Don't let anything stop you. Never. Not for one minute."

Grumm kept himself so high he almost disappeared. At that point I guess he'd braced himself to wait it out. He kept repeating, "All in the fullness of time," as if I were disputing him.

I was desolate. The worst was I didn't trust myself any more. I'd resolve to sleep alone, but after I'd got done my day with

Wilberforce– there's another tale, believe me– I'd need a few drinks, and by the end of the night I'd be in somebody's bed, like as not listening to some dreadful sob story about how the guy had lost his wife by having a fling with somebody like me. Some interesting characters I met.

Eventually of course the fence called and the Vlaminck had to go. That was the very day I decided to visit Elena. She'd written recommendations for me. Her house was always a refuge where I could take stock and pull myself together. She was a very elegant person, genteel without being naive or foolish. She was fond of me, I know, and I would always go away with a good feeling. She was a real pick-me-up, an inspiration and a lively conversationalist, very wise, kind and calm. She was sixty-five-ish and still beautiful. She never wore makeup and she always dressed very nicely. Her husband left her some money.

Well, she was drunk. I'd never seen it before. I didn't want to see it then. I didn't want a drink either, but she made me have one. She made me sit down and stay a while, just for form's sake. She was horribly slow and sloppy. I'd worn a beautiful pair of boots she'd given me, that I never could have afforded. I don't think she even noticed. After a bit she sat sideways and looked out the window. It was two o'clock in the afternoon. She was still in her slippers and dressing gown. Her wig was askew. I didn't even know she wore one. Her face was all pouched and red. Her eyes were watery. Her words were like moths on her tongue.

I was sick in my heart, sick in my soul. I could see her sinking into silence, losing her will to speak. It was absolutely appalling. The silences got longer and longer. I'd ask her a question. It was a great undertaking for her to answer. She said she'd stopped going out, she'd stopped reading, stopped going to the hospital– she did volunteer work in Hyannis– stopped everything actually but feeding her schnauzer that she always carried under one arm when she left the house.

I tried to commiserate, but she wouldn't respond. It was like she was beyond despair, as if I wasn't even there. Nor her either. I was terrified. After a while she talked out the window at the water, just meandering, making chat about nothing, about how beautiful deer eyes were, is what I remember. Apparently she'd been up in Maine, in a cabin with the Vice Admirable, this English leech she was attached to somehow. I didn't like to think about that.

Anyhow, he hung a gutted doe from a tree outside and when she woke from a nap and saw it she threw up. The VA was quite irritated. She said, "We can't all be soldiers, I suppose."

That, "I suppose," was so like her. Only once did she turn her head and look at me straight on, and I had the strangest feeling that she pitied me. On my way out she said, "It's always nice to see you, Veery. I'm glad you're doing so well."

I couldn't help seeing what a mess the house was. It was like a vision of hell. She was usually impeccable. I wondered if the Admiral had moved in or something. I never understood what she was doing with him. I thought: Is this what's going to happen to me?

I was in a state of shock, my only prop in this town– in my whole life– knocked right out from under me.

All I wanted was to get blotto. Just forget everything. I went to the Bradford, and ordered a rusty nail. I haven't touched one of those things in years. I must have been looking for lockjaw.

Bayou saw me in the window. He came in and said, "Want to have a last look?"

"No," I said, "I don't."

"It's going tomorrow. Come on, we're having a Bon Voyage party."

He looked a bit subdued. Of course I was bereaved, too, but that painting seemed the least of my losses. I felt like I was becoming a multiple personality monster, trying to minister to so many men. But I never said No to Bayou. So I pounded down my nail and we walked over to Grumm's mother's in the rain. It was drenching weather, with a lot of wind. The trees were thrashing. And it just blew into my head that my life and the whole world I lived in was a worthless botch best blown sky high. I should have had a stick of dynamite.

Grumm was there. And Katherine. And a bottle of vodka. And the Vlaminck. We all stood around like it was an opening. Katherine put out some cashews. Still, it seemed as hushed as a wake. With this pile of packing materials in one corner, just waiting for the last rites to end. I had no reason to be there. I didn't belong. There or anywhere.

It's so hard to gauge the reactions of youth. I might just as well have been thankfully looking forward to a more normal life, such as skipping town, like them. But what happened— I can hardly explain this— I simply became mesmerized by the painting, like I was stoned in some new way. I walked away from the talk— there was a third and fourth chair now— and it caught me somehow. I stared at it for the longest time. I'd already looked at it plenty. I knew quite well what it looked like— I can see it now— but this was different, some sort of coalescence in the eye. Deafening, too. It was a very powerful sensation, like leaving everything behind. I can still feel how stunned I felt, how exalted. I can remember in the abstract too what I took from it, and keep to this day– aside from the gratitude that comes of awe of human greatness– the sense that all things are malleable and one both. Is this mumbo jumbo? Where's Grumm when I need him?

We were sorry to see it go, all right, even Katherine. It became a solemn occasion, even while they slavered for the payoff. So, the long-awaited moment was a bit of a bummer, I never heard what the agreed-on price was. That's how much I cared, because suddenly they seemed like crazy strangers, and then I'd look at the painting and get separated all over again. It was like making my getaway.

From then on things went wrong. The next morning the fancy fence in Boston halved his offer, and by noon he'd withdrawn it entirely. Then there were endless wrangles in Katherine's living room about how to proceed– she'd developed quite decided opinions– and after that pretty much nobody went there except me. She would summon me, or they would send me to reconnoiter, and I would drink little sips of vodka in her living room and tell her I didn't know anything about anything and didn't really want to. I remember her looking at me quite cold-eyed, like a traitor.

Which was more or less warranted. I'd canceled the whole thing out of my mind. She never let slip anything I could take back to Grumm and Bayou. By this time I was nothing but an emissary or a spy. I was supposed to keep them all up on each other, I was a way to keep them all on the straight and narrow. I don't mean they thought any of them would sell the painting and abscond, only that someone might crack or say something careless somewhere.

It got more and more ominous. The rain never stopped. One of Grumm's little tricks came down with a baby of her own, but it had no effect on him. "She's an adult." he said. "I can't worry about the whole world. Abortions are easy."

They were now preoccupied with finding a new fence who would give them a price equal to their deserts. They refused to go back to the small-time thief in Providence whom they now considered to have fleeced them on the earlier paintings, and they demanded the Vlaminck compensate for that too.

Grumm said, "And for the wear and tear on the nerves."

"For our loss," Bayou said. "When the time comes. Right, Veery?"

I just nodded. I didn't say a word any more unless I had to.

The Vlaminck never got unwrapped. It stayed in its layers of plastic and blankets in a special wooden box Grumm had made for it, absolutely beautiful too. Even Grumm never went back any more. One day– or rather night– they packed up the basement. Bayou retrieved his table and chairs. The spotlight came down. I think they knew they'd never have it so good again. They were planning to rob another museum up-Cape– of course they didn't tell Katherine– but there was nothing there they really coveted, nothing that really took their fancy. Their ardor was gone. This was strictly business.

Things had gotten serious finally, and want of money owned them. And cabin fever. There was a lot of talk about palm trees and out-of-the-way, little beach towns in Puerto Rico where no one ever went, where life was simple and the people were nice. The minute they got rid of the painting they were all going to get out of town, they were going to scatter, even me, when June came. I wonder where I would have gone. People were always talking about leaving– it was practically an avocation– and some succeeded, generally on the lam or in a coffin, or so it seemed.

According to Bayou it would all have worked out if it weren't for Katherine. He says they agreed to hold off till the heat went down. Rumor was that some of the first paintings had turned up and certain dealers were being squeezed for information. He says Katherine disguised her voice as a man's and called the fence in Providence, whose phone was tapped.

Katherine claims Grumm played F.B.I. and called the museum to ask what company insured the painting. The curator said he didn't know, but he'd find out, if Grumm would call back the next day, and the cops covered the pay phones and caught him.

Grumm insists Bayou lost his address book at some stranger's party he wandered into when he was drunk. Someone took it to the police and they recognized some of the phone numbers and tapped his phone.

Of course the indictment got all snarled up. "Just don't lie," Bayou told me. Grumm said, "Deny everything." I was the ghost that never got called, never even got mentioned. In the end they didn't make much of a defense, didn't even try. Grumm was too flummoxed, Bayou too flippant, and all of them were too ornery. And unworldly. Katherine was half-right at least. She didn't get charged, but only because they both upheld her alibi that she knew absolutely nothing. The judge said, "Meet the son you raised."

And the Vlaminck? The Vlaminck went back to the museum, which moved out of town, too. The owner felt unappreciated. You could say I was the one who got to keep it.

The other thing I've never forgotten–a sort of second saving grace– I went to see Elena again. It took me about a month to screw up my courage. By then I hadn't the courage *not* to go. I meant to try to befriend her, after all she'd done for me. I was really afraid of what I'd find. I went about noon, for fear she'd be plastered if I went any later.

She was fine. She acted as if nothing had happened– or would-n't deign to give it the time of day. I was certainly too young to bring it up. She made me a nice lunch, and I went away very much reas-sured– I can't tell you how much it meant to me.

She's dead of course– out in the cemetery with her husband, whom I regret I never met– but I remember her quite clearly. She was like... what... a meadowlark? Freida would be a blackbird, I guess, Ruzo a sparrow, Brade a scarlet tanager, Bayou a grosbeak. Grumm a mourning dove, Katherine some sort of wren. You I'd hesitate to say– maybe an ovenbird, once removed. Twice.

Can you read that? I know– to you we're all magpies, parrots, cuckoos, crows. I shouldn't make light. The time is gone. People grew into themselves, like cages, wherever they meant to go. We were the last of the troglodytes. After that it was all feminism and CR groups. People coming out left and right. And whoever you were or whatever you'd done, tell all! The worse the better!

Mortification! The new glory! Not for me. I didn't want to gang up on men either. I just wanted one of my own, but that never hap-pened for long, and finally I got over it. After which I went from fag hag to recluse, and now it's years since I could put up with a lot of talk in my house.

My cat's enough. He's sixteen. But he still limps out at night and sleeps all day and he still gets chewed up every time some female yowls. And then I have to pop the pus out of his boils. Otherwise they get infected. I can't be taking him to the vet all the time. Not on my salary, with my rent.

He's my lion tiger, he leaves a carcass on my back doorstep every dawn, bloody little chunks of fur, for which I have my special broom. I guess it keeps him going, and I'm used to it. What can you do? Even domesticated mammals can't be made to change. Of course I would never geld a cat. Nor fix a female either, nor have one for a pet, I must admit. I never wanted children, thank god. I don't envy anyone. Not anymore. I've got my window on the woods, and a good pair of hiking boots. That's all National Seashore out there. Audubon would love it.

Of course I never dreamt I'd end up here. I didn't know any place like this existed, even after I'd been here a while. I doubt I ever would have come if I had, much less have stayed. I wouldn't have had the nerve. I wouldn't have known enough. Life's a risk, I guess. All surprise, good or bad.

Well, I don't know about you, but I'm going to bed. Coming? Pardon my humor. You know, we might have done once. So many years ago. We almost did, the night we met, remember? That would have been quite something! Can you imagine? We would have been too young. What use? I can't say I'm sorry. We never would have had this night. Still, I wonder why we didn't. Good luck, I guess. Shyness. Angst of incest. Pride.

THE FREEDOM OF SHADOWS

Rima's first marriage, an elopement in 1950, begot dire prophecies. Both were nineteen, the boy an Irish Catholic prole with an uncontrollable temper and half a dozen lost jobs, she a bourgeois Jew, sales-clerk in a department store, rambunctious herself and sweetly naive, eager to start life on her own.

Overnight the streets of Rochester became a hell, while the newly-weds, hounded by mounting debts, slid downwards from slum to ghetto. Every day they were bound to meet some meddling or mettlesome clan member, finally fled to South Boston, where an uncle of a buddy of his ran a boarding house. There, marooned in two rooms, they fought like savages.

A daughter, Nikki, conceived in a grudging embrace, born toward the start of their second year, led to no truce. The father, at odds with the quenchless monotony of his fate as a house-painter, harnessed behind bib and shoulder straps of white coveralls caked stiff with the same hated color, had always drunk to oblivion; now he began to beat Rima for having stolen his freedom.

One Saturday afternoon, while he was roaming the bars, she took the baby home to Rochester on the bus. Her mother welcomed her first grand-child with unmitigated delight, but Rima's father did not cease to regard his apostate daughter as dead, and refused to speak to her or permit her name to be spoken in the house.

Harried by raging phone calls, wretched at home, Rima filed for divorce, left the baby with her mother, and bussed to West Palm Beach, where family connections had an air conditioner sales and rental business.

Florida had always meant glamour to her, and it felt only fair to seize what was left of her fleeting youth. She loved the lines of pelicans sailing down the beach on still wings, gratified to see how tan she could get, oiling her lithe, blond body, basking in the glances of passersby. Half giddy, half shy, she was wary of complications, and kept to older men.

But she slept with too many, repelled by the pathos of pity, irked by their un-sooth-able worries and woes, shamed by their indulgences. Her innards rebelled and eventually she stopped dating, lived on cigarettes and coffee, at dawn found herself sitting at the kitchen table, playing solitaire, weeping because the cards refused to fall right, unable to go to bed till they did. Haunted by thoughts of suicide, she was deterred by fears of death's deeper solitude.

She was briefly distracted by a dental student, who bought her flowers, took her to auctions and concerts, and proposed to her when she got pregnant. She knew it for an act of honor and penance, and secretly borrowed money for an abortion.

He went home to St. Augustine for a few days to gain some perspective, while she, having followed circuitous directions to the anonymous door with no knob at the end of an unlighted lane in the suburbs, handed the gaunt woman in soiled, blue smock a sum it would take her six months to repay, consigned herself to what appeared to be the kitchen table, sustained after three hours of excruciatingly induced contractions an inadvertent glimpse of the maimed homunculus on its way to the garbage can, was then urged to rest for a minute, received a vial of pills to stanch potential bleeding, was escorted out a different door, found a parked taxi, and got home safe, her errand unknown to anyone. She recovered quickly, but felt removed from everyone and everything.

The dental student never called, nor did she call him. When they chanced to meet a month later, it took him three screw-drivers to admit that, though he was deeply fond of and would never forget her, he was now engaged to his old high school girlfriend. The tragic look on his rosy face made Rima laugh.

She met others, too many to remember, somehow all the same. It was not the life she had envisaged, but there seemed no escape, and she slept around more and more heedlessly, which led again to frenzied boredom, disgust, fear, and the resumption of chastity.

Tinged with hysteria at both poles, these cycles lasted until her twenty-sixth year, when she fell in love with Abe Katz, a labor organizer on vacation. He was a familiar relief after the gentile sybarites who had drawn her so far from her orthodox origins, and she was suddenly, completely happy.

Owlish and strong, with a beautiful, untroubled certainty of action and never a doubt about adopting her daughter, Abe moved her to his apartment in Queens, married her, bought a house, conquered his qualms and advanced into management.

Rima's now widowed mother, however, having moved to Los Angeles to rejoin her family, would not part with Nikki, who had no memory of either parent, a providential arrangement Rima accepted without regret.

Over the next decade Rima enjoyed a more consummated motherhood. Lillian and Morris were born in 1959 and '61. Abe, bent on security for them, worked long hours, eventually spending weekends at the Newark factory office. The babies were often Rima's only company, along with the radio, cigarettes and coffee. Once she dreamed she made love with Janis Joplin with jewelry on. She was bemused, but Abe was upset, as if she were guilty in fact. She had told him nothing of her past amours because of his strict conventionality, and therefore was dumfounded when one Saturday morning in the seventh year of her marriage she got a phone call summoning her to an executive session with the elders of the company Abe had served so avidly.

While he stood pale and silent, as if to receive a surprise award, she was presented with the evidence of a lie detector test that had been forced on him, handed in writing the name and address of his mistress, and told that both miscreants were thereby dismissed.

The woman in question, the comptroller, was not present at this event, which lasted but a bare minute, at least in Rima's dazed memory, and only in retrospect did it seem strange and barbaric. Fortunately no funds were missing; no legal action ensued; no permanent harm had been done, except perhaps to Abe's psyche.

It was the wholeness of his guile that stuck with Rima. She had never suspected; he had let slip no clue. Moreover Abe's secret life seemed to mean nothing, to have virtually no consequences, and soon faded in their mutual outrage at the humiliation inflicted on them. Her rival was hardly a threatening figure or face— careworn, spinsterish, unselfconscious— whom in any case Abe claimed to be relieved to be free of. He swore, without the slightest pressure from Rima, never again to betray her. She realized that she had reason neither to accept nor doubt his word.

Malfeasance made him. With almost triumphal ease he found in Manhattan a better job at twice his old salary, plus stock and princely incentives, but his alteration was complete. The last vestiges of class solidarity and anger at injustice vanished, his union bonds having snapped under the weight of wedlock, mortgage and the advent of heirs.

"Growth!" he vowed now. "Enterprise! Productivity!" He dressed ever more fastidiously, had haircuts by regular appointment, and a monthly manicure, gone his former shaggy, rumpled self. Now he expressed only pleasant platitudes, kept an eye on Rima in public, became a model of suavity, flawless in demeanor, even at home, always imperturbably reserved. Rima never knew what he was thinking; making love she could hardly tell when he came.

In the summer of 1971 they rented for a song a spacious house on the bay in Provincetown from silent partners of Abe's firm, Dal and Ida Shevell, who were going to Spain "for a change of venue." The Shevells spent much of June enjoying their own guest quarters, making sure the Katzes got acquainted with the right people and ways of beach life.

Dal and Ida were redoubtable partiers, forever rolling joints, inventing exotic cocktails, experimenting with mescaline and mushrooms, wafting from scene to scene. The Katzes acquired a blur of new names and faces to match each morning, while the Shevells held their hoarse, uproarious postmortems of the past night's novelties and escapades. Then, after a Bloody Mary on the deck, if the tide were in they went for a swim, or waded out on the flats till they dwindled to wisps.

By the time the Shevells left for Barcelona, histrionically bewailing their lot, Rima was half-delirious with joy. The pristine dawns made her want to weep. The elemental sea and sky reflected perfect fulfillment, and the long days on the beach with Lillian and Morris seemed idyllic, but as the pink and orange sunsets faded and dusk came on she suffered a sharp nostalgia for Floridian nights. Among people whose purpose was to spend not save money, for whom leisure was the rule, pleasure the goal, ennui the enemy, she found herself curious again about other men.

"Abe, you've got to take care of me now, I need you, you've got to look out for me," she told him quite directly one night. "We don't even talk anymore."

"I swam all the way to Cold Storage Beach and back," he said. "I'm tired."

"Abe, I'm in trouble," she said. "Something's happening. I don't want anything to happen."

He turned on the pillow and looked at her unblinkingly. "You're a big girl now, you've got to cope," he said turning his face away.

Eventually she slept, but woke at first light and walked the beach, wondering miserably if all this were merely in the cards. She never spoke of it, but her life once again was a shambles, and at blank moments her heart quailed. She was amazed at the incongruous finality of the incident, no more in fact than a single phrase. In a week it passed beyond forgiveness, and she sensed in herself a sort of turning aside, a distaste, an impatience, a weariness with this mannequin she had married, who drank abstemiously, patronized the children, and swam all day like an athlete in training.

Everything began to seem unreal. Abe was handsome and virile and preferred the company of women, and now Rima half-wished he would have another affair, but he was preoccupied. For the first time in his life he was making a lot of money and seemed to see a clear way into the future. He spent hours on the phone and more and more time in travel, the object of which he no longer made any pretense of explaining. She was glad to see him go, but despite her resolves the moment he got back she grew distraught. Lines deepened around her mouth, digging toward the lips, and she grayed from constant chain-smoking, at parties sometimes laughed so loudly at so little that he accused her of embarrassing others. She taunted him bitterly for faults she had once doted on, aghast at her new shrill voice, while the children's moon faces orbited on the edge of her vision. He refused to quarrel, said she was behaving irrationally, left the house. One day in resentment she asked if he wanted a divorce.

In surprise he asked, "What for? You're having a good time, aren't you?"

She writhed at this remark and worried about the morose children. Lillian looked after Morris, the neighbors frequently fed them, and indeed they seemed to enjoy leading the life of adults outside the house. There were dreadful moments when she saw them as no more hers than Nikki, knew she had failed as a mother. She dreamt, but never told Abe– never told him anything anymore– that having gone to a movie with the Shevells, they had rolled her on a gurney out in front of the screen, where she had given birth to a tyrannosaurus, then refused to nurse it and was ostracized by a circle of almost-familiar strangers, who began to grow scales on their lizardlike faces.

On the Fourth of July, hung-over from the previous night's bash, she and Abe walked gingerly into town and stood on the curb to watch the parade.

The majorettes couldn't catch their batons, even on the bounce. The disheveled band thumped and shrilled out of cadence and key, followed by a few World War II and Korean veterans trying to keep in step, then a troop of Cub Scouts with plastic rifles, after which all was outlandish, private, defiant– floats of psychedelic flowers and rainbow-colored dream-scapes, ostentatious freaks and flipped-out types in eastern robes, an Uncle Sam with a small, black mustache and a flag with swastikas instead of stars, an alligator on stilts, camp and drag, bump and grind, drug graffiti, peace slogans, hippie families gaunt as migrant farmers, a rollicking reggae band on a flatbed truck, which got grins and loud kudos from a group of otherwise impassive blacks, brown-baggers, staggering stragglers gawking left and right, seemingly unaware they were part of a larger procession. A motley, lethargic train of fun-seekers joined the end and then the whole throng flowed together to the center of town as toward a drain.

It was the nadir of an awful week. The Pentagon Papers, briefly suppressed, had resumed giving the lie to official pronouncements, appalling the faithful and doubters alike. The war was being lost; the boys were coming home pell-mell, drug-ridden and unwelcome; the whole country was disintegrating.

Tears burned Rima's eyes and she groped for Abe's hand in the crush. With sternly averted face, he locked his fingers hard in hers and she realized with a chill that his eyes too were burning as he forged a path homeward through the mob, both of them too demoralized to speak.

The next day they heard that a strayed marcher had fallen off the wharf around noon and drowned, and by sundown another reveler had succumbed to heroin in the men's room of the Town House Lounge.

On the 6th three Russian cosmonauts were found eerily dead in repose when the hatch of Soyuz II was opened, reminiscent of the hapless flickers caught behind the fan in the Shevell's stove vent the day the Katzes moved in. The children's eyes had stayed wide for hours, staring at the perched birds, lifelike and still.

"They got in where they didn't belong," Abe told them. "There's no one to blame."

"No one to blame, no one to blame, Rima's mind helplessly rhymed like a radio theme she hated but couldn't shake, and she dreamt of large insects blurred behind screens, dressed in space helmets and tubular suits.

On the 10th, about three p.m., while she was home alone, she heard a gong resound in the street. Then came a pounding at the front door, which flew open to admit a grim man with a pistol who pushed past her and rushed from room to room. She cowered in a corner of the foyer till he departed, ominously touching the muzzle to his lips.

She slid to the floor with relief, and another wild-eyed stranger burst in with a baseball bat. He had a policeman's cap on backwards, an open blue suit jacket over a bare chest, Bermuda shorts and flip-flops. "Did you see a man with red hair come in here?" he demanded.

Rima struggled to her feet and tried to describe, starting with the mysterious gong, but in fact the gun-waver had distinctly black hair, and at that point in her breathless account her interlocutor ran off down the street with his bat.

She was still shaking when Abe got home. He listened but found nothing to say. They never told the children, as the episode raised questions they could conceive no answers to, and it soon slipped from mind.

As if Rima had now to endure yet a third youth, the men she had met began to pursue her less and less discreetly, and one, a friend of Abe's from the old days, whose own marriage was crumbling, declared over cocktails that he knew exactly what was wrong with hers, knew to the last nuance what she was thinking, felt as she felt in all things. He said he too was unbearably lonely, ended by suggesting a tryst on Nantucket.

His lugubrious face seemed to weep even more when he smiled; she had liked him once, wished she could comfort him now, but had no illusions, and hoped he was too shaky to notice her wince of repugnance.

What had happened to him? His clothes smelt of ill-health and stale sweat, his hair and beard had grown long and unkempt, and he exuded a kind of sly, complicit woe, as if claiming her as kin in his ruin. He came to the house twice more, chiefly it seemed to drink, though he didn't scruple to renew his proposition. Then he disappeared; next she heard he'd been hospitalized, but only a week or so later she saw him hunching the street with a glassy-eyed girl who looked to be still in her teens.

Early in August, walking the beach, Rima chanced upon a man she had met at a party named Smitherill. He had talked nearly nonstop in a silken monotone, with an air of inviolable concentration, dominating every subject that came up, like an intellectual acrobat past caring for his audience— she felt sure he wouldn't remember her.

"I forgot your name," she said, smiling.

"John," he said. "And you're Rima."

"How nice of you to know," she said.

He bowed with aplomb. "I asked someone."

Without prelude or provocation he began discoursing on the black holes of space, shells of burnt-out stars collapsing on their cores of irresistible gravity till they explode in supernovas or disappear into reverse cornucopias of void that swallow even light, previews of the end of the present universe, when every atom will be compacted in the final paradigm, followed by nothing at all, or only another grand bang and then something else, or merely maybe more of the same.

"And doubtless this is the one possible world," he admonished. "That is to say, both best and worst."

"Are you obsessed?" she asked.

"I read it in the Sunday Times," he said, and went on with his explication, pedantic and dry, refuting objections she had not raised, till it occurred to her that he wanted revenge.

"And yet," he shook a finger, his eyebrows jumped, and little perplexed commas set off his mouth, "black holes project more energy than anything."

She shaded her eyes at the faint weirs afloat in the shimmering glow of low tide, said he took an irrelevant view of life, and suddenly he became all agreement. They sat down in the sand, gossiped about people it turned out they both knew, laughed frankly, their fingers touching over matches and cigarettes.

The next morning Rima drove Abe to the airport in sharp suit and bronzed face, eyes clear as a window on nothing. The girl at the counter greeted him with pert deference. A small, red plane taxied close. He and three other men, each with a valise, mounted the wing, bent and squeezed in.

The slightly rocking plane whirred slowly away, turned down an alley through tall, yellow cord-grass, vanished into silence. In a moment the whirring resumed, then roared, grew loud and louder, a flash of red skimmed toward the trees, disappeared perilously, stopping her heart till it cleared the shadow, rose steadily, turned black as a fly, diminished to a dancing spot on the blue, with one last, faint wave of sound was gone.

Rima was filled with dread. A neighbor was on her deck, holding a drink.

"Life's a bowl of shit," Nancy said.

"Really?" Rima said, deciding not to skip the drink. "What's the matter?"

"Ohhh," Nancy allowed, "Sammy."

"I just put mine on a plane to Chicago, and he can stay as long as he likes," Rima said pleasantly, and went inside to put on a bathing suit.

A week of perfect weather passed. She walked the flats, dreamy, almost content, picking up anonymous nubs and bits of sea-polished debris– bone, porcelain, stone– shaking them together in her hand like dice, dimly aware of earlier times and people long dead, then tossed them away to favor some new find, while the pure sun poured down, tingling her skin, giving her a sense of nearly intolerable well-being and sensual delight. At dusk she would loiter naked at the mirror, cleansed of salt, dazzled by her bright eyes and teeth, white buttocks and breasts.

Then came a spell of grey days— windless, humid, all colors, all distances merged. The beach was oppressive with rank smells and swarms of gnats, ankle fleas and ferocious, green flies that bit back of the knees or stung the armpits, couldn't be driven off, attacked until killed. At intervals in the stagnant haze a resolute few could be seen twisting and turning, flailing towels.

She took to strolling Commercial Street with its teeming bars and shops, its stalled line of cars and hordes of day-trippers, rubberneckers, thwarted sun-seekers, workers intent on getting somewhere, street and sidewalk so crowded it was like bathing in people, awash in a quiet hubbub of voices and feet.

Ragged kids sat on the curb like sparrows or wandered with sleeping bags, accosting each other, "Know anyplace I can crash?" There was always a bereft-looking girl with tangled hair and a thin kitten clinging to her breast. Everyone seemed to have a guitar.

Periodically one would thrum a careful, soft chord, bend an ear to appraise, then still the strings with gentle palm, and gaze off again into space. Saturating all was an odor of patchouli and incense, and a slightly-crazed atmosphere, as if anything might happen, as if the lemming mutterers might at any moment head for the edge.

Often the emaciated, hirsute young men looked quite saint-like, and once Rima happened on a poignant scene in the high school parking lot, where a burlap-clad couple was giving away their possessions— bed, chairs, bureau, records, dishes, shoes— with terrifying expressions of beatitude. A blended murmur of approval, awe and contempt came from the cynical or greedy or grateful, who made off speedily through the mob with their loot.

But the strangest, most haunting occurrence, was something Rima never saw, never had an inkling of. Amid the crowded noontime street a man's voice, startled to an unnatural tenor, cried out: "I don't believe it, I don't believe what I just saw, I don't, I don't, I just don't believe it!"

She spun round with her girlish gaze, stood while the throng jostled past, looked and looked but saw nothing of note, could not even identify the incredulous one, but she wondered wildly what he had seen, and it recurred as an intermittent worry that woke her before dawn or gave her pause at trivial decisions.

She had begun to spend her late evenings at a more or less perpetual party, which only got into full swing when the bars closed, then held sway until two or three or four a.m. in a spacious, summer house high on a dune, with the lights of Wellfleet winking through the grove of sinuous locusts that climbed the slope. The jerry-rigged place was all windows of different sizes, screen porches, tiers of little terraces built with railroad ties and lighted by lanterns. On wet nights there was always a robust, log blaze in the noble, boulder fireplace. A crew of attractive youths, offspring and friends of the host and hostess, kept the music playing, the liquor flowing, snacks passing, and no one was ever in want of anything.

MacKenzie Rex and his wife Venus were right out of Fitzgerald, as all were bound to observe, though elders thought the scene had a touch of the Gay Nineties. Mack himself was a man all charm, all grace, never at a loss to put the awkward at ease, and he always wore a fresh, white, dress jacket and rose cummerbund. On exceptionally hot nights he dispensed with a shirt, baring a shapely chest well-tanned and feathered with lushly-curling, silvery hairs.

Venus was the most animated of matrons, the slimmest, most silkenly-voluptuous and insinuating that could be imagined, yet good-hearted, down-to-earth and dignified withal, so that Rima felt less and less an ingénue as the nights flew by.

"They don't take part," someone said. "They set these things up to watch."

In fact the house was full of mirrors: one could hardly escape oneself, and a whole wall of the living-dancing room served as a screen for an ongoing film of past festivities, while an attendant youth went about unobtrusively documenting the current moment. A little nerve-racking at first, the effect soon proved addicting– total experience, all senses engaged– so that one was apt to become bored elsewhere, and head for the MacKenzie Rexes, once midnight had tolled.

"They work hard all winter. He makes a lot of money. They come here every summer. They just like to give people a good time," retorted a regular with asperity.

Such banalities were scoffed at by cynics looking for flaws, hoping to witness a downfall.

Certainly the Rexes were not libertines themselves. Though they always had a glass in hand it was always empty, and they were reputed to care only for each other, as the number and fondness of their children and their children's friends seemed to attest.

"All things human come to ruin," said faintly-smiling Smitherill. "What will happen here?"

Chagrins and triumphs went cheek 'n jowl, and one might get caressed or ego crushed or both before a night was out. The selection of young men standing around looked like rough trade, but proved to be well-spoken and genteel, at least until Cupid emptied his quiver. Rima found herself courted by a dissolute pair, Stoodles and Ponze, with whom it soon grew impossible to cope.

She enjoyed them sober, for they vied with gallantries— luxurious state of affairs— but toward the wee hours they invariably got bombed on the limitless cases of beer stacked in the two refrigerators devoted exclusively to liquid refreshment in the Rexes vast, comforting kitchen, where someone was always frying linguica and chopping onions and potatoes for hash-browns to go with platters of buttery, creamy, scrambled eggs and toast.

All in a trice, as if a joker had juggled a vase or a twerp twirled the chandelier, her swains changed utterly, forgot they were pals, gave chivalry a kick in the pants, no longer attended Rima in tandem, maligned one another by turns, and half-suffocated her with their demands.

Stoodles tended to wheedle and whine, then grovel, finally descend into piteousness and threaten suicide unless she yielded, while surly Ponze made imperial declarations, received rebuffs with cool, stoical gloom, but went on secret rampages, appearing a day or so hence with black eye or bandaged knuckles, once confessing to have bumped into a telephone pole, then punched it.

As soon as one stalked off to sulk the other popped up full of hope. It was like being caught in a vice, though gratifying not to have lost the knack of driving men mad, with little or no effort on her part— quite the contrary— and once glommed on there was no shaking them off. Bemused, she mocked her plight with the thought of going back to her mother, joked that a husband might yet have a use.

"You're cutting a swath through P-town," Mack remarked, and Rima suppressed a vestigial blush, though she still shook her head, reassured to hear nothing carnal in his voice, see only perceptive sympathy in his eye.

And later that night, to her amazement, she danced solo, shameless and bold, as if she were in her own bedroom, the next night with trepidation watched the scene reenacted on film, to such sincere-sounding plaudits that she felt flattered and proud, though she suffered a momentary, disconcerting thrill of attraction to the unfamiliar figure luridly gyrating.

All in all it was a strange, exhilarating initiation, as though all the old wisdom had been abolished, or somehow didn't count any more. A new age was being born and everybody could tell. Occasionally it even felt scary, as when The Angry Brigade blew up the top of the tallest building in London.

"What are they angry at?" Rima asked.

"Greco-Roman-Judeo-Christian mores," said grinning Smitherill.

"What's your sign?" inquired the rap-artist, read her palm, made some computations with the numbers 1, 9, 5, and 0, declared that she furnished further proof, were any needed, that Cape Cod Bay was the site of special spiral forces, that visitors from advanced civilizations had already reconnoitered the scene, that he himself was the receptor of inter-galactic vibes, and was even now making himself master of the lotus method of interpreting the messages of spirits from former times waiting to be reborn at both the basic and nine higher levels of awareness, his incredible powers stemming from ancient lore and the secrets of sacred texts like the Kabbalah and the Tibetan Book of the Dead, which combine all knowledge coded as enigmas beyond normal human powers, wherein even the lost runes of the Aztecs, North American Indian shamans' residual prayers and the magic dimensions of the Pyramids can be synchronized with the confluence of solar wind and lunar wave to make manifest and bring to the fore with imminence all the mystic unities, end human greed and strife, and promote eventual, if not immediate, triumph of tarot.

His ethereal voice ran flute-like on, never pausing, never returning whence it came. All these many marvels were doubtless pleasant to contemplate, and his disciples nodded and murmured as if they had parts in a choral lullaby. And what was the harm, Rima wondered, in reciting such malarkey if it made one happy? Did he really believe one word? What did he want? Not sex apparently; that, he said, was pre-spiritual.

Distracted, then attracted by aromas, he floated off toward the kitchen, and his circle dispersed, harmonizing an amen of om.

Most pot just made Rima drunker, but the passed joint, slim as a knitting needle, smelt like perfume. After a polite half-toke she was paralyzed.

"Viet-grass," said the lean soldier on leave with crew cut and tattoos. He sniffed the last, thickening fumes, pinched the roach, put it on his tongue, swallowed, stood up from the couch without using his hands, bowed from the waist, winked, and went away, saying, "Here comes reality."

A golden glow enclosed her. She could neither move nor speak, but only look about the room with awed interest in everything and a gulf-like sense of the unique importance of each moment. She began to grasp the point of recording, the fad for tiny cameras and bugs and TVs the size of wrist watches, the discrete particularity of the world. What if there were nothing more to life than the obvious? What a fix she was in, Stoodles on one arm, Ponze on the other, benevolent Mack in the doorway, and Smitherill, still as a heron, watching them all in the tilted mirror on the first stairway landing.

Respite came in the form of a blessed skein of brilliant days. The crazed street subsided. Even the MacKenzie Rexes' was deserted. Rima with relief went out at night only to swim at high tide, riding the calm swells like a boat adrift, listening to the slap of waves against the seawall, feeling herself one with the waters, went to bed early, rose at dawn, creature of light.

One late afternoon, while she was sunning on her deck, John Smitherill came meandering, eyes upon the sand. She hailed him, invited him up, strove with fierce, metallic laughter to goad him from his morbid trough of nihilistic ironies, forced talk of gratitude for the flawless weather, flirted and teased, posed and preened, until he made an offhand proposal, lightly spoke but phrased as a challenge, and she accepted.

Their eyes grated together like quartz, and stubbing out their cigarettes and downing their drinks they stole unsteadily upstairs in the silent, empty house.

She took off her bathing suit and stood looking wryly at his deeply-tanned, bald head, while he held the bedstead with one hand and tried to free his ankles with the other.

"My god," he said, "it doesn't take you long."

"Once I make up my mind I don't delay," she said.

They threw back the covers and took possession of the bed with lascivious nostalgia, though she noticed he never lost his preoccupied look. The act itself, so long postponed, yet so absent of ardor, hardly marred the surface of their casual cordiality. He rolled on his back like Abe and stared out the window. Some boys on the patio below were drinking beer and arguing who was worse, Calley or Manson.

"What are you thinking about?" she said.

"Death," he said.

"You shouldn't always," she said.

"Why not?" he said.

"Because," she said in exasperation, "you can't do anything about it."

"All the more reason," he said.

"Poor man," she said, "with your mind in a cage. Crib, I mean."

"Listen," he said, very grave, hushed, portentous. "It's the one thing you can count on."

"I have no doubts myself," she said.

"Look," he said, "at that round shadow on the ceiling. Ever since I came in it's been getting bigger and bigger, and now it's going to blot you out at seven o'clock exactly."

"You too?" she said, glancing from the shadow to the clock, which showed half a minute to the hour.

"Oh, no," he said with grim sincerity, "I'm going to live forever."

"That's the spirit," she said.

"The empty hourglass," he almost sang. "The cigarettes, the booze, the drugs. This is a true presentiment. What's left is your last thought."

"Don't be silly," she said and glanced at the shadow, which seemed to have grown.

"Goodbye," he said.

"Goodbye yourself," she said, and had the sensation of falling off a mirror, diminishing, diminishing, unable to scream, and the shadow convulsed.

Smitherill sat bolt upright. "Time to go," he said in a queer voice.

"Is it seven?" she said, reaching for her bathing suit, relieved to find she could still move.

"I've got to meet someone," he said apologetically.

"At seven?"

He nodded, busy with his fly.

"Are you going to go to bed with her?"

"God knows. I hope not."

"Then don't."

He laughed violently, like a bark, and led the way down to her deck, paused to part. "Another seven gone," he said. "You made it through another day."

"When I was a child," she said, "we used to play a game called Sevens."

"Rehearsals," he said.

Their eyes met but before he blinked she glimpsed his arrogant addiction, as in a dark pool the silvery, darting fish of his fear. He went down the steps to the beach and trudged back the way he had come, hands in pockets, head down, and she, sick with disappointment and disgust, waded out toward the weirs till the tepid water ringed her waist.

At ten, beset by the jitters, she walked into town. Every flower was in bloom, the moon was full, the night nearly as bright as day. A large calico cat came out of a hedge and strolled ahead of her on the sidewalk. Rima bent to pat it but it walked out of reach, regal and aloof. She followed, bending, but it kept walking away, tail high. A rosy, smiling young woman came the other way, knelt and held out her fingers. The cat sat before her and accepted a caress. "Friend of yours?" Rima said.

"Oh, no, I don't know her at all," she said, her eyes brimming with delight. "But what a beautiful creature. I feel honored."

"Two beautiful creatures," Rima said, and the woman blushed.

Walking on into the teeming town Rima felt a sense of finality. Intermingled throngs eddied both ways around a traffic jam by the Fo'c's'le. As she entered the bar two muscular men in tight tank tops with identically-dyed, blond hair, were inspecting the leather display next door. A rust-bitten Ford jounced to a stop and stalled. The driver hung motionless at the wheel, gaping at them through silver, one-way sunglasses, while his wife in holiday dress twisted to settle a back-seat tangle of kids. Rima was so close she saw herself doubled in his silver glasses, two startled women in orange blouses and white slacks.

Inside, panicky, she sat down on the nearest bench, and pretended to hunt in her purse. What the haunted-looking mutterer opposite blurted at her bowed head must have been some awful revelation, for when she glanced up he glared at her with dread. She shook her head absolvingly, puffed out her lower lip as a show of compassion, and fled to the bar, bought a schooner of beer and sat in a window, looking out sidelong, wishing she were invisible.

Ponderous-bellied in their old dress uniforms, chests festooned with sashes and ribbons, three members of a VFW convention up-Cape ambled by unsteadily, as they might have done once on the Champs Elysees, except they wore angry sneers. Long-haired boys and girls wandered like Samoans in the garish light. A woman in a flowing black gown went by on the arm of another in a bowler hat, who curtsied, spreading her tutu at someone in the next window. For an instant Rima thought she saw Nikki, and felt a strange, lonely regret. At the long, center table two boys with gaudy tans were interrogating four girls, who glanced at each other before answering. The Beatles frolicked on the jukebox.

Still miffed by the calico cat, Rima glimpsed another kind of life than hers, then warily focused on a fat fly on the thickly-urethaned, name-carven table. At first it seemed immobilized by the sticky surface. Then it took several, finicking steps and changed the angle of its body like a bomber on a turnstile. She bent to examine its repulsive, hairy head and geodesic eyes, then very carefully covered it with her hollow-bottomed mug. She watched it through the glass. It didn't stir, nor fly when she lifted the mug away.

She kept putting the mug over it like a dome. It kept not flying away, apparently enamored of spilt beer or dulled with surfeit or the onset of fall. Finally, somehow cheered, tinged with indifferent contempt, freed in spirit, Rima swept it into the air with a cavalier hand, fished out another cigarette, turned defiantly to the passing world, let come what might.

THE WEATHER

What can I tell you? It was one of those nights. Cerise died on Monday. Funeral on Thursday. Eddie was wrecked all week. By Saturday night he was so bleary you never knew what you were going to get, except it wouldn't be what you ordered. He was all alone on the bar because it's February– Cerise still hasn't been replaced.

She was Eddie's long-time pal, his mainstay. She'd been depressed for years. She always drank a lot, had a hacking cough she couldn't get rid of, kept going on pills, started losing weight and decided she had cancer. She refused to quit smoking or see a doctor, said she didn't want to know and didn't care. Then she got a big rent increase. It got pretty grim, what with this endless grey. You can only take so much, never mind the rain, rain, rain.

I think she just got tired, just didn't want to do it anymore. Not that I blame her. I don't think I saw her smile in the last two years. She tied some window weights from her landlord's basement around her ankles and slipped off a finger dock down at the wharf. Somebody happened to see it, but they couldn't get her up in time.

Eddie was in terrible shape. Which confirmed his wife's suspicion that he and Cerise had it on. Which they didn't. Which his wife would have known at a glance, if she ever came around. But she hasn't set foot in the Bradford in years, can't stand the smell of booze, so Eddie's home life's a shambles too.

I was sitting at one of the chess and backgammon tables in the window with Coffee and Malcolm and Warren Wender, finest kind, every one. Coffee– Coughlan Dice– he's huge, he's not that tall either, he has a big black beard, he's bald on top, and still wears those little round, wire-rim spectacles you never see any more. He's a sweetheart, a truly dear man, everybody loves Coffee. Malcolm's thin as a stick. He and I go way back, he's over me, I don't have to fend him off any more– or anyone else for that matter. Malcolm used to write for the wire services in Paris, he gave that up twenty years ago to drink in P-town. Warren's a writer too– or says he is– anyway he's always writing in a little red notebook that he keeps in his hip pocket. He said he goes through fifty a year. That much I can believe. Coffee's been working on a novel for as long as I've known him. I don't dare mention it any more, he always looks so pained. There's no point asking Warren anything, all he sees is death. It's his one love in life. The worse everything is the better to him. Fodder, he calls it. He never even smiles– though he laughs a lot. Sort of. You can't imagine him ever telling a lie. Anyway, whatever he says, it's never something you want to hear.

It was driving rain outside, gusts of wind like explosions, you could see the windows bulge and shine, shingles in the street, signs banging, not even cars going by. The whole town's comatose, no fish, no work, everybody down, dead broke, in a funk.

Hardly anybody at the bar, four or five guys around the pool table, waiting for their quarters to come up. I don't indulge unless I'm bored out of my mind. Some women like to play, have the guys cuddle up behind, reach around, brush those nipples while they help them point the cue. Any babe can look good bending over. The macho guys take it sooo seriously. There's a lot of ego, it's like being in the spotlight. As if anyone's watching.

Well, there's always Wallace Drake lolling around in his slippers, he does nothing *but* watch. He lives upstairs, doesn't drink, doesn't smoke, doesn't speak. He's supposed to be waiting for his inheritance. He's grungy, he must sleep in his clothes, his complexion's sort of mud-flat gray, I can't describe it, except he's repulsive. He's about sixty, an ancient sixty, his expression says he despises this place and everyone in it, can't wait to get his hands on that dough— and then what? All I can imagine is him standing around with his fists full of hundred-dollar bills. One time he happened to be right next to me, quite rank he was too— I says, "So how's with you?" He never answered, never even glanced at me, he's got the place all to himself. Owns it, you might say.

At the table in front of us there were these two young guys, I was half paying attention. Apparently they had 100 Quaaludes, which they were supposed to sell, but they'd already popped some themselves, and they were getting ready to fight over the rest. The one holding the stash said, "You'll be gonzo. You can't handle any more."

Janine's sitting across from him beside his buddy, rubbing the inside of his thigh. She says, "You've had enough for now, you can have one later. I'll buy you a beer, how about a shot of tequila?"

She's trying to keep him up long enough to get him home with her. They were both pretty ratty-looking kids. Janine likes her love as she calls it. She holds out her hand, she says, "Let me have one to keep for him."

The kid with the stash said," Fuck off, bitch."

Nothing fazes Janine. She says, "Give me two, one for me. Have another yourself."

Tad'll kill us," the kid's voice goes up like a flute.

The one beside Janine says, "He'll kill us anyway. We may as well take the rest of them."

Stash says, "We can save our ass if we up the price, skim some of that, too."

"Yeah. Don't panic. We'll get our share."

"Yeah," Stash says. "In pills." He sounded disgusted.

"So we might as well take these while we gotum."

"He'll kill us."

"I don't care, I'll be so high I won't even know."

"You'll be out cold by that time," Stash says.

"I don't care. Just give me my half."

And on like that. This shit is gotta cease, but I don't see it happening. Flip was Eddie's other sidekick. Annette went to Boston for two days. He'd tied off both arms. She blames herself for not having known. Eddie never knew either. Nobody knew. She thought he only did coke once in a while, you could tell– if he was ugly or nice. Jekyll and Hyde. I can never remember which is which. Like everybody I guess.

About ten there began to be some action around the pool table. Some flashy, new hotshot was winning every game. Whole line of quarters. People at the bar watching, sitting face outwards. He was a big, handsome guy, very well turned out, dressy in a casual way, great pair of boots, great belt, great head of hair, fine leather coat over a chair. He looked like the lead man in some mod western, strutting around the table, cleaning up the balls, he shoulda had spurs, you could almost hearum jingle. We couldn't figure out what he was doing here. Just blew in because he heard Dodge was the place to be in February? What a laugh!

But could he ever shoot pool! Brought his own cue, beautiful cue, inlaid with mother-of-pearl. It gleamed— not a really straight pool stick in the place but his— it unscrewed in the middle, goes back in a leather case, slickadee. He won every game. It was him against everybody else. You don't see that too often. Sooner or later the top gun loses. Nobody goes home undefeated.

He was good all right, no doubt about it, and he was good-looking, he had all the moves, he wasn't ever not doing a pose, but he wasn't making any friends either, he definitely wasn't Mr. Charm. He was more the intimidating type, he was loud and crude, he had a slightly bellicose edge, he heckled and hectored his opponents, sort of loomed over them when they went to shoot, like a schoolyard bully. He sort of swaggered even when he was standing still, chalking his cue. He more or less ran the table every time, and the regulars, they were all miscues, scratches and long faces. They couldn't make a shot to save their lives, cost them a beer a game, too. And he wasn't what you'd call a gracious winner. He'd say, "Who's the next bozo? Rack 'em up." And then he'd sink two on the break, you could feel people groan.

It got so everybody in the place was watching, everybody wanted to see his ass get whipped, but he wasn't into that. He rattled every player that stepped up so bad it was pitiful, it made you wince to see. They couldn't respect him either, he was too derisive. And they were all meek as mice— 8 ball all right. Everybody's behind that one in this weather.

Well, not Janine— I saw them all take one. I didn't see it, but I'm sure they popped another round or two, God knows how many. She knows how to get her way.

Dendred actually came close. He's Mr. Cool around here these days, he sank a couple of impossible shots, left himself a tough lie for the 8, last ball on the table, one of those shots if you make it you're liable to scratch. He could have played a safety, lived to try another day, but he felt he had to go for a clean win, not some long drawn-out tippy-toe game of safeties. He knew he had the guys' hopes up, they were rooting for him to rescue the local honor, so to speak. He kept walking around it, lining it up, then he'd straighten up again. And walk all around it again. Like his life depended on it.

Hotshot wasn't taking any chances, he followed Den around, leaning right up close, saying stuff like, "You don't have the balls to try it, you know you'll scratch. If you go for a safety, you know I'll knock it down wherever you leave it. You're outta your league and you know it. So shoot and make way for the next dung-boat."

Den kept setting up, this way and that, open bridge or thumb and finger loop. The cue goes swooping back and forth, like a hillbilly fiddle, like he would hit it this time for sure, but then he'd shake his head and stand up and study it all over again. Hotshot was yelling, "Come on, come on, Dingbat, get it over with, you know you're gonna lose."

Den got so frazzled– even his friends began to rag him– he changed his mind again, and when he lifted the cue, he was trying to be casual, he nicked the cue ball, and it rolled more than six inches, no question, more like a foot.

Hotshot howled, he literally howled, and then, insult to injury, he sank the 8 ball with one hand like a lance– Den was in shellshock– of course it was a close, easy shot, side-pocket, straight on, but he hit it an arrogant crack– that's real control– and it hit the back rim of the pocket and went down with that nice gallump! you get sometimes, very satisfying when it's your ball. You could feel the whole place dive out of sight like a life-raft with a torpedo coming.

The table behind us was these four Portuguese, New Bedford fishermen– you used to see them, not any more– they have such wonderful faces, all arroyos, they're built like barrels, black hair curling out under their cocky caps, they're completely engrossed in a game of checkers, all talking at once, completely serious, they smack the checkers down like it's curtains for the other guy, they never look up– no spectator sports for them.

There's a chess game going beside us. Barnie plays all day out of a book. Squeak's so stoned he doesn't notice Barnie's got no king. The instant he moves Barnie slides a knight like a bishop or jumps a rook like a knight, and Squeak goes back to scoping out his next move. Entertainment for all.

Trashette comes in. She's all disgusted, she says "The men at the Surf Club are either married or have six chicks apiece or hate women or are in love with each other and don't know it."

I nodded toward the pool table– he was a hunk, I had to admit. The guys should've introduced her. Trashette is not someone you'd care to cross. When Willie O'Dell fell off the wagon– actually he more like jumped– she stirred Antabuse into his cocktail and mixed plaster of Paris with his Metamucil, or so she says. Anyway she's single, and that's something I never thought I'd see.

Women leaving town all over the place. I could adore one of those fishermen. I think. Probably put me in the galley, keep me four-five days at a time out on the bank, no thanks.

Anyway there's no comfort like a dog. My Vinnie's sweet sixteen, he's reverting to his puppy-hood, the last few months my car smells like a pissoir, he can't walk any more, I take him everywhere. While I've still got him.

About eleven the rain let up and Little Matt came in. Hotshot's leaning his ass back on the table, eyeballing the ladies. Such as there were. No quarters on the table, no more takers, they're all had-enoughers, had to buy too many loser beers, and who wants to be degraded besides?

Matt walks over to check out the scene.

Hotshot says, "You're up. We're playing for beers."

Matt says, "Nah, I don't play pool any more. I'm too rusty."

Hotshot says, "This whole slum-bucket's rusty. Rack 'em up. I'm thirsty."

He already had more paid-for beers on ice at the bar than he could drink, but he wouldn't think of giving any back to the guys he'd beat them out off, he's the kind that likes to whip things in.

Matt said, "I don't feel like playing pool."

Hotshot says, "Come on Midget, get yer pecker up. That *is* yer name, init, Midget? Or you a dwarf?"

Matt says, "My name's Matt. Two t's."

"Tooties?" Hotshot says. "Matt the Twat."

Matt says, "Anyway, I'm not drinking," and he started talking to one of the guys.

Hotshot hauls out a five dollar bill and puts it on the rail.

Matt looked at it for a minute like he was thinking, then just shook his head.

Hotshot went over the edge a bit, gave Matt a whole barge of shit. By this time I think all he really wanted was just another game.

Of course he could've played freebies with the guys he fleeced. And let them drink some of the beers they'd bought, which by then they sorely craved. He could have acted half-decent. And been a big deal, heap big chief of the Bradford pool table.

Could'a been. 'Character is Fate.' Every writer I know quotes it. That and 'No day without a line.' Only Warren can spout that one with no squirm.

Matt says, "I don't want to play pool."

Hotshot says, "Yeah ya do."

Matt said, "I don't. I just told you."

Hotshot says, "You do, but you don't cause you're a pussy."

Everybody hoped Matt would just walk away. They figured he had no chance, plus he had no clue what he was up against.

Matt has a sort of gravel voice, he says, "I don't know anything, except you're in my face."

"So rackem up. I want your money."

I guess Matt couldn't take it anymore. He can't resist a gamble– the numbers, the ponies, football, basketball, whatever's going. He put out a ten and took Hotshot's five, says, "Rackum up."

Hotshot says, "Winners don't rack. Don't pay neither."

So Matt got foxed at the start. He pushed his quarters in the slot, the balls rumbled into the bin. He squatted, put them on the table, racked them tight, very careful when he lifted the rack away, base first, straight up, then pushed the front corner clear, and then that little flip in the air at the end.

Matt's a coal miner's son from West Virginia. He's all knotted and wiry, white patches in his grey stubble. He's got that kind of dyed-in, derelict's tan you get from always being in the sun. He'll do anything to keep outdoors, and he's got a face to match the

Portagees, only he never fished, he's scared of the water, won't even go for a row around the harbor.

So. Hotshot broke, hit it a good smash, as usual, dead on, the 3 went down, balls rolled all over the place. He ran the 9, the 15 and 13, finally missed the 7, but he didn't leave much, and when Matt missed his first shot by a mile the guys kind of looked away, they didn't want to see it.

Hotshot didn't take Matt too seriously, he didn't loom, he just wise-cracked to the guys moping around as if they were his entourage, like they never seen Matt before in their lives.

Quite a pair, Matt in his ragged sweat-shirt and green work pants that he never washed since he first put them on, he's got more jobs than God. I think Hotshot must've lost his concentration, or maybe it was the beer, or maybe he just didn't give Matt a chance, because he missed a couple he would have made before– the guys suddenly acting like the Red Sox won the pennant– but at the end Matt still had two balls on the table and Hotshot– it wasn't that easy an angle and maybe he was a bit careless– he hit it good and solid like he was making sure Matt got the point, and the 8 caromed around in the mouth of the pocket and finally just hung there, and Matt ran the table, never looked up once.

Well. We all enjoyed that. Matt picked up the ten and walked off. The guys vied to get their quarters up while Hotshot went to the bar and got one of his stock of beers, which he plunked down on the table Matt was sitting at.

Matt said, "I'm not drinking, I already told you."

Hot gives him a little sideways lift of the chin like, "Oh, yeah?" Then he puts a couple of quarters in, he took them right off the rail, as if now the other guys were nothing but the price of admission–

naturally no one spoke up. He racked the balls, laid out another five and says, "Your break."

Matt said, "I toldja, I didn't want to play in the first place."

"Best outa three," Hot says. "Step right up, Champ, it's Chump-time for you."

Matt said, "I'm already a chump about a million times over." He stood up like a weary old man almost and got out his wallet, dropped the ten, took the five. He really didn't want to play, didn't want to do anything, least of all put up with more mouth, but he couldn't not give the guy a chance to win his money back— and if he lost he'd be in for another game. So he had to win, and by this time of course he knows he's in with a shark.

Which reminds me, Jimmy Z got his old pal Diane to front him some dope and got her busted. He was dealing himself before the cops got ahold of him. There's nothing you won't do for the Big H. He'd broke his arm, no money, no place to go but Diane's couch, just him and his habit. Nobody's seen him since.

I mean, what do people think? Nuts dropping in out of no-where, What's-his-face, dead by the roadside with $1,600 in his wal-let, and a broken neck. I met him in the Bradford, too. One of those older guys— leftover hippies— who start off normal, then get men-acing. 'My name is I need a cigareet, I need another drink, I need a fix.' He ran on about reincarnation and doing people the favor of offing them to speed their changes, he wrote little poems on scraps of paper like 'Do Dharma Bums Need Guns?' He wanted to put that one down my bra. I picked up my drink, I was in such a tizzy I dropped my bag, spilled my junk all over the floor, mostly bills. I finally got relocated down the bar near the service station, he moved a couple of stools the other way and started hassling Debbie.

Anyway. Matt made the 9 on the break, but the rest stayed put, like suddenly all the balls were sticky. It turned into a very difficult game, very slow, with a lot of impossible combinations and safeties, which would have been boring in normal circumstances, sort of nudging their balls out in the open. Hotshot got back to mouthing and looming big-time, but Matt never backed up or backed down, he just held his ground, his face got darker though, which made his stubble look whiter.

Eventually it got very tense. Hotshot made some amazing shots, but Matt had better luck in his leaves, he was enjoying himself, drinking his beer. They got down to one ball apiece, Matt says, "Hey, shut up for once, willya!" and he actually did for once, but Matt still missed. It was a tough shot anyway. And then Hotshot made a long bank shot. It was a beauty. I never really watched a pool game before. Because I never cared who won. Guess I'm becoming a man— what else can you do with so few women in town? If you want to fit in. You have to live here to know what I mean— no aspersions on my drinking buddies.

Hotshot had that one last ball to go before the 8, which was right in the middle of the table, just waiting there, and he scratched— nobody could believe it— it had a little follow on it, it was rolling toward the side pocket very slowly— all the sound went out of the room— it had just enough legs to reach the pocket's edge and stop there for an instant, and then it dropped, and the guys all whooped, then shut up, looking mucho embarrassed.

Matt sank his ball and then the 8, easy shots. He even looked a bit embarrassed himself, disappointed to win that way. He said, "I just got lucky, you'd beat me nine games in ten." And he pushed the ten dollar bill toward Hotshot.

For a second there I thought there might be nice all around. It wasn't as if everybody didn't know Hotshot was the best. But Hotshot pushed it back, laid out another five and racked the balls like this time he meant business, he was certainly none too pleased, and he wasn't all that sober either. He was perfectly steady at the table, but not when he went to the bar. He came back and thunked another beer down in front of Matt, and says, "Break!" in a real nasty tone, just dripping contempt.

Matt says, "I toldja I didn't want to play pool. I already played two games with you, and that's enough. And I'm not drinking. I already got a D.U.I. pending."

Hot said, "So, get another. You're still a wuss of a twat." He bent over and pushed the beer at Matt, and belched right in his face, he didn't mean to, he didn't apologize either— that's pretty crass. Matt just closed his eyes and leaned away.

Getting dissed like that really put Hot in a pique. He took all the money and gave Matt a look that said, "Want to make something of it?"

Matt just stared off into space like he wasn't even there, he broke even anyway.

So then Hot makes like a sports announcer, "Okay. All right. I'm taking bets, he's two up already. Come on, come on, who's in?"

But nobody spoke up. All the guys headed to the bar or sat down with Matt.

You could see Hotshot wasn't used to being ostracized, glowering there at the table all by his lonesome. I guess he figured he'd monopolize the table— if nobody'd play with him, nobody'd play at all. But nobody went near the table.

So then Hot went to the bar and tried to sell Eddie back the beers on ice. Eddie says, "They boughtum you gotum."

Hot says, "They're mine, I won them."

Eddie said, "That's right, you can drinkum one at a time. Or you can give them back where they came from. But only one drink to a man at a time. That's the law."

I couldn't hear– Hotshot gave Eddie some grief, and a guy I know from Wellfleet stood up, and all of a sudden it got vicious, pushing each other and squaring off, Eddie's shouting, people backing out of the way, bottles rolling on the bar.

John Brown was on his way, but leisurely, he never hurries unless he has to, he's like one of those African gods with lowered eyelids carved in ebony, only larger than life, much larger. You never know what JB's thinking, except when he laughs he makes your ears ring and your eyes dazzle. He couldn't care less what happens till he gets there, but Marla saved him the bother, she rode to the rescue like the sheriff, the peacekeeper. Inserted herself right in between them and starts to make up to Hotshot, in no time they're playing serious kissy face and sort of swaying together, but then he wanted her to leave with him right off and I guess she wanted to finish her drink or maybe get a little bit more acquainted, they argued back and forth. She must have said something he didn't like, he got in another snit, went back to the pool table and hit the cue ball so hard it jumped the rail and sailed into some empty chairs, made a huge clatter, and John Brown decided the time had come.

Poor Hotshot. JB said, "You've had enough, you've got to go now." He's standing right up close, like it's a confidential chat, classified info.

Hotshot couldn't believe it. He said, "Whad I do?"

John Brown says, "It's not what you did, it's what you're not *gonna* do. So take a walk or something, and come back tomorrow night."

Hotshot says— he was pretty drunk— "I haven't finished my beers yet."

"That's too bad," John Brown says. "Come back tomorrow night, maybe you can winnum back."

Hotshot says, "Fuck you!" but it sounded more like giving up.

JB's looking out the window, he says, "Otherwise Eddie'll have to call the cops, and you'll be the night in protective custody."

Hotshot had to face it was a lost cause, but he never looked at JB again. He just unscrewed his cue and put it back in its case very... caressive, loving, like he didn't care who saw. Guys and their sticks. So that's him. Buthe's still got some things to learn. Nobody said any goodbyes to him, nor him to them. He might as well have never been there.

He got all the way to the door before he remembered Marla. He stepped back and looked down the bar and made a little jerk of his head at her that said, 'Come on.'

She just snuggled up against the guy he'd had the pushies with, and pouted her lips at him, Later for you, Bud.

By this time the dancers had all gone to Piggy's. Just us hard core were left. I was on my fourth, fifth Stoli, it might as well be water. Eddie gave out the beers, he sent a victory whiskey over to Matt. It got loud, high fives and laughing, like everybody'd won. Quarters lined up again. The kid with the stash is trying to get into the game, he doesn't have any quarters, so he puts up a Quaalude— more business for John Brown. So Janine gets her way, all three of them go out together, the guys could hardly toddle, she's in the middle, arm around them both.

Anyway Matt was the hero of the day. Somebody brought him another whiskey. By this time everything's on the house. Eddie's starting to look like himself again. Matt came over to say hello.

Coffee mutters and chortles into his beard, and finally he says, "Glad to see the gods were with you tonight. A splendid bit of sword play, Sir."

Matt said, "You know I like to win, but I don't even work at it any more, I don't really care."

Malcolm said, "Maybe you play better that way. Anyway you made our night."

Warren was just coming back from the men's room. He always looks like a funeral. Matt says, "You look like somebody who could use a hug."

Priceless the look on Warren's face, Coffee and Malcolm grinning like crazy. It's just a phase Matt's going through. He's getting his consciousness raised, he's getting sensitized, getting over his homophobia, growing his hair.

Warren let himself be hugged. He just stood there looking over the top of Matt's head with his eyeballs rolled up to the ceiling, he even patted Matt on the back. That's the nicest thing I've ever seen him do.

Matt said, "I better get outa here, before I start playing pool again."

He's heading for the door, but everybody's calling him over, and then two guys come and pick him up, one under each arm, and carry him back to the table, hero of the day, everybody's cheering, so he has to play another game.

"Well, well," Coffee rumbled. "A stellar night in the Dismal Swamp."

Malcolm says, "Slough of Despond."

They argued back and forth about Pilgrim's Progress, which I never read. To them books are like trophies, other guys collect bottle-caps or girlfriends or guns, whatever. Pretty funny, Piggy's used to be called The Pilgrim Club."

Coffee went for another round and I finally got a buzz on. Eddie just kept waving off any money, pouring from whatever bottle he happened to have in his hand, so people left him a good tip. If they had anything left. So I guess you could say it was a good night for the locals.

All the same— I remember one time in the A&P— middle of the summer— there was a woman in line at the cash register, endless line, babies climbing all over her, she says, "I feel like I been through the Veet Nam War."

That's just about the way I felt. At least I wasn't bored. Everything was all hunky-dory for a change, except next day we heard Little Matt got picked up again driving home, so now we hardly see him anymore.

WITS' END

Lasker told Ellen he'd be back in a week but two weeks went by, then a third, and he never even called. She didn't mind at first, glad to have him out of the house. All they did was fight when he wasn't working, and it was worse when she had a job and he didn't.

At last it hit her, *Oh, my God, he's drinking again.* On her day off she borrowed Edna's car, drove up to Gloucester and cruised the waterfront till she saw a bar he used to talk about.

Two grizzled elders were playing cribbage with arthritic deliberation while the bartender read a newspaper. She drank a beer and smoked two cigarettes, but no one came in. When the bartender glanced up she said, "Do you know someone named Lasker?"

His slightly-deferred, barely-perceptible jog of the head might have meant maybe.

"What time does he usually come in? I'm a good friend of his," she added deprecatingly. "I mean he's my husband."

The bartender looked at her. "He's in and out."

"Is he drinking?" she said.

"Just coffee."

Ellen began to relax. She felt vastly grateful. Getting Lasker off the booze was one of her proudest accomplishments. "Do you know where he's staying?"

The bartender shook his head like a tic.

The door opened to admit a lank, bearded man in a blue chamois shirt.

"Jaybo!" she cried, "I should've known you'd be up here, too. Have you seen Lasker?"

"Yeah. He's around. Pretty much."

"Is he working?"

"Yeah. Well," Jaybo said. "The job's over. I don't know."

"Where is he? Shacked up or something?" The moment she said it she knew.

Jaybo looked down at his toes.

"God damn it." Ellen banged her elbow on the bar, bent chin to heel of hand and tapped her front teeth with her fingernails.

Jaybo stood awkwardly, glancing at her and away. One night when Lasker was passed out and they were pretty far gone themselves they had stepped out to look at the stars and wound up screwing amid the August tomato plants– so spontaneous, so long ago, so embarrassing, that neither cared to remember.

"I know I shouldn't ask," Ellen said. "It's just female curiosity, I guess."

Three girls in well-fitted jeans and proud sweaters strode by the window with brash laughter. Jaybo swallowed, turned back to Ellen. "Buy you a drink?"

"Thanks. I'd better not. Actually I'd like about fifteen double zombies. What's she like? Is she beautiful? Is she young?"

"She's not so much." Jaybo fussed with his wallet.

"Yeah," Ellen said. "I don't even want to know. I've got to get out of here. I must be getting old. A few years ago I would've sat here all day and when they came in I'd be this shrieking banshee."

Jaybo gave his mug mournful half a turn.

"I shouldn't say anything," Ellen said. "She's probably a friend of yours."

"She's nothing to worry about," Jaybo said.

"Yeah," Ellen said wryly. "Tell Lasker I said hello."

Jaybo walked her to the car. She knew he felt bad, but what could he do? He and Lasker were buddies. "Take care," he said.

"On second thought," Ellen said, "don't even mention I was here."

She drove back to the Cape with the radio up loud, while daylight died. On suicide alley, the single-lane, no-passing road before Orleans, she could barely make out her faded, favorite graffito on the overhead bridge— *God's Country Rock Till You Drop*— and tried to swathe her heart-sick humiliation, jealousy and rage with the thought of swerving into the next pair of headlights.

She couldn't even blame Lasker. She might have done the same, given the chance, though she never would have let him catch her. But what never failed to amaze was how much it still hurt, how instantly wrecked she felt at this familiar, undiminished stab of betrayal.

Why did she never learn? Why had they stayed together all these years? It was like an addiction they couldn't kick. They could no more stand to be together than apart.

That was why they'd got married finally— to break the spell. Recalled now, the bravado of their wedding seemed all the more poignant for being sincere— she in the borrowed, antique dress with its erotic rustle of petticoats, which she had vowed to wear in fantasy at least once a week for the rest of her life; he suave as a boulevardier in the yard-sale, silk suit and his favorite tie with gaudy flamingoes roosting in the foliage of what close up proved to be a female crotch; the golden July afternoon blending into a mellow twilight of pink stars brightening in a lavender sky; the casual, communal feast on the lawn, passersby welcome; the garbage bag of Maine homegrown in the kitchen, joints the size of cigars; their tireless, fiddler friends making the street resound till ten p.m., the benign cop car creeping by, creeping by, no hassles the whole day, nor the whole night long.

They honeymooned at home, ate leftover tabouli, felt like blessed castaways. They were poor, but everyone was poor. Who needed money? Everybody was family and once the rent was made there was always somehow enough extra for all to eat, sleep under a roof, drink and smoke, and what more did anyone want than love and music, which were free?

She and Lasker were hardly hippies, at least in their own lexicon, though by the end of the Vietnam War who could tell a hippie from anyone else? They had gone to P-town in the summer of '65, stayed through the winter, then simply never left, rejoicing to have shucked the straightjacket of respectability, quit the rat-race, slipped the mean fear of inadequacy and failure that had dogged them both. The soaring gulls, at ease on still pinions, suggested a more essential security, the confidence that nothing mattered, that no real harm could come, so long as they kept clear of artificial rules and routine, valued life rightly, and kept faith with nature.

The winter town teemed with young refugees. The welfare system was liberal, the unemployment rate above 40%. Rebellion ruled and the good times rolled. They danced every night in the sweaty packed-jam at Piggy's, partied and lazed away the off-seasons; then, from June to Labor Day, slaved to pay the summer rent, grew frazzled and gaunt. It was like living in a vortex, exhilarating so long as centrifugal force held them to the steep sides, but the abyss always yawned. It dizzied Ellen to think how many had gone down, how often she and Lasker had nearly gone down.

The failure of love was awful, and ordinary. It almost seemed foredoomed. Who could stick marriage anymore? Their discontents and bickering had gradually resumed, followed by infidelities suspected but unconfirmed. They fought, moved out, moved back in, left town, came back. Reconciliations ceased to last or re-conquer the heart, grown secret and hard. They split up so often their friends couldn't keep track of whether they were still a couple.

Lasker's relentless drive, once he had relinquished drinking and drugs, was not the domestic boon she had envisioned. Now that the ethos of macho debauchery had lost its cachet, only work and more work could sate his need for excess. All his aggravated energy focused on making money, and he hated to see Ellen idle or adrift, nor did he hang around the house himself. He left early, came home for supper, went right out again, and when he wasn't working he was surf-casting or clamming, winning- never losing- at poker, so he always claimed, or tooling around in his truck. Not drinking didn't keep him out of the Bradford, where he played backgammon, or the Fo'c's'le, where he matched the guys Coke for drinks.

By the early Eighties new people were coming to town, people not in flight, nor in exile once arrived, people with nothing to hide or forget or recover from. It bewildered Ellen to count how many friends had disappeared, died or dried out and faded into reclusion, what few had got rich and wore rings and new clothes, or no longer spoke to people they used to get stoned with, how common the BMWs, how rare and conspicuous the old, oil-burning junk-heaps.

Everything was changing, rents rising, strings of condos springing up on spec, talk of Maine and Vermont, cocaine everywhere, heroin dealt out of cars on the street. Only Lasker remained the same. Well, the hell with him. She would winter alone and enjoy it, drink her fill, hang out at the Surf Club with some rugged fisherman or eager-eyed young painter– right in the middle of which, of course, Lasker would come home. Oh, the bastard! If only he'd called she wouldn't have worried, wouldn't have gone to Gloucester, wouldn't feel so demented now.

As the car topped the rise above Beach Point, the lights of Provincetown came into view, the "diamond necklace" that had thrilled her the first time she saw it, that ever after always made her heart beat slightly out of control with sheer anticipation; but this time it held no mystery, no promise of refuge, only a cold glitter in the distance, a lie for the tourists. The real town was dingy, sordid and sad, with winter coming on.

She thought, *I don't want a lover. For once in my life all I want is peace and quiet. I could try and write my children's book. I could actually do that. Finally!*

When Ellen drove in Edna came smiling to the door. "I didn't expect you back till tomorrow. Was Lasker there?"

Ellen sat down wearily, stiffly, and told her tale while Edna sliced a zucchini-walnut bread and poured some tea.

"So what are you going to do?" the older woman asked. Her children grown, she was long-divorced, and had had a succession of lesbian lovers, the last of whom had recently left her, "to play", in the current coin; so now she was single again. Her neat little house with its irregular windows and nooks was cozy and warm, her liquor supply always ample.

"I think I'd like to cry," Ellen said, "but I don't want to."

"Mad, sweetie," Edna said, "is what you ought to be."

"Oh, I am. I'd like to rip his balls off," Ellen said with a grimace. "What I really should do is go out to Ohio and see Jason. He's my oldest, dearest friend, he's a very good painter. He's gay. He's the only man I ever got along with. We were always going to collaborate on a children's book to celebrate our childhood friendship. I was going to write it, he was going to illustrate..."

She shook her head, squinting back tears. "Of course we've only been talking about this now for twenty years."

"I think you should get out of this town," Edna said. "You've been here too long. Go somewhere else, get a new life."

"Where?" Ellen demanded. "There isn't anywhere else. You know that."

"What do you mean?" Edna said indignantly. "There's everywhere else."

"You've been here longer than I have," Ellen said.

They sat looking out the window into the dark, and it dawned on Ellen that Lasker might never come back. A sleek black cat jumped into Edna's lap and let her knowing fingers knead its spine till its purring trilled and it stood stiff on all fours, nose and tail stuck straight up.

"I guess I'll go home," Ellen said hastily.

"I'll give you a lift," Edna said.

"Thanks, I'd rather walk," Ellen said, getting up with a groan. "It'll give me a chance to stretch my legs. My back's been hurting again."

"See you soon then," Edna said. "I'll be here."

Ellen limped glumly down Commercial Street. She had slept with a woman once, but it held little interest for her, and nearly cost her a friend when she declined to repeat. Women were too soft, too much of the same, too intimate, too sentimental, too nice. *I couldn't stand that,* she thought, and laughed aloud with chagrin.

The stars were clear, the harbor quiet except for one yelping gull– then silence. A few roses still bloomed but the trees were bare. She tried to find her rightful zest in the sharp change of season, felt only dreary resentment. She'd worked all summer with hardly a minute to herself. Now that the world was hers she couldn't enjoy it.

In the middle of town two bushy-haired guys tumbled out of the Governor Bradford and rolled in the gutter, punching each other feebly and growling. Her heart sank when she saw it was Billy and Jimmy Z. "What are you guys doing?" she hissed. "Here come the police."

Across Lopes Square Patrolmen Washburn and Damos were advancing in step– but slowly, slowly– hoping the combatants would wear themselves out or flee. Neither seemed in danger of injury and Ellen walked on. "Here come the cops," she called over her shoulder, but they spasmodically rolled up onto the sidewalk, then seemed to fall asleep. *And this is only November,* she thought with foreboding.

Her back was shooting pains down her left leg by the time she reached her street in the West End. The lights in her apartment were on and her spirits soared that Lasker had raced her home and was penitently, impatiently awaiting her. She ached with fatigue, need for a bath, and a long, warm, secure sleep.

But no, it was Katrina and Steve, whom Ellen hadn't seen in three years, since the legendary week they had met, wed and fled to Vermont, one of the great escapes of all time in the eyes of veteran observers. What the pair had in common none could say, except they had got each other out of town. Katrina, whose horrendous decline had been hidden from her in an alcoholic haze, had drunk no more; and Steve, a native, was finally free of his mother's domineering rule, and happy up north in the woods. He loved to hunt and fish, hated the ever-longer summers that crowded his home town with hordes of aloof strangers.

"Can we stay with you for a few days?" Katrina said. "Steve's mother's dying."

"Don't say that," Steve said. "I keep telling you."

"Anyway," Katrina said, "she's in the hospital, full of tubes. The doctor says, 'I don't know how aggressively we should treat this.' She's eighty years old, everything's gone: heart, kidneys, lungs..."

"She's only seventy-eight," Steve said.

"Seventy-eight," Katrina said in exasperation, and opened a fresh pack of Camels. "Nobody lives forever. Steve can't stand to stay at home without her there. He thinks it's bad luck."

"You can have the other bedroom," Ellen said. She made a pot of coffee and they sat at the kitchen table till midnight.

"Steve believes in Magic Thinking," Katrina said. "You think something, and then it comes true."

"It's worse when you say it," Steve said. "It means you want her to die."

"I don't," Katrina groaned. "I just want what's best for her."

Ellen gazed at the floor with her pained clown's smile.

Steve slumped in his red and black checked jacket, chin on chest, eyes half shut. None of them had taken their coats off yet. They had drunk all the coffee in the house and now were starting on the tea.

"Why can't people accept death?" Katrina said. "We're supposed to be rational beings. Steve always used to say she was the bane of his existence. The truth is, she waited on him hand and foot."

He lurched up suddenly and reeled into the extra bedroom. The springs jounced and they heard a long, despairing sigh. Katrina made a face and shrugged. After a minute Ellen went in, pulled his boots off and put a blanket over him. He had covered his head with a pillow and she patted his shoulder. "Get some sleep now," she said and shut the door, wishing she could go to bed herself and sooth her back pain.

But Katrina was going full tilt. "What I'd like is for him to show a little strength," she said. "He bosses me around, but he's completely helpless. His mother spoiled him, so I've got this big baby on my hands. I really need him to show some strength now. Or what's a man for?" she demanded.

"*Chercher la femme*, I guess," Ellen said gloomily.

"He'd never look at another woman," Katrina said.

"Well, that's good at least," Ellen said.

Katrina laughed with contempt. "I had to go to Vermont to learn what reality is. I woke up one day and said, 'Who's this middle-aged, fat person in the mirror, and who's that jerk she's with?'"

"You look great," Ellen said.

"But seriously," Katrina said, "everything's changed, but nobody's noticed."

"I know what you mean," Ellen said.

"That's our last cigarette," Katrina said, crumpling the pack. I'll roll the butts if you have any papers."

"I don't," Ellen lied.

"Then it's bedtime," Katrina said. She washed the cups and emptied the ashtray. "How are you, by the way?"

"Oh," Ellen said, trying not to quaver, "I'll tell you tomorrow." She got in bed and lay on her side with her knees drawn up, which gave some relief, but she couldn't fall asleep.

She thought, *Maybe I* should *have married Jason—* as Lasker always taunted her when she got bitchy— dear, kind, beautiful Jason. They could have had a happy, Platonic home and no troubles, but not in Dayton.

Both hated their birthplace. Jason had always talked of leaving, but he had stayed, and next month— in eleven days, she counted them out— he would be forty. The soul of responsibility, he had worked in the Civil Rights Movement, and during the Seventies, little as he liked a public role, had acted as a spokesman for gay political circles.

He had a good job, a house, a car, insurance, the whole bourgeois panoply except a wife, but he was always depressed. It choked him to say he was a commercial artist. He was a success by the standards of the world he despised and endured, a success of sorts in the real art world, if the opinion of his peers and critics counted, but his shows seldom sold anything, the canvasses piled up in his studio, and he painted less and less.

On the wall opposite Ellen's bed hung one of his earliest, mature works, a somber oil of two old women sitting side by side, hands folded in their laps. A gleam from the street lit their white faces like a single pair of eyes in a black void, like a glimpse of his long loneliness. He couldn't abide the gay bar scene and had grown solitary as the years passed.

She thought, *I absolutely* must *go home for his fortieth birthday. It's a Sunday, too. What great luck! I'll go on Saturday and take him to dinner at his favorite place. The minute Katrina and Steve leave I'll give him a call.*

She woke at seven, exhausted, distraught, thankful at least she had another day off. Her guests were gone, and she skimmed the *Globe* in her bathrobe. Page 1 had a picture of President Reagan— *The National Cuckoo,* Lasker called him— waving, boarding a helicopter. The lead story purveyed the revised Pentagon doctrine that tactical nuclear war-fights were winnable, within the limits imposed by the mutual catastrophe of all-out exchange, nor would NATO losses be so dire as the timorous feared. Page 2, the Iranians: a sea of shouting mouths and shaking fists. Page 3, recession. Page 4, teen-age suicides. Page 5, a mysterious disease characterized by failure of the immune system.

At noon Katrina called from the hospital. "Would you believe?" she wailed. "Once they've started dialysis it can't be stopped. Now she'll probably live for months. Steve's convinced himself she's going to get better."

"Oh God!" Ellen said.

"He's driving me crazy," Katrina cried. "I'm just beginning to find out the kind of man I married."

"Oh God!" Ellen said, coming undone.

"I'm sorry for all the turmoil," Katrina said, chastened by her tone.

"Never mind," Ellen said, "I can stand it if you can," but the rest of the day went to waste. She tried book after book; not even

Colette could ease her anguished furies. She harangued the dog and cat, let them in, let them out, went to the store for cigarettes, never for one moment forgot Lasker.

At dusk Katrina and Steve drove in and sat down at the kitchen table. "She's dead," Katrina said. "She just stopped breathing. She must have wanted to."

Eyes shut, hands in pockets, Steve slumped in his coat, collar up, knit cap down over his ears.

"I had to call the funeral home for him," Katrina said. "His brother's flying in from Ft. Myers tomorrow. I'm sick of this. I need a rest. I've got to get some air. Come for a walk with me."

Ellen opened her mouth to speak sympathy to Steve, but his stolid bathos blocked her and she followed Katrina out the door in silence. Intermittent jabs pierced the muffled ache in her coccyx and a chill wire of fire jiggled the length of her left femur, ceased for a few steps, then jolted her with a deadly bolt. She flinched and caught her breath, unable to attend to Katrina's world of wrongs.

"Nobody can stand the truth," she was saying. "Why can't people accept death? What's the big deal? Since it's inevitable. I have no trouble facing it. It's perfectly natural. Life's bad enough."

"I've got to stop a minute," Ellen gasped.

"Let's go in here," Katrina said.

"Katrina!" Ellen said apprehensively. "This is a bar."

"I know," Katrina said, leading the way. "I never liked this place. It's too gay. At least I won't meet anyone I know. I'm just going to have a Coke."

They got sat down at a window table. The only other patron went tilting past them toward the door. He had a bright red face, a dazzling white crew-cut and an expression of petrified fear.

"Endy!" Katrina cried in delight. "How are you?"

He lurched to a stop, gaped at her with despair. "My health is very poor," he said, got the door open and staggered out.

"He doesn't even know I've been gone," Katrina said with aggrieved surprise.

"He looks like he could use a vacation," Ellen said.

The waitress came, a grey-haired lesbian in a discreet cowboy suit and boots. "Yes, ladies?"

"Just a Coke, I guess," Ellen said.

"I'll have a rum and Coke," Katrina said.

"Oh God!" Ellen said, facing the futilities. "I suppose I'd better have some rum in mine too."

"I haven't had a drink in three years," Katrina said. "Actually I never spent a sober day in this town."

"I don't think you should do this," Ellen said.

"I'll only have a few," Katrina said. "It probably won't even affect me."

Ellen laughed with gruesome rue.

"What an awful day!" Katrina said.

"Well, it's over," Ellen said, appalled by how feeble she felt, how undermined, how helpless to intervene, console or even care.

They had another round, which went down unregarded, and the waitress brought a third, Katrina looking out the window all the while. In the blustery night a few dead leaves scuttled along the gutter. "It's still a magic place," she said. "I just realized I still love it here."

"Yeah," Ellen admitted, "it gets in your blood, all right."

"Not only was I not sober when I was here before," Katrina mused, "I was not married either."

"Oh God! Ellen said, banged both elbows on the table, clutched half her face in each hand, dug her fingernails into her cheeks. "Hadn't we better be going?"

"I think I'll just sit here a while," Katrina said offhandedly. "This is a great window. Tell Steve ... well, you'll think of something, I'm sure. Say I ran into some old friends."

Ellen made her painful way home, thinking that death was supposed to bring people together, exasperated that Katrina heeded no troubles but her own, nor felt compunction at using Ellen to deceive her husband.

Steve was sitting at the table like a bent nail, just as they had left him. To Ellen's version of their excursion he made only a mumbled grumble, and she retired in haste.

Next morning when she got up he was still sitting there, baleful and blank. "Kat never came back," he said.

"Oh God!" Ellen said, escaped to work and fended off thoughts about Lasker. With reckless rage she wrestled the rained-in cans of slop down the ramp, while the owner of the restaurant smiled benign approval.

She got the worst one done with never a twinge, and stood there, hands on hips, congratulating herself on her unwonted luck when, without having budged, she was struck by a ghastly bolt that turned her face blue and made her armpits drip.

"I've got to go home," she whispered, untied her apron, let it fall, edged one foot ahead at a time, stunned by the magnitude of her problem. She felt electrocuted and brought back to life, but numb. After a few blocks the absence of pain began to be elating, and experimenting with a lengthened stride she decided that her back had simply cured itself with a final, supreme spasm.

All her joints felt newly oiled and she seemed to float. "I'm on my way," she chirped jauntily," to see Jason in Oh. High. Oh. And leave these P-town blues here, right here where they belong."

Steve was still sitting at the table, expelling gas from both ends, his rank socks competing.

"No Katrina, eh?" Ellen said.

"She's got the car keys," Steve said. "Everything's locked in the car. We're supposed to pick up my brother at the airport at noon."

"She'll be back any minute, I'm sure," Ellen said.

"That woman will drive me insane," he said.

"Maybe you should go look for her," Ellen said, and nodded firmly at him.

"Oh, I can't," he said, and his eyes took on a glaze.

"Why not?" Ellen said.

"I'm so weak," he said. "I haven't eaten anything in two days."

"There's food in the refrigerator," Ellen said.

"Oh, I couldn't," he said. "I couldn't eat."

Ellen didn't want to be cruel to one who'd just lost his mother and whose wife had run off, but she was also determined not to feed him, and hungry herself, which posed a dilemma, not to mention her desire for privacy and a bath.

"But now you're hungry?" she probed.

"Yes," he said. "I guess I could eat something."

"Well, make something," she said. "Scramble some eggs."

"I'm not really hungry," he said.

She gave in and made him a three-egg omelet with green peppers, mushrooms and tomatoes, a taste of Tabasco and a cooling dollop of sour cream. He wolfed it down and looked around for more.

The Washashores

"Now," Ellen said, nodding at the door, "go find Katrina."

"That God damned woman will drive me insane," he said.
"You'd better go look for her," Ellen said.
"I'm not going to go, you go," Steve said urgently.
"Me?" Ellen said. "Why should I go? You go."
"I can't," he said, and his eyes glazed over. "Go find Katrina for me. Tell her when I get her home I'm going to shoot her."
"You go," Ellen said.
"No, you go," he said, sank into his clothes, diffusing a fetid smell.

Ellen surrendered. She had lost her appetite, as well as all hope of a bath. She was furious at Katrina too, for having dumped him on her, and where was she? Ellen had found her once, tripped over a knee-high picket fence, with a gashed throat, drenched in blood.

"All right. You win. I'll go."

Steve said dreamily, "When Lasker gets back will you ask him to help me do something?"

"What, Steve?"

"Lasso Katrina," he said.

Ellen went. Her leg started to ache again, tears blurred her eyes. Past Cookie's she hobbled without looking in; Katrina was banned there forever for some long-forgotten fracas. Nor would she be in the Cove, soon to close for the season, nor the A-House, all gay men, and surely, after last night's debacle, not the Crown & Anchor again, but possibly the Old Colony, Bradford or Surf. But first she would try the Fo'c'sle, likeliest of all, where the kindly sun balms the morning, and the days flow together, years on end.

The Fo'c'sle

- 155 -

And yes, there she was, half visible in the shadow within, one bench back from the west window, looking bedraggled and shaky, with a schooner of beer and a pack of Camels.

"What a night!" she said. "I'm afraid to remember it."

"Katrina!" Ellen wailed. "You've got to help me. I can't deal with this guy. He's your husband. You've got to get him out of my house."

"Oh, how can you ever forgive me?" Katrina cried with a sob.

"Don't worry about it," Ellen said, "but you've got to move over to his mother's house. You also have the car keys, and his brother's plane comes at eleven."

Katrina groaned. "I just remembered I nearly died the last time I was in this town."

"That was your only time in this town," Ellen reminded her.

"I'd better go," Katrina said with a distracted face, drained her beer, stepped leerily, gingerly into the street.

Ellen rested a while, testing the urge to have a few beers herself and chitchat with the bartender, who after all had never left any doubt of his warmth toward her. They could play the jukebox and enjoy the empty a.m. together; then she could get them some scallops for lunch, and the day would ripen as people drifted in for the long, sociable afternoon, with a night of generous possibilities to come.

But heartache blighted even fantasy. Another time she might have welcomed a fond flirtation, but she was frazzled past all pleasure, and soon grimly set out for home, pain jittering down her leg. Fear and discouragement owned her, her only hope a hot bath.

As she came in sight of her house, Steve and Katrina were just getting into their car. He rolled down the window, waited for her with both hands on the wheel, knit cap down over his ears, eyes straight ahead, revving the engine.

Katrina leaned across him and said, "We got his brother. He's going to take care of the funeral. We're leaving. Thanks, Ellen."

Steve popped the clutch; they sped off, spraying Ellen's ankles with sand, braked at Bradford, turned, roared engine, screeched tires, went.

Marveling at her good luck, Ellen got herself into the bathtub, and the phone rang. In frustration, afraid to hope it was Lasker, she climbed painfully out of the tub, got sat down at the kitchen table, and on the ninth nerve-racking ring picked up and said, "Hello?"

"How are you?" said Jason. "It's me."

Ellen's heart overflowed, tears of grateful joy bathed her face. "We must be psychic!" she exulted. "You've been on my mind all week. I'm so glad you called."

"I'm afraid I've reached a point," the dear, considerate voice said, and went on dispassionately to describe how he had stretched a canvas for the first time in a year, then been unable to enter his studio again.

"I realized it was just another road to nowhere," he said. "Last year I spent a month with my sister in Minneapolis. I thought it might help. She's happily married, with a sweetheart of a husband and three kids. It only depressed me all the more to face my own failure after that.

"I wound up in the hospital again— I never wrote you— and then I got a new shrink, who changed my medication, which turned me into a zombie. He insisted I keep on with it. I quit him finally and I'm off everything now except for valium as a last resort, but I really don't know where I'm going from here..."

"Art is your life!" Ellen cried in consternation. "You just have to get back to it."

"I'm tired of the rejections," Jason said. "After two whole years of holding it Doubleday finally sent back my *Alpha Bestiary* with note saying it was very good, but it would be impossible to sell such a book unless the artist had a national reputation— which I will never have."

"You will," Ellen said, "you will," but for the first time she wondered.

Jason said distinctly:

"If you meet it on the Forest Floor
The Somber Feathered Finderboar
Will stun you with its pungent breath
Then claw or tickle you to death."

"I'd give anything to see that plate," Ellen said.

"Very handsome creature, very sinister," Jason said, and his voice picked up with pride.

"But you need to get back to oil painting," she said. "That's your real métier."

"I know," he said. "I've got literally hundreds of canvasses gathering dust. And people pay perfectly horrid prices for decorative crap to put on their walls."

"You have to start from scratch again," she said.

"I have a good life, you know," he said. "Once a week I bring my grandmother over and she sits on the stoop and watches me work in my garden. That makes as much sense as anything. I'm sick of Ink Incorporated. If I have to hear another racial joke I think I'll quit."

"You should sell your house and move down here," she said. "I know you think it's too frivolous."

"My old enemies," he said grimly, "solitude and futility."

"You should try P-town," Ellen said, but knew he never would. He liked to visit, but that was enough for him. She remembered his last sojourn in Utopia. She had inadvertently found herself walking behind him down Commercial Street. Several young men in tank tops were leaning out of a second-floor, guest house window, commenting, caroling on the passing anatomies, with catcalls, laughter and applause from bystanders. Jason, doubtless deep in reverie, awoke to a chorus of, "Nice heinie!"

Ellen could almost see his hackles rise. She'd let him tread on alone, rigid with outrage and disdain. P-town was too rich for him, Dayton too poor.

"You have to fight your battles at home, I think," he said.

He always ended thus– stoical, steeled neither to win nor be defeated– and after fervent farewells, hortatory, sanguine as ever on her part, heartened and grateful on his, they hung up.

Ellen eased back into the tub, full of dull dismay. His call had made her happy, even if he did sound worse than usual. To her he had everything– talent, beauty, brains, grace– in spite of his disappointments and inveterate complaints. That he relied on her to bolster his ego had always gratified her pride, but today, for the first time, she felt a jealous chagrin, his woes having grown so vast apparently, so overwhelming, that he never thought to ask after hers, though of course, as both well knew, those could always be encompassed by the one, fatal name: Lasker.

But, apart from his strict family, from which he had always been able to find respite at Ellen's house, why was Jason so despairing?

He had not been unhappy as a child, nor in youth; he regretted being gay only on his fundamentalist parents' account, but not long after she had left Dayton— she could not precisely pinpoint when— he had begun to refer to himself, ever less lightly, as "a miserable wretch."

Twenty years ago he had been the last person to talk to her father, a sensitive, bookish gambler who idolized Mahatma Gandhi. The two— one barely more than a boy— sat up late, drinking whiskey, discussing suicide; Jason had conceded that in some circumstances it was justifiable, and early next morning before anyone else in the house was awake her father had gone down in the cellar and shot himself.

Neither ever alluded to this old bond of grief, though she knew he blamed himself. She blamed no one, least of all her father, the first love of her life, nor Jason, the second, both idealists to whom life had somehow proved intractable.

But Lasker, the third, the resilient, rambunctious one, for whom life was never enough, who seemed to thrive on havoc, why was he the one to whom fate had doomed her? Why? How had these things come about?

It struck her now, up to her scuppers in the luxury of almost too-hot water, that everything might yet be different, if only she chose, if only she finally had the courage, to leave Lasker.

Jason needed her; Lasker never had, or at least not in the way she needed him. She could go and live with Jason, cheer him up, help him get back to painting again; they could do their long-lamented children's book together, and be happy in a normal, steadfast, stable way.

And suddenly she realized with incredulity that she had neglected to tell him she was coming home for his birthday.

She must call him back the minute she got out of the tub. The more she thought about it the greater and grander grew the idea of leaving Provincetown, until suddenly it revealed itself as salvation for them both. Meanwhile, Jason's house was large and sunny, with a nice kitchen. How wonderful to do some real cooking for a change, what pleasure to pamper someone who would not disappear the minute dinner was done, who would sit amid the dishes and talk, as they used to do. And a garden! What joy! To be loved, cherished, listened to, cared for! Who needed sex? And anyway, who could ever be sure, given the chance, what might not happen in the long run?

She wove a rich vision of bliss in Dayton with a vindictive thread of Lasker coming home to find her gone. She thought, *I can't wait to call Jason. He'll be so happy.* But a shadow of constraint crossed her mind, as if he might not be so pleased by the idea, yet she knew he surely would. Still she felt a need to hurry, to act decisively, lest she lose her nerve, and she recalled, with a chill, the ever-reverberating dawn that had pulverized her mother's widowhood.

The soap had floated away, drawn to the far end by the running water. She bent forward with the combined purpose of retrieving it and turning off the faucet, heard herself scream before she knew why, then involuntarily continued screaming in a strange voice that distended her throat, squeezed free of her maw like a gigantic, black bat unfolding its wings, buffeting, blinding her. She slid back in the tub and tried to writhe, but was paralyzed, and the unbearable pain went on and on and on without diminishing while her will dissolved and she prayed to pass out.

Then it stopped– respite of silence– but terror and humiliation gripped her, cold sweat traced down her brow. The water was getting hotter, rising toward her chin. She dared not move lest the pain revive and she slide beneath the surface and drown. She could cry for help, but who would hear in the empty house on the empty street? Her feet were scalding; steam clouded the mirror.

She thought, *I can't just give up;* and in desperation, warily, secretively, not to provoke the black bat, she budged one foot, felt a grisly twinge, and lay back gasping, till the water began to spill into her ears and lick her lower lip; angrily then she tried to sit up, and screamed in that stranger's voice. The sweat froze her face; her feet seared in the roiling torrent of near-boiling water, while a gruesome end approached.

But after all the deadly medium buoyed her, as did mortification at the image of this ludicrous, lobster's fate. By dint of minuscule adjustments of position and cautious explorations of limits, after many alarms and despairs, she got a heel and a knee under her, took a deep breath, clenched her eyes, and rose straight up, pink and dripping.

She hardly felt human however, gone her goddess days when Lasker marveled to behold her naked. In bed with her knees pulled up, she no longer minded her aching coccyx, but her whole left thigh was numb. Bitter intuition told how problematical it was that she would be fit to travel in time for Jason's birthday.

But what else was ahead? Suppose the unbearable pain came back? Suppose it came and stayed? Where was Lasker, now she really needed him? She could just see his swashbuckling swagger, his suave insouciance, as he reinvented his life and wild times for his new, wide-eyed, young cherub, made a myth of his witch of a wife, if he even mentioned such an ogre. The name Ellen probably did not exist up in Gloucester. She slipped into sleep and dreamt the world had tipped and she was sliding off.

In the morning she awoke so stiff it took her an hour to get to the phone to call her employer. "I think I did it moving those barrels," she said.

"I know the routine," Halburd said blandly, cheerfully, completely canny, "I really don't need you right now anyway."

"Halburd," she said. "I can hardly move."

"So let me know when you're feeling better," he said. "I've got more help now than I need, as is."

Scared, she made her arduous way back to bed. The cat and dog jumped up with her. Sometime in the sweaty, dream-ridden afternoon Tringle put his head in the open window, looking for Lasker.

"You're still here," he said.

She hadn't seen him in five years, or was it ten? Where had he been? He hadn't changed at all. When he heard about her back he said, "You're a Virgo, aren't you? Your mercury's retrograde."

"I thinks it's stuck there," Ellen said.

"Never happen," Tringle scoffed. He ran on, as ever, rapping happily about the stars, the oscillations of yin and yang, the ancient, secret signs. "What I can tell you?" he asked.

"Nothing," she said, "I'll be fine," but things got worse. Edna was out of town or incommunicado. No one else dropped by– not that she wanted company– and finally she took a taxi to the doctor, who gave her a prescription, told her to move as little as possible, rest on a hard surface till the pain went away.

With immense effort she filled bowls and pots with dried cat and dog food and water, and put a quilt and blankets on the floor midway between refrigerator and bathroom.

To eat or answer calls of nature now exacted absolute attention or else the screams recurred in that puppet's voice she came to loathe. She dozed or brooded while light suffused the darkness, swelled, held sway, faded, gave way again to night. Turning her head she could see mounds of dirt under the stove and dead insects with their feet up in the air.

On the second day her back felt slightly better and she groped about the house for a minute, but was so depressed she lay down again at the first twinge.

Her spirits went on sinking. She hardly ate. The pills made her groggy. She kept thinking about Jason's birthday– a funereal occasion it would surely be, with only his grandmother to help him celebrate, his parents still deeming homosexuality a mortal sin and art pure frivolity.

Ellen grew glad she had not told him of her birthday plan; to have to cancel it would only have got him down. She would call again when she felt better; it wouldn't do for both of them to be in the dumps at the same time; and now, as she thought about it more closely and calmly, she wasn't quite sure what she wanted of the future. She could start with a casual trip to Dayton and see how that went. The old, bitter riddle bedeviled her still. Why couldn't he have loved her, in the first place, as she had him? What hope was there for them, at this late date?

Every day she thought, *Tomorrow will be better.* But it was worse. She had known depressions, expected to hit bottom and start up, but the plunge accelerated. She began to hate her own existence; even her will to hope vanished.

By the third day her back was undeniably better, but still she lay and watched the changing light. She could smell herself. Every failure, every flaw, every dark folly of her life pointed toward this awful, empty consummation. Where had the years gone? For what? Jason had painted his paintings at least, but she had invested herself in Lasker, was locked up with him forever, never could trade Provincetown for Dayton, not even for Jason, nor could Jason ever take P-town for more than a week at a time.

P-town, where she'd meant to make a life of theatre. When was her last role of any size? Dear God, ages and ages ago, gone with her favorite director and confidante, dead at 52, of some unknown ailment. So many of her friends' signature flamboyance had goaded Lasker to open hostility, finally spoiling her pleasures of being someone else, however briefly. But she had been good, everyone said so, "a vivid mobility of face and an unbridled, comedic range," one review had crowed.

She had been good, good, good, she had, she had. Strange to feel those ambitions now so deep in the past she no longer seemed to care, unsure at the moment if that in itself was a good or a bad thing.

In the morning she woke suffocating, with the cat crouching on her chest, the dog breathing down at her. Their worry was so palpable that she caught a glimpse of her own plight.

Revulsion got her to her feet. She was so mortified she didn't notice the lack of pain. Her back seemed a dim episode in a distant past. She was up, vertical. That was the main, the only thing, in fact, and she had lost some weight for sure– the proverbial silver lining.

The dog pranced, eyes agleam; the cat stretched complacently, yawned, sat back, began to lick its flank. She was ravenous and laughed aloud shakily. A sciatic attack, a strayed husband! What was all the fuss about?

She began to think, freely, clearly for a change.

The sun streamed through the windows. It was going to be one of those wondrous, warm days, mellow, over-ripe and still, with a thrilling hint of something unwholesome on the balmy air, one of those hallucinatory days of late fall that last and last, that grant the attentive a glimpse of eternity, nostalgic gift of the green, motionless bosom of the Gulf Stream, almost a promise of no winter at all, but only endless fall and early spring.

She heard the postman. Two letters came through the slot. Her heart leapt to see Jason's elegant calligraphy on one— was it his birthday? She tried briefly to count the welter of days. His sister's mélange of print and scrawl spoke from the other envelope.

Jason wrote, *Dearest Ellen, I have lost faith and want to leave. I'm sorry to do this. The catch is I can't live for others and don't want to for myself any more. I hate to leave with you this horrible thing.*

His sister began, *This is the hardest letter I've ever had to write.*

Ellen was dully not surprised. The letter told of Jason's death four days before. He had left notes for his friends on his drawing board, had stapled a sign to his door: ANY FRIEND OF MINE DON'T COME IN. CALL THE POLICE.

Someone broke down the door and found him, hanging from his storage loft.

He had willed his body to medicine, his paintings to anyone who wanted them.

Ellen lay back down on the floor. For a while the network of fine cracks in the white ceiling held her eye, proceeding from nowhere to nowhere, branching and re-branching, source-less clusters, soul-less and complete, but still there was no denying the consequences of the distracted phone call. One word of her visit would have saved him. All his calls over the years led only to this one failure to speak.

In deaf and blind calm she trekked to the liquor store, and lay down on the floor again. She kept thinking, *I've got to go see Jason and talk this over.*

Toward dusk, steadied by vodka and the exhaustion of all tears, she brought out the box of his letters, cards, drawings and memorabilia, and began to go through them piece by piece, the accumulation of twenty years and more, in case some clue awaited her.

It all came as revelation, was somehow all the same, unchanging, a familiar reflection of her own letters, as they must have been of his, which always began with the weather— looking out his window— night or day, half a page at least, rapturously portrayed.

Then came fervent thanks for her last letter, saying how much it meant to him, how he depended on them, like links on an anchor chain. Next came good wishes in her struggles for self-mastery, hopes that her relations with Lasker had improved, or were terminated, once and for all, that soon she would get back to her interrupted career.

Then followed accounts of what he was etching or painting, how hard he was working, how tired he was, how dismaying his fickle health, how frail and groping his ego.

From year to year he chronicled his regimen of pills and diet, bewailed his bouts of depression, his Calvary of herpes and shingles, his allergies, and respiratory and intestinal infections, his incredibly high blood pressure.

At first with boyish joy, then increasingly baffled remorse, he recorded his ardent romances, so full of expectation, so soon cooled, that always left him lonely and demoralized.

Time and again he said he longed to have a good cry with her, *to even the odds,* as he put it, always closing with the words, *Wink at the Sun & Moon for Me*

On his most recent postcard of the Alhambra he had complimented her on her beautiful handwriting and asked for the make of pen she used, but she had yet to answer it.

At midnight she went to the window, saw no star, nor moon, knew what she must do. It was the only way to keep faith with them both, the only possible redemption, the only true path.

Loath to do herself violence, she tried to think where she could get some pills without implicating anyone. Heart clement, head clear at last, she pitied whoever must find her, thankful at least that it wouldn't be Lasker.

The vodka was gone. She made it to her feet and found on the top pantry shelf a last inch of blackberry brandy, left from some forgotten festivity or dolor, tipped it down, slow as honey, rinsed the bottle, stood it in the dish rack.

She thought, *I'd better get on with this,* and a bright, exacting light stilled the room. She was surprised, impressed after her lifetime of doubts, by how strong, how resolute she felt as she delved in the drawer by the sink for knives. One of them she knew was very sharp, the black-handled one Lasker used to fillet fish. At the grate of the blade on her thumb she threw up without warning, easy as a baby.

She lay back down and dreamt of a children's book. Jason had always said, "You write, I'll illustrate." It was the size of a monument, covered with strange hieroglyphs, laid flat in the grass of a vast cemetery that stretched to the horizon. Two children were walking toward it, hand in hand.

As she approached them they turned. It was her and Jason with grotesque, adult grimaces. She woke on the kitchen floor, head pounding, palate raw with bile, bereft of all but loss, an exile in her own home, alone in a posthumous world.

THE DUDE

I f I did or didn't do it don't matter anymore. I don't even have to care. Cause of three hours ago I'm quitted. I'm innocent. I was worried for a while, I was scared. I coulda spent the rest of my life in jail. Fifteen months was long enough, half a million bail, $17 to my name. Nobody came that whole time, not even Skolly and Chaz, nor Skip either, just Hedrick, the court lawyer. Ma wouldn't set foot up north. On the phone she said, "I don't know who you are, you're not my Jimmy that I raised."

"Maybe not," I said, "but I'm me. I do know that." All I remember is she sat through every one of her divorces watching the soaps on TV about yelling, screaming marriages coming apart. By that time all her husbands had split, my father too. Who could blame him?

But I'm out, I'm in the clear. It was all circumstantial. The jury cried, but they had to let me walk. Three days they wrang their hands, three nights I never slept. "Thank you," I says. "Thank you, thank you." I made the sign of the cross, I was in tears, too. I couldn't hardly hear myself. The judge was always telling me to speak up— he didn't say nothing then though.

Hedrick, he just looked at me. Not sad exactly. More like he pitied me, or his own self for doing a dirty deal. He knew they never had a case. He didn't feel too good, I guess. He believed me though. Said he did. Nobody knows, that's the truth.

The cops was shocked. They didn't even have another suspect, no one in reserve. You'd think they'd have a backup, in case they got beat. Cause If I didn't do it who did? They don't know. Nobody does. I'd like to know myself.

I'm going take a rest and celebrate, drink a quart of vodka, pop some pills, what kind, who cares? I'll take what comes, codeine, amphetamine, Sominex, Percoset, then I'll smoke an ounce of dope, get laid by every twenty men I meet.

This sure ain't Palmetto Lakes. I ain't never going back there, I'm staying right here. Her niece in the paper says, "This isn't the quaint little fishing village it used to be, the elderly of this town are petrified now." They oughta be, they'll get their dessert too, just like everybody else.

Seventy-nine, she was old enough. What's the big deal? Some dude couldn't stand those hymns all day long, that keyboard coming through the walls. That skreaky voice. I don't blame him, I couldn't take it either. Who could? Drove me down the boiler room, I could still hear her though, like she came through the pipes. "How sweet the sound." Bull-dicky.

Give her a little tap, somebody did, lotta little taps, ten at least the coroner said. Mush he made a mess. Don't bother me, Death, I'm only 27. Still good-lookin. Whaaa tcha got cookin? How about? Cookin. Somethin. Well. Still got a few years left. Then I'll pay my dues. Less I live to be a dirty old man. Can't see waiting around too long on that.

When I hear people talk about God. All that love not war crap makes me puke. There's no peace cause there's no God, less He's a frickin scumbag worsen me. That's circumstantial. Any idiot would tell you that.

The Washashores

I feel good, I feel great. Not a cloud. When you're young at heart. Too hot for this frickin three-piece suit though, don't even know where it came from. Never wore a vest before. Who'd ever think it was me? Not even me, less I'd been there in court watchin myself, three whole days, all the court house jackals crowding in to hear the verdict. They couldn't wait to see me take the dive, but I busted their balls, you could hear their breath go out when the fore-man said "Not Guilty," like a big frickin prick fizzled down to nothin.

I'm glad a that, I'm proud of it. I look a million bucks, too, all shaved and showered. Last real shower I had, no, no, never mind that. Don't go pickin your nose, pokin your hose. Then's then. Now's now. I'll ask Skolly and Chaz to let me have their couch back till I... If they're not home I'll... They don't lock their door, she did though, dead bolt. Yeah.

"Yeah, right here. Here's just fine. Thanks. A lot. Hey, you fool around? No? Sure? Sure-sure? Too bad for you you prissy fuck."

Not bad looking, who the fuck's he think he is! How come he's got the BMW and I'm hitchin and hoofin, humpin this suitcase with nothin in it, everything I own, that's what I'd like to know. Won't always be this way. Maybe.

Too hot, longer walk than I thought, much longer, legs don't hardly work any more. Hey, I only lived here a little while, three weeks the papers said. How'm I sposed to remember where every-thing's at? I was fucked-up the whole frickin time. I don't remember a frickin thing. Don't even remember *not* doin it.

Sometimes though. Little flashes. Naturally. Cause I've heard so much testimony, read all the transcripts till I'm brain-fed. I been taken over in my mind.

That's why the judge sequestered the jury, the newspapers was full of lies, what a laugh, they got my whole frickin rap sheet all shuffled up, Florida, South Carolina, Maryland, Long Island, they shouldn't of published any of it, I shoulda got off right there. I'm a hustler, I'm a B&E man, I'm a burglar not a murderer. Wouldn't mind if I was. What's the difference? I'd still be me. Thieving's not so bad. Livin by my mind. I'm a sharp cookie, how about cookin...?

Frick, I'm not going near that house again, it's too far. Anyhow Skolly and Chaz aren't even there any more, they left town, told some reporter I ruined their lives. They shouldn't of said that. What they got to bitch about? Look at me.

Somebody killed the old lady, that's for sure. Maybe they did it, hell no, they never had time to hurt a flea. Go to work, come home, eat, suck, fuck, snore, no wonder I couldn't sleep. Add up their money all weekend, can they afford to do this, buy that? They're too nice anyway, they felt sorry for me cause I didn't have a place of my own.

I really wonder if I coulda done it. But if I did who ransacked her house? Furniture all tipped over, everything smashed, blood everywhere. Her niece said she didn't know if anything was missing. Maybe she bagged the jewelry, I sure didn't. If I did they never found it. Me neither. She was going to a church potluck supper, she was looking forward to it her niece said. How would she know, she live on the frickin phone with her old biddy? Could be, could be, it rang and rang, I can still hear it. Quit it, quit it right there, Dude, don't even listen.

Old ladies like little things, little bottles of perfume, little tea-sets, they keep everything neat, they love antiques, they eat cottage cheese and Campbell's soup, watch the birds and squirrels out the back window, their days are numbered.

I was real nice to her, put my manners on, my charm, I was helpful. Sometimes I feel good. She might of left me in her will. I said I wouldn't charge to fix her screen, that's how that lowdown worm got in, all those locks, what was she afraid of? How could anybody harm an old lady like that?

Why? Hey! Happens all the time. Just read the papers once in a while, Dude, people get off on that shit, right? They lap it up. I don't think I probably did it. But even if I did I'm in the clear. Anyway I didn't. Didn't. Didn't. Didn't.

Yeah, yeah, I'm in the clear. Why should I have to swear to everything all the time? It's over and done with. It don't even exist any more. So don't worry so much, you're in the clear. You hear? You're in the clear.

Yeah. I must've been tappy the whole time. I didn't have no meds, nothin to cool me out, I couldn't get no rest. Tonight I'll sleep like a rock down a well. First time in…

Frickin life I've had, never asked for noner this. I feel like that blind wretch like me. I drank all day, I even went to the priest, I told him I'd been in prison, I'd just got out, wanted to find peace with my God. All's he could say was he felt incapable of providing guidance, I should go back to my home-town and seek help. In other words, Get the frick outta here.

So I went back to the Town House Lounge. What was I spose to do? I kept going back all day, drank more beer, had some gin, plenty a gin, Skip was on the bar so it must have been night, yeah, it was dark, I remember that all right. Well, it was December, now it's spring. Right? If you say so, Dude. Who were those two frickin guys that testified I mentioned something bad I did that I was ashamed of? I never said what it was– course I wouldn't say, I got time hanging off me like Spanish moss, probation violations, assault on a police aide, things they don't even know about, no murders though. No, I'm a B&E man, Dude. I'm a con man. Whaa-tcha got cookin?

Those two guys were fucked up worsen me, the little one said a demon came out of a guy one time and threw itself into the fire, he's the one who said I seemed to be under the influence of something, he couldn't say what cause he was drinking all day himself. Yeah. More alcoholics here than I ever seen. Try and detox this population. They said we went to two, three, four other bars. They couldn't remember. Sounds like reasonable doubt to me.

Prosecutor never asked me straight out if I did it. Hedrick neither. I told the investigators I didn't do it. Four apartments in that building, anyone coulda done it. I got it all out of the papers. How'd I know anyway? It's all over, I got to get God into my life. Like a big frickin prick, whooee! And then?

Skolly and Chaz left for work. What'd I do? I felt like shit from all the stuff I did the day before. Or was that later? I was desponding, I'd been depressed, Skolly and Chaz said so, too. I was fixin to put me out of my misery, do it for real.

Woke up next morning when Skolly and Chaz said there'd been an accident upstairs, the cops wanted to know if they'd heard anything. Course they didn't hear anything, they weren't even there, I know cause I called from the Lounge, I even said so in court, there was nobody there.

Coulda been somebody upstairs though. Bloody bathrobe and nightgown she had on. And those bloody jeans stuffed behind the sheet-rock in the basement, Skolly said he knew they were mine from the frayed cuffs, cause he did my laundry. Whose jeans don't have frayed cuffs? Coulda been anybody's, like her blood on them, type O, mine's A, none on the hammer, no fingerprints nowhere nohow, no flies on me. Same with that strand of hair, the F.B.I. guy said it was mine, my expert really socked it to him, said the lab stuff wasn't conclusive, coulda been anybody's. No proof at all. Hedrick asked the landlord's wife, "How'd you know he just took a shower? You see soap in his hair?" He got a laugh out of that. She said I made her nervous, I talked a lot. I always talk a lot. No crime there.

I went over to Skip's, I found his stash. He kicked me out when he came back, he didn't want anything to happen in his kitchen. I asked him to call my mother, tell her I'd found my peace. I couldn't remember her number, what name she was using. I was gobbling a handful of pills, spilling all over the place, Skip crawling after them. He didn't want his dog to get them. I was convulsing when they picked me up, strapped me to a stretcher, special delivery to Cape Cod Hospital, they pumped me out, then twenty days observation, all I did was lie around, I needed a rest, just wakin up's hard work these days, dumb-ass shrink. What'd he think I was going to say? All he got out of me was I understood the charges.

Armed robbery, breaking and entering while armed with intent to commit larceny. Dismissed for lack of evidence. Where's the evidence I killed her? I don't even know myself. Because I didn't kill her. My looks, people don't suspect, they're shocked when they find out. By then I'm gone. I done a lot of time in jail. Lotta different jails for a young guy. I might have to go back some day. Live under oath. Furniture all tipped over, everything ransacked. She had her bathrobe and nightgown on. She was going to some church supper.

I been in worse fixes than this, no you ain't Dude, no you ain't. Yeah I am. I'm out. What if God starts pickin a bone with you? I got the worry wart, I got the habit, I got to kick it. I hate needles, some people don't even wash, I keep myself clean. In the sight of the Lord. Yeah.

She shouldn't of screamed. Cop that found her, he broke down, his kids played with her. What kind of grownup plays with kids? She was going to bake them a gingerbread house. I can't believe this shit. Any of it. Can you? No.

I'm not a bad guy, I don't think I'm such a bad guy, I'd never do nothing like that. The landlord said he was grateful he never had to see it. Bet he couldn't wait to raise the rent. My trade's a thief, a damn good one when I'm straight. I got my pride like anyone else, but I never did anything like that. Never.

The whole world's a rotten filthy slimy crud of a bung shitting bellybutton mung dung. Give it up, gotta give it up, get to a church, different church. I'll burn it down. I would if I got convicted.

Cause I didn't do it, couldn't of done it. Impossible for me to be there that time, that place. All this is making me freak. Hot in this frickin suit. I couldn't a been there, I didn't have the opportunity. I mighta had a motive. The prosecutor was just trying to convince me in my own mind. Did a better job on me than he did on the damn jury, the paper said you could hear them yelling at each other every time the door opened.

I wonder what else I left down that basement, cops would have found it by now anyway, I'll go over to the station, I'll say, By the way. Whatever it was. I want it back. That'd be a hoot. Course I knew her, can't say I liked her, yer honor.

Yeah. Rigor mortis come and gone when they found her. I never knew that before. Twelve hours in, twelve out, like the tide. I could not have been in that place at that time. Hedrick says, You couldn't of done it. How's he know? How the fricks he know if I don't?

I had alibis up the ass, that's why. It was all circumstantial. Tracks in the snow, comin and goin. Bottles of milk on the porch. Milkman musta been there. What milkman? I ain't no milkman, never touch the stuff. Three times they asked the judge what reasonable doubt means. He didn't know either, he just went in circles, he says, "Convict this sucker," but they wouldn't, they couldn't, they didn't have the balls. They knew I'd come give them a lead enema. Yeah. They can't touch me, they can't double my jeopardy. Next time I come I'll pack a gun.

Hedrick says, "Please don't convict him on these imaginary screams and a strand of hair." Course not, when I heard them I wasn't upstairs. I was downstairs asleep, just like Skolly and Chaz said in court. Under oath. I must have been dreaming, I was certainly fucked up, I mean to the moon, Dude, like I sat bolt upright. Skolly and Chaz said it was just a phone in some other apartment, it kept ringing and ringing, I thought it was screams, I knew it was, can't tell me it wasn't screams. They couldn't hardly calm me down, I knew something bad was happening to that old lady, whitest hair I ever seen. Like a ghost. Prosecutor said I was dreaming those screams, but that was no dream.

So I couldn't a done it. Who did? Never mind, Dude, you don't even want to know. Who'd do a thing like that anyway? You wouldn't even want to meet him. Yeah, I would. I'd wring his neck. I mean I'd suck his dick and then I'd wring his neck.

Here we are. Nobody here? What the fuck I care? "Hey, Skipster, whatcha got cookin? You day shift now? What's a matter? Ain't you gonna gratulate me? After all I tipped you? Just kiddin. You know what I want. A big frickin Stoli. On the house. Hey, I mean it, I got it coming."

"You got an I.D.? We don't serve non-humans."

"Hey, Skipster, don'tcha even know me in this frickin suit? I'm your native son. I'm on the loose like a goose. I'm cookin."

"Some places you'd have fried."

"They don't do that any more. It's inhumane. I wouldn't mind the needle."

"Right in your eye, people looking in, ready to pop the champagne."

"Hey. Gi'me my Stoli, preash."

"You're barred."

"What the frick for?"

"What the frick you think for?"

"Hey! I got a right. I'm out, I'm quitted. You didn't hear? Three, four hours ago? I got off. That's all she wrote. Rod been around lately? Randy?"

"So you beat the rap."

"Yeah. Must be on the radio by now all over everywheres. Give me my vodka. Thanks. And a beer chaser."

"So what're you gonna do now you're a celebrity?"

"Know anybody who's got anything? Smoke? Sniff? Pop? Whatever."

"I don't know anything about anybody. Except you."

"I could use a job."

"Town's just opening up. You oughta be a hot prospect. Put you in a shop window like a mannequin with a hammer in your hand."

"Hey, come on, Man, don't make jokes."

"I wasn't joking."

"I didn't do it, I didn't do it. Okay? Somebody murdered somebody, but it wasn't me. "

"I don't care who did it."

"You don't?"

"Why should I? I've done worse."

"Don't brag."

"To you? Are you kidding? With your mouth?"

"You just want me to say I did it. But I won't cause I didn't."

"That wasn't your bloody shirt?"

"What bloody shirt?"

"If you don't know I don't."

"They never found no shirt."

"What'd you do, eat it?"

"Come on, come on, gi'me another."

"One more and you're outa here."

"What's the difference, she was just an old lady, she was going to croak anyway."

"So are you."

"Life's lookin up, you know? It could really be beautiful. When you're young at heart. With a million bucks. I'm sicka being poor. I gotta get a job, line some things up."

"Hammers?"

"For Chrissake, shut up. All you people tryna put me at the wrong place wrong time. Hey, that's where I live. Walk a mile in these shoes. Two miles, must've been. This frickin suit's hot."

"You oughta take that tie, go hang yourself in the head. You know those pipes? You just get up on the toilet seat and step off. That's what Trixie Judd did. He never did anything to anybody but himself. It was people that did him."

"What the frick I care about him? This here's bout me. Me. I tried to kill myself at your house, remember? I musta been in a bad mood. I never killed no old lady, but I done plenty."

"Such as?"

"I kicked my mother down the stairs. Nah, I didn't, I wanted to though. Not any more. Dorothy's Gift Shop, I mighta done that. Nice clean job. You'd never believe me if I told you I done that."

"Did you?"

"Yeah, but don't tell anyone."

"Why not?"

"I wouldn't want it to get around."

"Why not?"

"What d'you mean, Why not?"

"You swear you did it?"

"Yeah, why not? Hey, what're you doing?"

"I'm calling 911."

"Hey."

"This is the bartender at the Town House Lounge. I want to report a guy in here who claims he did the Dorothea robbery. Yeah. No. Okay. Will do."

"You didn't really do that. I can't believe you really did that. Gi'me another. And some more beer. And some of those chips."

"Here you are, spiked with my special drops. Lay you out straight. You don't know what sick is till you wake up."

"You wouldn't do that to me."

"Yeah, I would."

"No you wouldn't. You're a friend right? I might be dead if it wasn't for you."

"I been thinking about that. Dumbest thing I ever did. Well, here's your pals. Gentlemen! Nice to see you.

"You son of a bitch. I don't believe this."

"Where is he?"

"Right there."

"Him? This here's Mr. James Pickard. Couldn't a done it, he was up in the Barnstable House of Correction."

"Then he's a liar."

"Tell us about it."

"Well, thanks anyway. Always nice."

"I can't believe you did that."

"Doing my civic duty. Why'd you say you did that job if you didn't do it? You already had your fifteen, you want another?"

"It coulda been me. I was just tryna find out. What the frick's goin on. Where is everybody?"

"Won't nobody come in with you here."

"Bullshit. I'll have one more for the road. Brim it up, pleash."

"You're done. I told you. You're killing my business."

"What d'you mean?. I'm just sittin here mindin my own."

"People see right in through the window."

"Nobody know me in this frickin suit. Buncha bananas out there all rowing with one paddle."

"You're shut off. I told you."

"I just want to have my drink, then I'm going away."

"You pass out you'll wake up in hell. That hammer be right there beside you."

"That's my prick, Dude."

"Okay. That's it. I told you I did something worse than you. I did plenty, nothing like that though. You gotta go, or I'm going to puke."

"Why'd you lie to me? Tryna prove you're bettern me?"

"Get out or I'll sic the cops on you for drunk. They'd like some action. Bored outa their gourds, nothing to do. Just shining up the thumbscrews. Get the fuck out. NOW."

"Hey, I thought you were my friend."

"I'll make that call. I'm making that call. Nine. One. One to go."

"Frick you, Skip, you frickin phoney. Ratting me out. What a laugh. Cops can't touch me. I busted their balls and they know it. Little Bar at the A-House be better anyway. Nicen dark, jukebox, some cute guy, some hunk, little peace and quiet. Wake up in hell. He shouldna said that. That's no way to treat a friend."

Frick is it ever hot in this frickin suit. Where'd it come from? Where'd anything come from, Dude? Where'd I come from? Yer mother's bunghole, Dude. Why couldn't I been born somebody else? Wouldna made no difference, Dude. What d'you mean, I wouldn't be me. Yeah yer would, Doood. Hah! That's not what I mean. Whad I mean? I mean I need a bottla vodka. And some pills. I need to sleep. I haven't slept in. And a place. Consistent with. A struggle. Yeah, must've been. A blunt instrument. At least ten. Multiple fractures of the skull and multiple lacerations to the brain. Consistent with. Some son-of-a-bitch, you son-of-a-bitch. Whynt you shut up, I've heard all this before.

If God's so good why the hell don't he kill the bad people?
Cause he wants them to kill each other. Save Him the trouble. God
don't fool around. He cool, Dude. Yeah. Hey, whatcha got cookin?
How about? With me. Oh my Oh you. Can't convict dreams and a
strand of hair. What the frick. Nobody here either.

"What's cookin, Dude?"

"It's pretty early. We just opened. My name's Jimmy actually.
What can I get you?"

"Big frickin Stoli straight up. And a beer back."

"Yes Sir. Seven dollars."

"I may as well run a tab. I'm going to be here a while. I just got
out of jail.

Oh. Ah. Well. That's good. I'm glad you're out, Sir. It's nice you
got such a nice day to regain your freedom."

"Too frickin hot."

"Actually it always seems quite cool in here. I always bring a
sweater. You could take your jacket off."

"I never took this jacket off in my life. I never had it on neither.
Hedrick must've got it for me. My lawyer."

"Well. It's a fine looking suit, Sir."

"Too frickin hot. What's with the Sir? You been here long?"

"I try to be courteous to the public. After all, I'm here to serve
you, Sir. Actually this is my first week. I lucked into this job. One
of the regulars got sick. I've only been here a month. I've been staying with a friend."

"Brimmerup, please. You don't know who I am?"

"No Sir, not really. I don't think you should have another. Not
right away. You've got quite a start on the day."

"It's my day. Far's I'm concerned. All mine. Please. Have a little class. Gimme a break. I'm a nervous wreck. I just got outta the can. I don't even have a place to stay. You really don't know who I am?"

"No Sir. Not really."

"I'm James Pickard."

"Oh. Well. We're both Jameses."

"No we ain't. You got nothin on me. I used to be Jimmy. Gimme nother Stoli. Preash. You really ever heard of me?"

"Well. All right, Sir. One last. That'll be eleven dollars. You can do without the beer."

"Yeah, yeah. Here's blood in yer eye. I'm cookin. I beat the rap. I'm a pro. I'm slick as a dick. Come in the head and you can sit on it. I got a bomb on my burner I'd like to get off on."

"I'll ignore that, Sir."

"Okay. I know. You're too sherry for that. Cherry. Gi'me one for the road, I'll be on my merry. One more once."

"No, that really was the last. I'm afraid you're getting inebriated. I can't in all conscience."

"Why you think people drink? Lemme bring ya up to date, Kid. I mighta killed somebody but I got off. I'm not guilty. That don't mean I'm innocent, but I'm not guilty. As of three, four hours ago. I'm out, I gotta celebrate. Brim me up."

"I can't serve you anymore. I'm sorry. Why... how could something... like that... happen to you? Someone you were... intimate with? Pardon my asking."

"You can read it all in the paper. I was headlines fifteen months ago. I'm not proud of it. I been through hell."

"I'm sure you don't want to talk about it."

"Why not? What the frick! I got nothin to fear. Prosecutor's the one doin the talkin. Him and the cops. They're talkin the talk. I'm doin the walk."

"Not to pry, but who did you kill? And why?"

"Whazit to you?"

"I'm interested in people."

"People. What's the big deal about people? I offed some guy. Gave me a hard time. Put it this way, he wasn't hard enough. No big deal. He's dead, dead, don't bother me. Fuck I care? Hey Dude, don't make it bad, sweet sang, swing low I sing of thee sweet peace now blind I see no flies no flies on me. Thank God Thank God Thank God I'm free."

"Sir? No, no, Sir. Sir? You can't sleep here. You'll have to go. You should go home. That's eleven dollars, Sir."

"All I got six, change."

"That's all right, Sir. You keep it. Just go."

Frick you little prick. Woozy walls and door hang on. Wo. Wham my head. Ah shit! Ow. Ow. OW. Okay. Kay. Big lump already, no blood though. Nobody saw. Woops. Hands and knees, gotta get up can't crawl Up. Up. Wo. Wish I could puke, sleep on my feet.

Cross, just get. Car better stop, sue their ass. Stare like I got two heads. Scuse, scuse me, sorry. Frickim. Who they think they are? Lean here till whirlies quit. Beach this way, path between, weeds, been here before, old rotten wharf, some guy who.

Now sit down, sit, slip off, don't jump don't fall just drop. Eee Zy. Oooof. Made it, made it, all the way. Blind now free. Hungry. Gotta puke. Some wrong with me. Skip maybe. Why'd he say that?

Hard walk in sand. Here enough far enough. Lie down tide comen take me away never get up again no sweat. Sand nicen warm in this suit. What's that? Biting me. Sit. Up. Not so easy. Nothin on my hands, nothing in my hair. Nothin. Nice view. Here far enough.

Shoe come off. Where? Don't need, don't care. Dues all paid. Curl up. Wasn't me. Swing my song sweet chariot. Wasn't. Isn't. Couldn't been. Hedrick said. Judge and jury too, what's the fuss? Even if it was I'm different now, I'm new. Time to move on.

Well, Dude it's just you and me now. I don't like you. That's you you don't like. Whynt you shut up for a change. You shut up.

That look on Hedrick's face. Still can't figure. Lookin down at me like. Like Whatchagodcookin. Why If I did I? She shouldn't of screamed. No I. Course I. Didn't. Didn't. If I don't believe my own attorney. Couldna done it. Downstairs in bed those screams no dream, no frickin phone either.

Shoulda got up, gone up, saved her ass, tap that guy, eyes pop out roll under the table. Blind peace. Such white hair. Mother Mary Jesus please God let it be over all over with forgive I forgive. Didn't mean her any harm even if I did so let go cry at last let go let go warm piss ahhh good long fart too squirt ahhhhh glubblegush lumpy hot love my own can't stand nobody else's who can? Shat myself. Don't even have to care.

Sleep stay by me. Now no more. Evermore. Safe in sand. Tomorrow I'll...

When he came to he got cleaned up, found a job, volunteered at the Soup Kitchen on weekends, never again missed early Mass, confessed his sins and sinned no more, went back to Palmetto with money in his pocket, made amends to his mother, never drank another drop, never popped a pill, allowed himself to smoke filter-tips on occasion, not more than one or two with morning coffee and one before bed, worked 24/7/365, did a life of good deeds, became someone everyone looked up to, helped the young, cared for the old, stood up for the weak and poor, was credited with making peace between people of all races, all creeds, all walks of life.

It was not always easy to be James Pickard but he kept true to his Dude, and it was rewarding because men came his way with respect. He was a living miracle though nobody knew it till he died quite young of overwork and the whole congregation, let in on his hard life, overflowed with amazement, love and gratitude, and scattered his ashes in some scenic spot, put up a tall monument in the church-yard in honor of his service to all mankind as a sign of his high acclamation by his fellow men and women both.

So it wasn't such a bad day after all, in fact it was a pretty good start on all the rest of the days of his life– so No, no, he really wasn't a lost cause, cause, after all, you just never know.

BOOKS AND THE PHANTOM ZERO

Books, the kids all called me. Books, hey, Books, whatcha readin? Sixty years ago. Little chuckle-heads. Books, Books, Hey, BOOKS!

Walking home, nose stuck in my stupendous find. Eleven was I? Twelve? Lurid cover, slavering buccaneer, wide-eyed wench with deep cleavage backed against a wall, crucifix-like arms out-flung.

Smirking old codger— about my age now— suddenly blocking my way, snatched it. "Let's see how you soil your mind, your father'd spank you if he knew. Bad Boy. I may spank you myself. Would you like that? *Crime and Punishment*, eh? Is it good? Show me, show me where."

He bent it till the binding cracked. I snatched it back and ran. Fifty cent treasure mixed in with drugstore proto-porn, more parsimonious of flesh in those days, what joy, my first taste of Dostoyevsky, then Tolstoy, Chekov, Pushkin and all the Russians.

Still never leave the house without book in hand, though passing eyes now never glance, tits a glut, title nil, author less. And I my own nadir, fuming, dim-eyed, corpulent, slovenly, uncouth, officious, pompous, pious, morbid, melancholic, hectic, all-too-often-idle prig.

Well, well, well, but who but me's doomed to travel on New Year's Eve? In transit from Albany where I'd gone to hear eulogized an august pedagogue, whose lectures now fifty years past watered

my own scholarly grains, whose nightly, late-lighted window re-
buked my student turbulence.

A millennium preceded him to the grave. Long he tarried by a
bedside shelf of richly-bound familiars– Sophocles, Dante, Shake-
speare, et al. Loathsome, merciful senescence veiled his estate's de-
preciation from him, whom his panegyrist, a nonagenarian himself,
rightly styled *Interpreter of the Great Documents.*

A dismal chill stole through the chinks of the stone chapel. Few
we were, a drab, shabby remnant hunched in our overcoats. I sat
unsung among them, dour wits, arthritic limpers, dripping noses,
no less decrepit, though far more gracious, more reconciled than I.

I did not stay for gab of where they'd got to. They looked quite
jolly, I had to leave.

Only in dire dream indeed would one be found in the Hyannis
bus station on the night of December 31st. Alas, such was I, absent
from my desk amid this evil epoch known perforce as The Eighties.

Rows of plastic seats bolted to metal beams, bare walls, assaul-
tive fluorescence, two huge NO SMOKING signs and butt-littered
floor. In the last twenty years, one by one, lunch counter, news-
stand, free toilets, all social benignancy, all easement to serendipi-
tous acquaintance, have been abolished, the place reduced to limbo,
the most forbidding the human genius could devise. SCRAM was
what its aura spelt.

Well, well, wrong to slight its cheerful side and season, when it's
graced by rosy, round-rump girls in piquantly-flimsy halters. What
truth can equal a summer séance of female radiance and youth?

Desolate the waste, empty but for three derelicts— more habi-
tating than waiting— who looked, I must say, but little unlike myself. Despite my rolling majesty afoot, my extravagant gestures and

portentous periods, seated, silent I cut but a negligible figure. I nodded each a grave greeting as I sat down, but none ventured to respond.

One was drunk, his purplish face expressing— I thought— sly defiance; haunted-looking and gaunt, the second kept revolving his head, muttering, as if to confute a swarm of spectral accusers; but the third touched me with hope— even of deliverance, given the depths of my gloom— by his ruddy countenance and bright white hair. Arms folded, he gazed straight ahead with aloof reclusion, ready to face the cold.

Meanwhile I mortified myself by surveying the follies of the past year, renewing my futile vows: to think only true thoughts, to work only to universal purpose, to defeat despair, combat misology, to do and endure all I dread. And to finish, finish, finish my damnable, abominable, 900-page diatribe of a novel— call it a novel— and to that sole end eschew opiate poesy of nostalgia.

Well, I am nothing but furnace and sewer, blown by appetites and sloth. The vice of self-colloquy has sapped my will, I read without compass, grub after news, shirk— nay, flee— that vast, blank void of final pages, but half a hundred, more or less, unmarred as yet by pen of mine.

Notes, yea, bales of notes, from which I spin vile verse. To what end my fruitless doodling? A pity there's no hell. Heaven's pillars I'd pull down and scrawl outrage thereon. 'Pon my word I would.

For proof— were one needed— that round the globe this festival of End and Beginning tends to the macabre, picture how two women shuffled in, mother and daughter they looked, older and younger, larger and smaller, shaped the same, bulky as Brueghel peasants, faces hidden by long scarves worn hood-like and tied beneath their chins with chains of knots.

Oblivious to all, they went resolutely to the pay phone, took positions on either side, moved not, spoke not, but stood in still tableau of obstinate dejection.

As if at the end of all strength, mother at last lifted receiver, daughter slid coins in and dialed, while mother gathered breath. Then both bent foreheads together like a little chapel of faith in hope, and waited, listening, listening, intently listening, till temple thuds drove my dry heart to heave up a prayer for some joyful voice to answer.

Reluctance failing, a doleful tug-of-war began, daughter finally, gently guided mother's hand to hang up, and they trudged out in mournful procession, the door held open for them by a silver-haired man in elegant evening wear, who, once within, dithered about, pronouncing in tones of bemused perplexity, "I don't know who I am, I don't know who I am."

My fellows observed him— if at all— with blank indifference. He made a circuit of the room, repeating these words to thin air, then with sudden, decisive step strode to the ticket counter and spoke them to the dour woman there, who sat still as a stuffed dodo, whereupon he made a sort of social amends, raised eyebrows and shoulders in unison, affably, negligently bowed, then backed a step and strolled about like a model of debonair nonchalance, till a sudden squall of half-quarreling black youths burst in, three boys and two girls.

They filled the place with din, loud and louder, goaded by the morgue-like atmosphere and torpid inmates, whom they contemptuously ignored. The girls tried to calm the storm, yelling at them, then at one another, for blaming the wrong one. The boys absorbed the artificial light and loomed, but the girls dazzled, their sequins glittered, sleek boots shone, proud eyes flashed. Their swains meanwhile were all cuffs and slaps, challenges and scoffs, few words among them except "Fuck this or that shit."

The kick-boxing soon grew too obstreperous for the girls who sat down to a fervid tête-à-tête, keeping an upward, wary eye on their parlous cavaliers. We whites looked on sidelong from our allotment with which they had as little to do as we with theirs.

The boys were hindered in their need to fight. None dared contend wholly with another for fear of an unoccupied third, and they sparred and kicked and feinted with ever-rising, shrill derision, each against all against each.

Finally the biggest loped to the Coke machine, poured coins in, punched several stuck buttons, then rocked the heavy dispenser bang-crash, crash-bang, till the girls together shrieked "Quit-That-Shit", and he came back and tried to tear one of the fiberglass seats off its steel beam while the other two watched with chivalric respect, and the girls hid aged faces.

I longed to see the orange boomerang shape wrenched free and flung– at whom I knew not– but it wouldn't budge. The youth looked sixteen, strained till his cheeks gleamed and his beautiful hands displayed every articulation– strange scene, dressed as he was in fedora, emerald ski pants and spurs.

He bent ever-steepening effort, nerve, sinew, heart, soul, brain, every cell of his being concentrated on moving that seat even one iota; and failing, failing, failing, finally loosed a scream that started deep in his guts, burgeoned like an unbearable cornucopia, spilled, gushed, flayed his larynx raw and charged the room with tragic pitch of homicidal verge.

The ticket-seller behind her glass picked up the phone. The screamer turned in small and smaller circles, hands on hips, panting, the pentad become a shielding quincunx, him the center. Born black, myself must surely long since have been dead of my tongue, if not of my impotent pen.

The back door opened. Dangling his nightstick, gazing up as if for stars, a paunchy policeman entered, paused on his heels, gaze slowly descended, coming to rest at last on the ticket-seller.

The kids fuddled and bumbled together; then, with sudden, languid eloquence sauntered out the front way, the leader last, glancing sexual scorn over his shoulder at the wan ticket-seller, who flicked her eyes toward the three bums, amnesia man and me.

The cop made for us. Two bums shuffled for the door like ducks before a neighbor's dog, but the ruddy one strode with upright gravitas, as though he and he alone chose to elect departure. Amnesia man, clad in the dignity of suit and tie, delayed till all were gone, then followed them into the dark.

The ticket-seller announced the Provincetown bus— last of the year— and dimmed the lights. I raised aloft my ticket, with the other hand hoisted my ancient portmanteau, so capacious and imposing, if virtually empty, and in my usual stately manner advanced, notwithstanding many mutters and sundry jerks, straight toward the stairs to the charnel house of a garage where the bus idled, in billows of exhaust, wheels frozen in rainbow rivulets of grease.

Well! Imagine my amazement, if not the pathos of my delight– impoverished soul, whose Mermaid Tavern has lately sunk to insufferable gentility, in short to victuals, waiters, tablecloths! — when I saw that the bus held four passengers, smokers all, all seated on the aisle, up front.

They spoke naught, while I, manifestly senior in age, corporeal stature and cerebral command, arranged myself close behind them. None had acknowledged my boarding, nor now deigned to meet my eye.

As if I and I alone had kept them waiting, the strange, morose driver— not my familiar, friendly Henry, with whom I had beguiled so many melancholy forays to and from the world away— hissed shut the door, released the brake with a hideous creak, precipitately backed us out upon the road, and roared into the dark like an irate plane on a short runway.

At first I feared to damp all social fires, my aspect such that I am oft addressed as Preacher, or shunned for a mortician. My clothes, however harmonized, bear a guise of gross anachronism, incongruity and decrepitude, garbed as I am severally by women I consorted with so long, long ago.

But their confab never was suspended— as though I indeed were none of them— nor anyone at all— while we whirled through the night, the dragooned driver grimly bent upon a speedy end of this last leg of his unwelcome run.

What I gleaned of the two forty-ish passengers at diagonals across the aisle from each other, both of a type, quick and slim, with cramped features and restive fidgets, gave me to dread that I might in time be called to give them each a thump.

"Help yourself," croaked the one who was dying of throat cancer, plucking a pack of Camels from the mouth of his bulging duffle bag, opened wide as a gargoyle's howl to show that it held nothing but cartons of the same.

He obliged his fellow passengers— except me— with a light. He had done nothing, he would do nothing, to hinder his malignancy. He loved to smoke, it was the only thing he had taste or talent for, his sole source of gladness and content. He would sooner die than change his style, meant to smoke for all he was worth, and let the cancer go its way, it too self-doomed. He cared not for life, nor death either, while he still cared for nicotine, and after that he would care for naught at all.

The other was a killer— if you please— or rather a self-styled acolyte in that line, who planned to try again, if not this very night. He felt he would succeed henceforth, he had a gift, he'd had it in him from Day One: kills were his fulfillment. He had started with worms before he could walk, soon progressed to crickets, minnows, moths and birds, cats, dogs, geese, cows, horses, pigs and sheep— these he slaughtered secretly, a trackless stripling of stealth, and, it went without saying, a crack shot— in ripening manhood slew countless hundreds of wild creatures, endured humiliating renown in the petty, Nimrod world of mounted trophies, while inwardly he crawled with chagrin that he yet had killed no human kin.

Poor luck and worse technique had ruined his debut, but he had babbled so persuasively he proved himself insane to dim official-dom, became a model inmate, a saint-like soother of the truly mad, obsequious to his keepers, till he was deemed reborn, a gentle penitent.

From his first day of captivity, to this very day of his release, he had busied himself, plumbing the certainty of contingencies and how to circumvent them, exploring all the elements of escape. While his fellow felons read law he studied criminology, to pay his debt to society, by never taxing jail again.

He planned to kill but one man at a time- common gallantry forbade dispatch of children and women, where, anyhow, was the challenge in that, where the pleasure, pride and glory?– he abhorred mass murderers, their greed and grandstanding, their crudity, the odium they bred.

A single, unrequited victim provides a universal thrill of vicarious revenge, a communal store of gratification open to all who dream of secret retribution— as who does not? — while the killer enjoys the shelter of the motiveless, but multiple kills provoke unease, bring exponential risk.

He recited the pantheon of names- not to be sung here- of artful killers whose careers spanned decades, and baffled even seers, but eventually had succumbed, conniving at their own downfall, from masochistic conscience or want of wide esteem for their fantastic feats, so much like Death Itself, near supernatural.

He had meant— still meant— to surpass them all, and retire unknown at his hundredth kill, at whatever age, but not one day sooner.

Without doubt he was a clever fellow, duly chastened. Now matured, he spied the towering legend he had vowed to build, weighed with care the burden he had taken on— a hundred kills unscathed– he wouldn't count his first fiasco, that later died of clumsy wounds– - nor did he begrudge the years in jail, to which he owed his ripening. He knew one enemy, and one only— wide-eyed surprise— which he lived to see in other men, but never in himself.

The third ranged far above it all, a decrepit white-haired sage, who owed his light to a single line– *Sentience is Pain*— which, like a tune heard in the womb, grown clearer by the year, had brought him to enlightenment, then led him prophet-like to bruit his gospel to the world, That after all its ages of vain pursuit of purpose, the simple fact lay out in plain view, That the universe was a whole near-unto perfection, in all its manifest, pristine garbs, with only the one lone flaw— pain, call it by its rightful name— which reached its evil apex in humankind, which alone thinks upon itself and gauges wrong.

Thus in these his golden years he went from place to place preaching restoration of all animate phenomena to their lost azoic state, when every atom was naturally at peace each with each. What mercy Camel Man and Killer proposed for self or others could little rectify the universal perversion of infinite futility.

One holistic measure was wanted. The dominant species of planet Earth had yet to glimpse its condign destiny, but clear-eyed science, once it grasped the simple principle that all extinctions were but one, could quickly re-establish the natural harmony of perfect, total insentience.

As to tainted sites elsewhere, in other galaxies, such were beyond his ministry, if not beyond a fervent prayer that none but Earth were or ever would be so afflicted.

"But the trick, the real stickler," said he, "will be to make sure the curse does not spring up again from hidden germs, and breed a more pernicious strain of pain, resistant to human remedy."

Therefore elite cadres must remain some while extant to tend the veritable armies, navies and air-corps of robots designed to treat in perpetuity with extreme prejudice every sign of recrudescence of life on earth, in air or undersea.

The whole operation would be directed by an impregnably-armed, special command of robots that would provide defense against rebellions of apostasy or faintheartedness among the dying cadres— once all other life was successfully stamped out— who might be tempted to re-infect some hapless planet elsewhere.

The fourth of my fellow passengers, a moon-faced Tsimshean from the Bering Strait— with black cowl of hair and winsome mouth permanently curved with benign delight— merely smiled the more he heard. He had fished in every sea, he said. There were not so many fish as once. No stranger to the Mayflower's first landfall, he once had helped string Thanksgiving lights on the Pilgrim Monument. "I'll bet I'm the only Indian who ever did *that*," he laughed with flashing wonder. "I must have thought it was a Christmas tree."

In him I placed my hope— for hope I must. And in myself, of course, that figment I impersonate. What have all my bluster and fustian composed but a string of thin poems that stitch my pages like sutures of a droll surgeon or drought-ending lightning streaks above the Serengeti?

Them I survey with pity, orphan offspring of my flight from prose, my dalliance with rhyme. 'Twas my novel that was to justify and encompass all. Well, well, not dead, not done.

Verily, verily, though was I loath to ride that rattling, clattering bus hurtling toward the end of one and start of yet another infernal annum. We were all smoking like fiends in hell, I my own, hand-rolled brand, that they turned from with contempt. Above the puffing driver half a faded placard blared: NO

Camel man marveled without complaint, "I thought this was a free country."

"No more," said Killer. "Everybody's a slave of everybody else. Except me, and I'm one of a kind."

"Who makes these rules? Let *them* leave the room," the sage decreed.

Inwardly I smiled— for the new seat-belt law was due at the kissing knell, but half an hour hence. If I ruled here, as rule I ought, I would rule all, down to the least nebbish or nut.

Neither have I car, nor can I drive. Where therefore should I go, beyond last rites of the justly renowned? I live for my epitaph. That at least I'll leave till last. And sign it with a match.

"I'm proud I was born in this country," declared the driver, "but sometimes I wonder."

"They're after our guns," Killer warned.

"Nothing's the way it was," said Camel man, with nearly wistful note. "I used to hate that bottle bill, now I care not a nickel's worth of anything."

"In Montana," Killer enlarged with outraged disbelief, "they're going to ration firewood. It's American to burn."

"Nothing should be done about anything," Camel man concluded, tossing his butt in the aisle.

"They're taking over the country," Killer agreed.

"Serves them right!" said the sage.

"Give it back to the Indians," said Camel Man.

The Tsimshian smiled with distant interest. "Canadian health plans are better," he said.

"Everything's out of kilter, queers everywhere," Killer said. "The only good people are black, the blacker the better. And we're the ones that made them good."

"It's Women's Lib," the driver summarized. "My whore of a wife made a fortune in drugs and left me with our debts."

The wry Tsimshian revolved his head in a circle both ways, and smiled more than ever.

The driver vaunted his harsh heritage. His father beat him with a baseball bat, and shot-gunned the heads off his dogs.

"In Nam when I was shooting people I kept thinking about that, and I went right on shooting. When I got back I says, 'Hey, Dad, I got you to thank for being alive.'

"He didn't understand. He was glad to take the credit though. Hey, that's life, isn't it?" he allowed over his shoulder with bleak glee. "We're in The Final Days. The signs are everywhere."

No one said him nay, nor knows how long we've been here. I am truly capsized, with no one but myself to right. Aghast at everything, I beseech leave of nameless nothingness before I squash a bug. Well, the less fit for existence the more arrogant.

My Tsimshian laughed, "I'm waiting for those UFOs to give us the word."

"Won't be no surprise," Killer said. "Difference is war."

"Tell me about it," the baleful driver said.

Killer said, "I can tell you more than you might want to know."

"We still got free speech," the driver said. "Don't wait on my say so."

"Words are nothing," Killer said. "I'd have to show you."

"Civilians!" the driver jeered. "I'd run the lot of you right off the rud."

"Kindly wait till I finish my smoke," said Camel man.

"Let us all remain seated till we reach our destination," chimed the sage.

"Talk is cheap. Rum costs money," remarked the Tsimshian in his cheerful, musing tone.

Clement exclamations united the five— grunts, half-coughs, sighs— humble sounds of verities accepted.

Ruminating Killer said, "Some bozos aren't worth killing," indubitably meant me, who offered him no thumps. And why? Why is what I'm trying to tell you, *mes semblables*, if any. Tongue gnawed to cud, teeth gnashed to sand, my purple hearts are rusted down to rubble.

Once inexhaustible of strength I now can hardly hobble. Excess of eat and drink, and fleshly inactivity, have dimmed even memory of my green years of book-packed knapsack, day-long walks and gay, robust companions. Where, O where, has gone my love of life?

False love? Where my strength? Illusion. Youth's defiant consolation in suicide's resort pales before enormities. And the Grande Dame died. O, my dear Auxilia Lomes, my last and dearest confidant! Time takes all.

"The world's too small," the driver growled, and all the more I missed my friendly Henry, who nodded at my every trope, and drove this road day in day out, nor ever sped nor slowed. "The end times are come."

"No, no," the driver insisted. "I mean *right* here. *Right* now. It's spreading everywhere. One of Khadafy's agents might just be on this bus."

I felt their sudden mass of glance, and quailed at anarchy, Wheelchair-bound Achille Lauro passenger tossed into the sea, hostage shot and dropped from hijacked plane to tarmac, TVs all tuned to body's bounce, bounce, bounce, had one a mind to sit for it. Bloodlust and imbecility employed to entertain.

It galls me to concede— if I ruled, as rule I ought— I would know no better, than to bide the shame of circumspection. Stranded amid mass folly, shall I not contrive my own *auto da fe*, lone cipher self-brought to naught?

In the headlights a white apparition appeared. The bus stopped with a skid of gravel, and a young woman boarded. We rolled on again, but slowly, silently, possessed by thought.

She wore no coat, but only a white frock in the frost, as she stepped from the woods, out of the pitch-black night, far from any human sign. She was fantastically, exquisitely beautiful it moment by moment dawned, too beautiful at first for amorous cupidity, though grow such folly must, and all too ruinous soon. But who the devil was she?

I sat pyramid- like in the desert. As a child I learnt with gladness there was no providence; it clarified, swept clean, let wind sing or whittle how it would. What was left to want or lose?

Smiling as if she were pleased by every circumstance, she stood by the driver, holding the pole.

"Where to?" said he without regard for route or fare.

"I'll let you know," said she, "I know the way."

Camel man offered his pack, but she declined with sweet smile of thanks.

"Let me show you," said Killer, "the finest kind of a time."

Her look gave veiled regret that she was elsewhere bound.

"You ought to have a coat," said the sage, and reached for his own on the rack above, but she only smiled deprecation of the cold, and he sank back shyly in his seat.

"You must be going *somewhere*," the glowing Tsimshian said.

Him she favored with closed eyes, then glanced appraisal of my worth, a terrible, due regard.

Well, I know not who she was, nor what, divinity or dream, at least no less than respite from the furies, ageless her countenance, her form uplifting to behold, and wise too she began to seem, sublime in self-possession and gracious show of radiant solicitude for each of us.

One must submit, submit, with endless thanks. Before our enchantment could be made mortal she with hand on driver's shoulder slowed and stopped the bus by woods no less dark than those she'd come from, and taking leave of us one by one with grave and speaking eye, stepped down, was gone, while we rolled on bereft.

"I'll never figure that," said the driver, finally treading on the gas. "My wife always said I was an ugly mug no one could stand to look at."

"I could party with her," Killer averred, "forever."

The sage demurred, "Frivolous dereliction."

"Only never is forever," said Camel man.

Laughless, Killer resumed his sneer.

"I couldn't care less," said Camel man.

"Nor I," said Killer. Like opposite bishops they were, who always agreed, but never meant the same.

Sheer progress in morbidity am I, nor need I seek. All things imbue my soul. What existence have I beyond my piled pages, small loss or gain in a hapless world? I can do nothing, even with myself. I take my stand. I lock my hands behind my back. The stars— my stars, I sometimes dream— rain down on me, all disasters at my back, am blood and mud and toppled towers, distillate of rues, butterfly and jackal, all resistance gone.

I have crossed the blazing hills, gone down the misty vale where dwell more dead than living friends, the land of endless elegy, what the Portuguese call *soudade*.

"They'll blow it all to smithereens one way or another," said the driver, sounding sooner right than spared.

"They'll botch the job," said the sage, "and make more grief than peace."

"There ought to be another world," said the Tsimshian. "We might just be smart ants."

"One is too many," said the sage.

The bus rolled, then roared, rolled, then roared through Truro, North Truro, up and down Corn Hill, where the Pilgrims stole the Pamet's winter storehouse, rolled, then roared, in the moon-bright, star-vast night, around the bay, the diamond town aglitter, and I bereft of gladness, a shameful fall from my inveterate gaiety at first sight of home, who never had one else.

The bus swept past Beach Point onto Bradford while Killer leaned into the aisle with anxious, darting eye. Smoking man chained up. Muttering Sage mimed his lines.

The town slept, no revelers in view, till the bus skirted Lopes Square, and three men in tuxedos– one red, one blue, one white– came dancing arm-in-arm in hats and canes, then two more lurched in strange garb like Halloween. Another sat on the curb with bloody face. Here and there some dullards trudged, heads down, hands in pockets. A cretin band boomed from the Governor Bradford.

The driver rushed us off. All dispersed without a word, as if we had not shared a moment's journey. Well, the year was not yet up. Time remained for final follies and accounting.

Making my stately way west, overtaken by all, noticed by none,

I spy Times Square in every living-room I pass, but no book, much less bookcase – menus the favored reading here – nor is there promise of solace down my privet-hidden lane. Weary, weary, my tall stairway quakes with indulgence of my hungers. None will come to bring or take a kindly cup. None but me will be regaled by anything I do or dream.

My window looks down into a tiny cottage with a stockade fence, where two rotund women summer, who never speak to me, so lithe a reed myself. They are just hastening out in their cowboy finery, taking leave of a dilatory guest, who remains at the mirror, adjusting her pirate cutlass, glancing over her shoulder, till they have gone from sight, then delves through every drawer, every nook and shelf in the house, till finally, grimly she locks the door, steps forth empty-handed on the trail of her hostesses, better luck, she hopes, ahead.

Indeed, I am indeed downcast. As who in sanity is not? I grasp at straws, flotsam and jetsam, my frail bark gone down beneath me. I see it glimmering from sight, and none to mourn, not even I. Well, well, what's lost but pride? Good riddance to rubbish! All things human come to naught, all hopes must fail. Ever it was, ever must it be.

I stare myself a trance, take belated stock, summon my Phoenix. Time is nothing. Around me, shelved from floor to ceiling, every wall replete, the ages speak from a thousand spines. Here is all I am, here I hoped by right to dwell. I lift my eyes to the fiery alphabet. Downcast?

No. No. Not I, not I, and many not, the best never. So many eons from the slime, so many yet from the final cold, where is due despair? Betray the girl in the white frock? More stupidity!

Reverence too be damned!

To toast all better selves, I fetch forth my bottle iced the day I left for Albany. 'Tis time to make my pledge, that I have never yet not broke before the infant hour was up.

Gold tinfoil and wire-wrapped cap removed, with ceremonial, slow deliberation, deep in piety, millimeter by millennium, I thumb the cork toward the future.

Resistant– as it always is and ought to be– the stubborn cork sticks halfway up. I set the bottle down to flex my feeble digits, good for naught but pen. Then like a boy with high expectancy, I bend again to my bathetic task. Instantly, with not a touch from me, the festive report rings out.

Black lights I see, my large tender nose hurts like blazes, I bleed buckets, inauspicious splashes down chin and front of my un-changed, white funeral shirt.

I gaze at distant dishcloth. Then, loath to leave my window, I forsake niceties, half fill my glass, hold it high, rage some while more at everything, not least at what I am, am not, am no longer, never was, then bow to all shames past, concede nothing to the future, still drip-dripping drink down a drought of red bubbly, pour myself a new dilute.

Outside on my high porch, vermilion glass in hand, I find a di-amond night, white frost on my railings, a whisper of surf, in the air a thrilling hint of snow, am suddenly reinvigorated, rapture-able and resolved, avid for my life of desk. Weary of peninsula weather, you are weary of life.

Three blocks away, plangent voices of young women rise and stream to me like galaxies. The countdown starts. *Ten. Nine. Eight,* defiant, vindictive, the dire milestones dismissed, disclaimed, traduced, loud and louder, reckless, remorseless, histrionic, individual and vibrato, then shrived, gathering, eager, conjoined, *Seven. Six. Five. Four*, a joyful march to the crescendo of the phantom zero, Happy New Year cries long ring up, till raw and breaking hoarseness sounds.

They rescue me, so they do. I wish them wealth of courage. Well. Well. No more doodling, no ardors but in prose. I'll start to finish, I hereby vow. Damn gravity. What remains, remains to see. What's to lose but pride? Not dead, not dead, not done.

Let the brave young women lead, as thankfully they ought.

GOOD SAMARITANS

The fabulous tints of a rare, balmy Provincetown spring were lost on Maria Nore. The world was too awful, and she was growing old.

In appearance she had hardly changed, a small, quick-walking, white-haired widow of an Anglo-Saxon specialist, long an ornament at Mt. Holyoke. At sixty-five he had left her for one of his students, a more motherly type, but had ceded her their summer house and money to insulate it, then kept up a vigorous correspondence with her from London till his death. She had remained solitary, never allowed herself a word of regret for being childless, despised her occasional loneliness.

In time, her legacy dwindled, she sold the house and its contents and moved into a tiny attic apartment in the West End, which, though cramped, had a wonderful skylight on the bay and suited her sense of propriety, the only real loss her large library.

Callers were usually sated with infrequent visits, as the attic angles cracked one's skull, the exactly arranged herds of glass, African and Asian beasts looked poised to leap from every nook where an elbow longed to repose, and a disconcerting air of pristine order reigned.

Oddly, the wallpaper and woodwork replicated the colors of her favorite lavender-and-green, plaid jacket, black pants and blue sneakers, so that in her own home, when she was still, she virtually disappeared, except for her flame of white hair.

Despite reclusive habits she kept up with the progress of the human project, and did her part by writing letters to the editors of newspapers and magazines. Sometimes she typed discreet, chiding notes marked *Personal, not for publication,* in hopes of broadening an influential view without offending its holder. Or composed wry diatribes against the blind materialism that was ravaging the planet and defiling the common soul. She tried to mitigate her tone with praise for humanitarian efforts, and always ended by expressing faith in the clear-eyed, internationalist youth of the day.

Seldom to be met on the street without some somber periodical demurely but firmly pressed to her heart, she would intercept one, no matter one's errand or haste, and laying the tips of her fingers upon one's wrist would spin forth her moment's concern– the nuclear doom, the disappearing rain forests, the virtual, general folly– always starting, in a little girl's voice, with the plaintive, phantom phrase: "One simply doesn't know what one ought to do."

Like stones thrown in a pond, her words rippled out till the whole surface was agitated. She leapt from one catastrophic topic to the next as though bewitched, and once caught it was nearly impossible to escape, for she had a way of fixing one's eye– the issues were serious, after all, likely fatal and she was eloquent– speaking so urgently that it felt wrong to walk off in medias res, yet no end ever came in view.

"She'll chew your ear to a bloody pulp!" an old friend once exclaimed in a weary moment, then made amends next time they met by standing blandly in the cold rain for ten minutes while she castigated the fomenters of religious strife in Sri Lanka.

Spring, for Maria, was always a sort of halting entrance into exile. The growing, weekend hordes and reviving sybaritic past-times, isolated her. She loved the bleak winters, the rain, mists and wind, the casual meeting of friends on the street; but at length the sun strengthened, the town swarmed and familiar faces disappeared in full-time work. An annual milestone along this road in late May was the removal of the coffee table from the Cove Grocery, where neighborhood women gossiped in the off-season.

Maria was reading the papers and having her afternoon tea for the last time, acutely minding her imminent expulsion, for the place provided a cozy nook halfway to town, and company in small doses.

The day's papers were not unusual– certainly there was no good news– but somehow they brought her to tears. Wars, famine, refugees, racism, sexism, class-ism, age-ism, rape, robbery, murder, militarism, mayhem, and in Utah a man who reported having been taken aboard a transparent spaceship of pure spirits that communicated with innumerable other planets by telepathy.

Tears drenched Maria's cheeks. She choked down an urge to scream, took off her glasses, blotted her face with one sleeve, put aside the *Times*, *Globe* and *Monitor*, and with grim pertinacity began to scan the Cape Journal– thinking that here at least things were not so dire– and met the exhilarating sight of her latest letter to the editor, her only effort of the month, entirely forgotten in her general dismay.

She took unfailing pleasure and pride in these publications, worked long and hard over them, signed them Alpha Frend, and kept a willed faith that no matter how insignificant, they weighed in the balance at least for a better local world. As she read, her lips formed the words and her look of critical attention became one of perplexity, then disbelief, then horror.

She read it again, at every sentence stopping to glare wildly around like someone about to give up and drown, but no one was in the store but the new girl, who was busy out back.

Maria turned the page and sat slackly for a while, at last roused herself, left the papers all in a heap like a collapsed tent. She seemed to have shrunk, and the step down to the street jarred her bones. She went homeward slowly, eyes downcast, and did not see a block ahead the great, familiar girth of Coughlan Dice.

The would-be author was out for a stroll, or rather a magisterial waddle, toes out, back on his heels, while his eyes roamed pleasantly. He was wasting his day off in the usual way, had long since ceased to hope to do otherwise, and was experiencing the pure happiness of leisure, with drinks in the offing.

When the sun set he would sit down to his books and browse the night away, and then, next morning, he would be back in the clattering kitchen amidst the smells and the sweat, the shouts and bonhomie, safe from his avocation.

It was amazing how much he loved food, amusing how much he drank. At forty he had grown decisively huge, and lapsed into the scholar's life, passive, fond, dubious, sentimental. The more he read, the less he wrote, the larger he grew, he noted with melancholy un-surprise, and lately grey hairs had invaded his broad, black beard.

Shiningly bald, he had a benign air and English manners, adopted in youth, but now so natural— substituting "By your leave" for "Excuse me" and "Oh, I say! For "Wow!"— that he was nonplused when anyone mocked or mimicked him. A welcome sight in the bars, he secretly loved men, but had never kissed one, nor for a long time had any intimacy with women, since a little spring had weakened in him unnoticed and resignation set in.

Why didn't he finish his novel? He tried to attract himself to the teaching job it might win him, but the prospect filled him with re-pugnance– all those needy or indifferent eyes. He would fail them, he knew. And why should he leave P-town, when he was so happy and at home here? He had escaped the rigors of respectability, and could live as he pleased. Did the world need his book? Did he not need to finish it? He had lost the desire for fame, as well as all but occasional pleasure in the labors of composition, yet the box of manuscript that waited year in, year out underneath his desk re-mained the center of his psyche, all he truly was, or ever would or could be.

Wearisome, these clotted knots, and Coughlan was out to enjoy this day. He stooped to explore the configuration of needles around the roots of a scraggly pine, sniffing the dank odor of muck in the gutter, reminded of his childhood when things were so much more mysterious and exact than they had ever been before or since, and glancing up suddenly under bristling brows beheld Maria Nore coming straight on, head down, muttering like a maniac.

Coughlan's heart quailed. For years he had refused to flee. He was too portly, dignified and kind, and he liked Maria Nore, but today he felt unequal. He almost hoped she might go by oblivious, but he was too big to miss, too ponderous to budge, and she gave a startled jump as his toes came into view and nearly bumped her chin on his belly.

"Oh, Coffee!" she cried. "You can't imagine how glad I am to see you."

"Likewise," he grumbled. "How are you, Maria?"

"This Poor Little Thing"– so she inveterately referred to her-self– "hardly knows what to do. Perhaps you can tell me how to get out of this galaxy. I'm at the end of my rope. I think perhaps I should just slip the leash."

"Ah-ha, oh-ho," Coughlan said nervously, playing his fingers upon his vast vest. "Where do you think you'd like to go?"

"Mars," she said with such certainty that he took a sharp look at her.

"Be rather warm there?" he said.

She made a weary, dismissive gesture. "I think to die," she said, "is the best I can do."

"Not yet," Coughlan said judiciously. "Death is one thing; premature death quite another."

"I agree," she said. "But I think my time has come. I'm just taking up space. The world will be well served if I get off and leave my pittance to some good cause. What I'm wondering is: Do I have the courage?"

"It's too soon," Coughlan said. "How old are you?"

"I'll tell you how old I *feel*," she said. "When I woke up this morning every single cell of my body was solid, aching gravity. I could think of only two sensible courses: one was never to get up again, the other was simply to walk off the end of the wharf. I wouldn't have had to get dressed for either."

She gave a little shrug of humility. "I finally got bored feeling sorry for myself, and what with one thing and another, here I am. But I can't see a reason to stay one day longer."

Coughlan felt a chill. She batted her eyes and spoke in her usual flirtatious lilt that belied the enormities of her everyday conversa-tion, but today the old, formal irony was gone, as if actor and role had merged, or parody turned real, and she had a gaunt, vague, frightened look.

"Ah-ha, oh-ho!" he exclaimed, preliminary to heartening, helpful words, but none came. As the silence lengthened and the sweat popped from his forehead, he felt the ignominy. From behind steel-rimmed glasses he stared at her in consternation, but she never met his eyes and he could see she really had slipped a bit.

"I have dizzy spells," she said. "I'm light-headed half the time. I'm losing my mind."

"Really?" Coughlan brightened. "You always were rather mad, Maria. You are simply achieving perfection."

"Not crazy," she said disconsolately. "Just dim."

"Dim?" Coughlan said. "What d'you mean?"

"Senile," she brought out.

"Ah," he said, and fell silent again while the disgrace grew on him and dragged his spirit down.

"I've always tried to live according to reason," she quavered.

"Of course," Coughlan said, and mulled. Was this new or only old? Did the ancient wisdom still pertain? *Best never born. Next best a timely death.*

"And besides, I can no longer bear it," she said on a firmer note. "Why must folly always prevail?"

"It doesn't always, does it?" Coughlan said, feeling the ground under him again.

"Why look who's here!" Maria cried, her gloom transformed by the shyly-passing woman with infant-in-arms, who stopped and after an expressionless glance at Coughlan held it up for Maria to kiss. The rosy little thing was full of sly delight and kept grubbing its way out of the dirty wrap the woman had slung around her neck.

It didn't look quite right to Coughlan. It had a mammoth, mature face, albeit not a hair, and was the woman its mother, sister, aunt? She was wrinkled and bent, yet young, and her dark skin and black shawl drew his mind to Greece again, but she only beamed at Maria's cooing compliments. The baby's features formed one expression after another uncannily adult, and its tensile fingers ceaselessly grabbed and instantly released everything in reach, Maria's glasses, ear lobes, chin and nose.

"What can one believe in anymore?" she demanded when they had gone. "I sent a letter to the Journal on the ocean issue and someone– I hesitate to think it was the editor himself– changed it little by little all the way through till it said just the opposite of what I meant."

Coughlan knit his brows, slowly, very slowly swelled with indignant disbelief, rumbled, chuckled, exploded with obscenities loud enough to be heard for three blocks.

Maria had never seen him in such a snit. It both mollified and appalled her. Faces appeared at windows. Why does he let himself get so fat? she wondered, and began to worry he would work himself up to a stroke.

"Well, it's not important," she interceded. "He's a nice young man, he means well..."

"He's a scoundrel," Coughlan roared, "a blackguard and a twit," his muse now in full cry, "he's a rascal, a blighter, a scalawag and a shit, he's..."

"But what I really can't understand," Maria broke in, "is how the world goes on." She began to recite the news item by item while Coughlan offered intermittent exculpations in the form of explanations.

"To be expected," he kept muttering, "under the circumstances."

He wished he could run, wished he could find an excuse to disappear, but there was nowhere he could decently pretend to be required. He heard, he could nearly see, the frail thread of her voice getting stronger, regaining its familiar, inexorable momentum.

"And why do people have to be identified as male, female, straight or gay?" he heard. "We ought to evolve to adopt each other's characteristics."

Next she expounded on how technology having outrun evolution, what were needed now were matriarchies, but had barely uttered a prelude to what promised to be a considerable discourse, when she noticed his despairing eye and clenching her fists at her sides, nested her head for a rueful instant on his great chest, entangling her hair in his beard.

He came to a sort of agonized attention, mortified at being caught, and she walked off quickly and turned the corner. He went on toward town, in penance straightening his posture, lengthening his stride.

Cindy Gillies, sneaking from her door, spied him passing her alley and thought enviously, Look at Coughlan go! He's really stepping out! Go, man! And suddenly seized by hope ran after him and grabbed his arm.

"Can I talk to you for a minute?" she said. "I'm in desperate need of advice."

She had never spoken to him before, but she knew his name, had seen him everywhere so often over the past few years that he seemed an old friend. He looked to her like sanity itself, security, wisdom, help.

"By all means," he said gallantly, then wondered. She was a perfect stranger to him, about twenty-five, in a sweatshirt and grime-shiny jeans, with a hectic, shrewd, pockmarked face. She looked like anyone at all and he stood gazing at her while his apprehension grew.

"Come to my house for a minute," she said. "We can't talk here."

He followed her down a path between two high, unkempt privet hedges and up some dark stairs to a padlocked door on the second floor of a house completely invisible from the street. Once inside she re-locked the door with the same padlock, a big, industrial one that gave him the shivers. Why was she locking them in?

Futon in one corner with a colorful quilt over it and three velvet cushions, a portable radio, an open wardrobe of what looked like thrift-shop finds, a decrepit bureau, a shelf above the sink with lots of teas and a bottle of brandy sadly low, a fish-box by the bed with books of a depressing taste– Magister Ludi, a complete set of Tolkien, an anthology of Zen poetry and a frazzled I Ching– and nothing else but two wooden armchairs, into the most commodious of which he wedged himself, and glanced at his watch.

"What would you do," she said fiercely without sitting down, "if you were being tortured to death?"

He feared she must be mad or high. Her distended eyeballs glistened and stared and she sat down and shot up like a spring and pulled her chair close and bent glaring at him.

"I mean it's day in, day out," she said. "I don't even know how to begin."

Coughlan settled his chin on his chest, buoyed by his consoling bulk of beard, and considered her patiently through his little, round, steel-rimmed glasses.

With an hysteric grimace she shook her head long and violently, as if she had hornets in her hair, then sat portentously still, her mouth wide open, struck dumb, then leaned till her nose nearly reached his, even in retreat, and hissed, "These two guys, Frankie and Bill, they live downstairs, they're out to do me in."

Coughlan lowered his eyelids judiciously, then raised and held them steady.

She sat back and said, "I haven't had a night's sleep since I moved in three months ago. They play disco full-blast till dawn, seven days a week."

"Earplugs," Coughlan ventured, irked by her mannerisms, looking to depart.

"They thump on the ceiling by the head of my bed with a two-by-four. They spit at me on the street. They work themselves into a frenzy every night after the bars close. They take a lot of drugs and hammer on the pipes and yell threats. One of them has a gun—he showed it to me. I mean their main occupation is terrorizing me."

"Why?" said Coughlan, taken aback.

"I have no idea. I went down the first night and knocked. I intended only the friendliest of complaints, but they both squeezed into the doorway with looks of such diabolical malice I could hardly speak."

"And then?" Coughlan said reluctantly.

"My whole life became a phantasmagoria. They slashed my bicycle tires, they threw firecrackers at my dog that was dying, they broke in when I was gone for a few days, and stole my liquor and dope and defecated on my pillow. They howl when they catch me in the hall."

"Perhaps you require the assistance of the law."

"Ah, yes, the police. They've been here a dozen times. Frankie and Bill are great actors, they always seem to be asleep when the police arrive. They deny everything.

"I even had them before the Magistrate. They showed up with this loud lawyer, my landlord and his wife, who're friends of theirs, plus three other witnesses I've never even seen before. They claimed I was psychotic, that I was a well-known trouble-maker.

"The Magistrate couldn't figure it out, but he finally issued a restraining order, which they trampled on the steps when we got back from court, wouldn't you know, at the very same moment.

"They wouldn't let me in the house, so I ran to the nearest phone booth, but they went indoors and got their call in to the police first and said I'd threatened them with a knife.

"So the cops came, I demanded they arrest them. Frankie and Bill were saying it was all my fault. I was enraged at the police, I yelled, 'You feeble, fucking assholes!'

"You know they would never have let that go on if I was a townie. I kept demanding my rights, they didn't like my yelling at them either. Finally they just gave up and drove off. Now they hate the sight of me, they keep having to come over, but nothing happens. One of them said, 'If you repeat this in court I'll deny I ever said it, but *you* should get someone to beat them up.'"

"Who are these people?" Coughlan wondered, hard pressed to believe her.

"Slime Eyes and Diarrhea Face, I call them," she asserted grimly. "They're gay, they used to be pretty but they're getting wizened fast. And they're madly jealous. If one of them even glances at another man there's such a row when they get home that the whole house shakes and next day you see them limping or bandaged or bruised. They're about thirty but they've still got all their adolescent energy. They're like some kind of horrid twins."

"What purpose have they in tormenting you?" Coughlan asked, alarmed that such monsters might really be right downstairs.

"I truly think it's because I'm an independent woman," Cindy said. "I tried to make friends with them right after that first night. I even invited them for tea, but they just came up and prowled around and left. They never spoke one word."

"Pleasant fellows," Coughlan allowed.

"If you only knew how many bored or indifferent or useless men I've told this to!" she exclaimed.

"You decline to move," Coughlan surmised, eyeing the compact space and airy windows.

"Wouldn't you?" she said. "I've been camping in dumps for years waiting for a decent year-round place I could afford. I love this place. I called the landlord even before I called the police. He said he couldn't believe anything like that about Frankie and Bill. They're both extremely well- mannered, they can be completely charming. They may all be in cahoots. The wife's a nut. The day I moved in here I thought I'd made it into heaven."

"Splendid flat," Coughlan agreed. "It looks like Kimball Tardiff."

"Doesn't it?" she said. They gazed in silence at the bare board walls collaged with finely wrought designs of painted or stained or raw, scrap wood, bits of furniture, pilot house and machine parts, all manner of dump salvage, whimsical gadgets and gizmos that mimicked real things.

"I was really just getting into my drawing," Cindy said, handing him her sketchbook. "They wasted my whole winter, that's the worst of it. There's great vibes here– if it weren't for S.E. and D.F. down there."

"Resident Porlockians," Coughlan murmured.

"Would you like a smoke?" she asked. "I have just about half a joint of very fine Columbian Gold."

Coughlan didn't favor pot; it tended to frazzle him. He would have liked the brandy, but there was so little he was loath to ask.

Deftly she rolled a needle-thin joint, leaving not a speck in her tin box with its two kinds of papers and hash pipe; he meanwhile leafed through her novice drawings, untutored, trite female faces, sexy figures and fuzzy dune-scapes.

They smoked the dope down to a last fingertip of ash, each glancing out a different window, while she reposed in the safety of company, and he wondered how to escape.

"Could your father not be of use," he tried.

She shook her head. "All my family have disowned each other."

"Just as well," Coughlan sighed, "oft as not."

He began to stand but found he was stuck in his chair, and after several clandestine efforts to free himself relapsed and gazed at the hypnotic walls.

"I also write poetry," she said.

Coughlan warily received the notebook she opened for him and skimmed some pages. She was no poet though the surrounding doodles were luxuriant and dense, and he studied them while pretending to read. Then he tried to get up again, pushing down on the arms of the chair.

"I hope you like them," she said. "I like sharing them with people."

A guilty sense of his own pathos quelled any polite response. Not only was he not at his desk where he belonged, he was not even outdoors imbibing the balmy, blooming air. How far he had gone from his own innocence and vows this strange girl's illusions reminded him, and he felt how tricky life was, how wretched and unfair.

"Well," he finally expelled in a great, bluff sigh, "I wish you luck with your muse. Myself must sally forth into the realms of day," and he struggled once more with the clasping armchair, getting free at last only with her help.

He made his careful, panicky way down the dark stairs, still calling "You're Welcomes" to her cascade of Thanks for coming up, for listening to her woes, the unvoiced appeal sounding between each exchange, till the outside door closed behind him.

What could Coughlan do, after all? He was relieved to be back on the street. It was almost 3:30, a good hour– as if there were a bad one– to belly up to the bar at the Governor Bradford. He went onwards, puffing with vexation.

Frankie and Bill were slumbering in their bedroom. The Hulk and Sharlane lounged on the living room couch half-dressed, groggy from the night before. Nineteen and seventeen, they were staying with Frankie and Bill while they tried to decide whether to look for a place in P-town or go on to Santa Fe in the Hulk's van.

"They're a pair of cool queers, all right," the Hulk said, grown fond of their supply of Quaaludes.

"They're letting us stay here for free, remember?" Sharlane reproved. She had grown up with Frankie's younger brother in North Andover.

"So what? They're still queer," said The Hulk, who came honestly by his name, straight from the comics, movies and TV. He was massive, clumsy and shambling, with black, impassive eyes, sloping shoulders and soft, luminous, white skin like a woman's. He was too smart for school, but didn't want to learn anything. He had watched with interest Frankie and Bill's war on Cindy. "Because she's a bitch!" they had explained to Sharlane.

"You ought to rape her," The Hulk had said, and laughed to see the revulsion on their faces. He himself had caught several glimpses of Cindy and got a hard-on from thinking about her upstairs all alone.

Sharlane was a working-class tomboy and called herself The Hulk's sidekick. When they first met he had carried her everywhere for months effortlessly, uncomplainingly, proudly, while her leg was in a cast. She had to use crutches only when he was out of earshot, and one night he had carried her half a mile through the woods to a beach party and back. It had nearly killed him but she had wanted to go real bad. "For me he's a pussycat," she told her friends

Now that she could walk by herself, Sharlane no longer liked The Hulk so much. He had the van and the money his father had given him to see the country with before finding a job— but he had begun to go berserk when he drank. It was like trailing a tornado, and the odd thing was, he never seemed mad. Only a week before he had chain-sawed down a row of fir trees in front of the house they were staying next to in Hingham. Luckily no one was home and they were leaving anyway.

"I figure it's art," was all The Hulk would say. He could do ludes or coke or smack or LSD even maybe and nooo problem, but not gin and beer. Last night though he had been fine, grooving on Frankie and Bill, who brought some vodka when they came back from dancing at the Back Room, and then laid open their medicine chest.

Sharlane yawned around the dark, plush, fastidious apartment with its bluish lighting and never a beam of sun. "Want to go out?" she said, but he didn't. Lately all he cared about was partying. She made her way barefoot down to the beach. The stillness disturbed her. The air was cooling, the sand was cold, and the swollen bay, at flood tide, for the moment glowed like gold.

We should have been here since noon, she thought with disgust, and turned back to make The Hulk come for a walk, but stopped to watch a cat and dog that were tensed as if to spring, glaring, noses almost touching through the chain-link fence between them.

"Go to it!" yelled a boy on a bicycle, grinning at Sharlane. No teeth were showing and both seemed to be waiting to see which side Sharlane would take.

"Stop that!" she said to the dog, which lowered its head and rolled up meek eyes.

"Come on," she said to the cat, but it only looked more truculent.

Cindy, hearing no stereo, tiptoed down her stairs. Her bicycle was locked in the rack at Town Hall, so far undiscovered by Frankie and Bill. She meant to ride around till dark, hope to meet with a more susceptible male, the bigger and meaner the better– risk of the single life– but if nothing turned up, she would rack her bike again, then pray to get home safe, padlocked in against whatever the night might bring.

As she reached the bottom of the stairs, Frankie and Bill's door opened. Her heart stopped cold with revolted rage and disappointment, then started up again with huge gratitude when only The Hulk came out. She began to taste a slice or two at George's Pizza, and a beer. Then somehow she couldn't get by him. He was as big as the man she needed, half-filling the dim, dingy hall, but she never looked up at his face, intent on getting outdoors, lest Frankie and Bill appear. But whichever way she moved he moved, too. She laughed good-humoredly, but The Hulk merely breathed. She tried again, with a dreamer's sensation of entering a nightmare, and found his arm across the door. "Excuse me, please," she said.

Both doors of the Governor Bradford were wide open as Coughlan strolled in and took a stool halfway down the bar beside Teresa. "Hello, Coffee," she said sourly. "Want to hear the perfect Good Deed Brings Bad Luck story?"

Nodding, he doubted. Teresa looked as if she'd had her usual snootful, eyes watery, pouchy cheeks drooped. She always seemed to him half in love with gloom.

"I ride this bicycle," she said, crushing her empty pack of Pall Malls. "You know my old contraption that wobbles in both wheels even when I'm sober? I was peddling out to Beach Point, this cop car pulls me over. It's Mac, he says, 'Tomorrow's the day we auction off all the unclaimed bikes. You can have the one you brought in.'

"It was this beautiful, new ten-speed with all the gears and little, thin tires like razor blades. I'd found this great bike and turned it in.

Not everyone would do that, a mother with a raft of kids. I don't have a cent, as you well know."

She gaped up at the ceiling. "I hadn't had it twenty-four hours and it was stolen. I'm so mad I'm in a frenzy. I can never afford a bike like that. My old one came from the dump."

"Someone like yourself may turn it in yet," Coughlan said.

"Ohhh, no," she shook her head stolidly, obstinately, with pure self-abnegation, "that would spoil the story," then sighing, she eased off her stool, "I've got to get some cigarettes."

The Hulk wouldn't let Cindy go. He didn't speak but kept his mouth open and breathed evenly, audibly, in and out.

She nearly hissed for fear of alerting Frankie and Bill, who seemed somehow to have spawned a monster, "What right do you have to keep me here?"

He almost smiled, as always surprised at people's assumptions. He wondered how long it would take her to learn about rights. He had no plans exactly, just a vague notion to capture her for a while and give her a bad time.

When she tried to force her way by he grabbed her and threw her bruisingly against the stairs, where she stayed, half-crouching. Now, he thought, I'll train her to love me.

Teresa came back and lapsed into absence. Coughlan looked around uncomfortably; the beer burned his stomach. He resolved to smoke no more pot, which always darkened his view and frayed his nerves. Outside the day had barely started down, but something drab and grim overlay his reflections, and the sociable pleasures of the place were not yet at hand, it being still a bit early and Teresa no help.

Two boys were playing pool, and his eyes were drawn to their buttocks and intent faces. These longings shook him with a clash of old despairs, and he decided that food might improve his mood. As he crossed Lopes Square he saw Suzi Q sashaying between bars, her face ablaze with sensual delight. "Ooo-Wee!" she called, giving him a giddy, little lurch of her hips, "watch out for this weather!"

He produced a grunt of good will, entered the Wharf Lunch-eonette, took his favorite table and began to peruse the menu for something new and piquant.

The Hulk now sat down beside Cindy and caressed her gently, with a connoisseur's hand. He touched his chin to her petrified shoulder, and said, "I didn't mean to hurt you."

She sat still; it was horrible, but it was safer than resistance. He turned her away and massaged her back and shoulders. "What are you afraid of?" he said. "I like you." He felt her gradually relax and his penis began to ache.

"Come on!" Sharlane insisted. "Quit it."

Grudgingly, with enormous exactions, the cat turned away, one step at a time, never taking its eyes off the dog, which waited till it had gone six inches, then lifted its upper lip and released a faint growl.

With the same profound deliberation the cat turned back to the fence and crouched again with its nose to the wire.

Sharlane laughed so sincerely that both animals laid their ears back.

"Come on!" she cried gaily. She patted the cat goodbye, but it evinced no pleasure, eyeing her steadily with dignified intelligence, and she surmised it had grown tired of being barked at.

When she entered the hall she had a confused impression of The Hulk and Cindy necking on the dark stairs. He stood up, smirking, and Cindy scrambled up the stairs, shaking so violently she could hardly get the lock open.

"You bastard!" Sharlane said. What a slut! She thought indignantly, losing her sympathy of the night before.

"I don't like the way you're getting to be," she warned The Hulk after they'd had half a bottle of wine at the kitchen table. She didn't feel much like a walk any more. "You want her, you should go get her."

"Will you stop!" he whined. "I don't want her, I was just on my slavery trip. Leave me alone now. Let's go get something to eat."

"I'm not hungry," Sharlane said. She slopped a glass of wine in his lap, and filled it up again. "You spoiled my day."

"Just shut up," The Hulk said, the smell of Cindy's hair in his nostrils. His wet prick throbbed at the thought of getting control of her in return for protection against Frankie and Bill. Why should they have her, after all?

In the month since Sharlane's cast had come off, The Hulk always seemed to have some scheme in his eye, but this was the first time she was jealous. Until P-town it had always been them against the world, but now, to her furious amazement, she slapped him dizzily harder and harder, till with one cool clip of the heel of his hand, he knocked her out of her chair, she stabbed his knee with a handy fork, and they made a shambles of the apartment.

Cindy heard their murderous voices spiraling and shivered for Sharlane. Frankie and Bill pulled the blankets over their aching heads and laughed.

Coughlan dawdled but in the end settled for his old favorite, the fettuccini. All smiles, the gay host and chef coddled him fondly, left him with a fine half-bottle on the house and the salad, a pale delight of plumped lettuce and lacy onions glistening in a divine Roman dressing, and he despised himself with good cheer.

But the wine burned his stomach worse than the beer, and he burped with chagrin. The place was empty but for two tables with normal-looking couples who had suspended their repasts, and a fourth table where, elbows amongst their plates, a middle-aged man and woman were kissing with their eyes shut, oblivious to their grinning audience. The waiter stood by to rescue the wine should the table tip.

Obviously it was spring. The man sported a long, leather coat and new pants brightly, hugely plaid; she wore a voluptuous sweater, turquoise bracelets and Mardi Gras beads. They would sit back dazedly, eat a studied bite, and look up. Their eyes would swim again and drown, and after an interlude of dreamy goggling he would strain off his seat and she, trying to demur, could deny him nothing for long, and leant to meet him.

Coughlan reflected that this was a common aberration of short duration, that a certain percentage of the human species was always so engaged.

Somehow the thought heartened him and he tore into his salad with grave gusto, making the lettuce fly and the sauce dribble in his beard. An extra-large plate of creamy fettuccini arrived in time to forestall impatience, and down it went in little more than a minute. He looked up bereft and found all eyes– including the lovers'– glancing away with smiles. He felt like eating half a chocolate cake and a pint of spumoni, but succeeded with a semblance of casual mastery in declining dessert over the protests of the chef, arising without upsetting the table, passing more pleasantries and bowing himself through the door.

Too soon on the street, he felt elephantine and still hungry, desolate too that his day off had gone so awry, there being now nothing left of his little outing but the tiresome walk home. Not the pot but himself was at fault for his state of mind— how stupid to have felt he could do that strange girl some good by getting high with her— high indeed! He reviewed and renewed his revulsion against her tormenters, damned the police, grew resentful of the girl's quirks and misfortunes. Majestically he made his slow way homeward in the middle of Front Street like the Queen Mary he hoped, not the Titanic, effortlessly parting the oncoming shoals of tourists, incommoding those in his wake.

Cindy, terrified by the crashes and screams downstairs, called the police, disguising her voice, and said someone was being killed at Frankie and Bill's.

The temptation to maim Sharlane was overcoming The Hulk. She, recognizing the remote stare she had heretofore seen directed only at others, fled into the parking lot. The mud puddle there was wide and deep with a week of rain. He chased her down and considered drowning her, imagined grinding her face in the gravel at the bottom, knowing he wouldn't really do it, almost knowing it, goading himself to the edge, cuffing her face back and forth with one hand, the other arm clenching her neck.

It was twilight but the blood was visible to Jimbo Sandeo who— dressed in his best, toting fifths of Wild Turkey, J&B and Stolichnaya— just couldn't see letting some bum beat on some chick.

"Hey, come on now," he said in the tones of one used to dealing with the public, "you're friends, aren't you? I thought you were friends."

Whereupon both began to revile, punch and kick him, driving him into the puddle, scattering his bottles, and spattering his suit with blood, he wasn't sure whose.

A patrol car arrived and was left running in the narrow street by Officers Damos and Evans. Damos said suavely, "We had a call there was a disturbance here. Would anyone know anything about that?" Evans studied the disheveled trio, surprised to see, at this address, none of the usual culprits.

"He was beating her up," Jimbo panted. "Look at me, man, I'm on a date."

"He can do anything he wants to me," Sharlane shrieked

The Hunk gave her a glad clout on the shoulder and guffawed at the cops.

"Maybe you'd better come and have a little talk with us," Damos said gloomily to The Hulk, thinking to separate them all, and handcuff him if need be. Jimbo they knew.

"I'm not going anywhere," the vainglorious youth averred.

Damos, casually advancing, tried to seize his wrists, but The Hulk flung him in the mud, then turned intrepidly, though not in time to keep burly Evans from getting a hammerlock on him. Damos regained his feet and all struggled mightily up to their ankles in water and muck, with The Hulk crying in a clear, carrying voice, "You're going to get your asses sued," and Jimbo shouting from dry land, "I'm going to press charges, I swear to God I'm going down to the station right now."

Another police car came, but had to stop a block away in the stopped line of cars. Horns honked and the street filled up with fumes. Edgy, Coughlan came upon a growing band of onlookers just as the two new cops rushed past him into the fray.

Infused with valor, bellowing about his rights and calling upon one and all for help, the Hulk refused to be dragged from the mud. The grappling, gasping mass lurched toward the sidewalk and the mob fell back around Coughlan with his deep repugnance for violence, acquired as victor in a fight with his best friend in grammar school.

Now the cops managed to tape The Hulk's mouth, but still couldn't handcuff him, and the clump of feet trampled in circles like a drunken behemoth, pausing at moments to catch its huge, ragged breath.

Sharlane had withdrawn from the brawl, her heart dull with thought for the future. All this was old apples from her mother's bushel of bad boyfriends. "No more!" she said, and glanced with involuntary, sulky appeal at Jimbo. He was sort of cute in his exasperation, his sleepy-eyed, seen-everything look, but he glowered indignantly back at her only for a second.

Cindy peeped out her window, praying somehow Frankie and Bill would get killed, or at least jailed, but they were still abed.

The line of traffic grew back toward town. The blinking blue lights swept round and round. Their radios talked unintelligibly at intervals, like queries, going up and up, but never an answer, then static, then an instant of silence, then another ascending phrase of garble, and static, static again.

Coughlan looked in the open window of the first car, thinking to move it a few feet to the curb and let the traffic through. "Good citizens that we are," he rumbled to Baro who, hands on hips, forward on his toes, was morosely watching, "we ought to park this."

"Oh, no, buddy," Baro said with a short shake of the head. He was a grizzled fisherman, strong as a rock. "Don't ever touch nothing of the police,"

"Maybe you should be the one to do it," Coughlan reconsidered. "You're a native, they know you."

"Oh, no, buddy." Baro shook his head.

"It's only sensible," Coughlan said. "Cars will be backed up to Town Hall."

"That's too bad, buddy," Baro said, and shook his head once more, to make sure Coughlan got it.

All Coughlan's instincts called on him to move the car and help disperse the mob that was gathering, chatting with itself, becoming a thing in itself. Flute-like cries and laughter espoused the warm weather.

He felt cowed, sad shame heated his face that he dared do nothing about this noxious traffic jam, even with clear reason on his side. Idling engines, car radios– all tuned to the same station– honks, door-slammings, oaths and derision were audible all the way back to the Shawmut Bank. At the crux even bicycles were bollixed on both sides, blocking pedestrians, too.

Coughlan lumbered out of the way. The handcuffed Hulk, foaming around the tape, was forced into the back seat between two cops, and one got in front. The fourth closed the door and the car edged forward slowly, slowly, then developed a series of jerks as if the driver were jumping the clutch, till the rear window shattered in a shower of little green chunks of safety-glass, and a triumphant foot emerged and was brandished like a flag.

Then, until the patrol car turned the corner, sounded the un-mistakable, slightly-liquid impact of flesh and bone meeting flesh and bone: steady, measured, deliberate. Splack. Splack. Splack. Splack.

Jimbo's stomach rolled queasily and dissolved his desire for re-venge. "I don't care, I'm not going down there," he said grimly aloud, and waded into the puddle, hunting for his bottles of booze, more and more miserable at the ruin of this, his night of nights.

He had spent the winter in a quiver of desire, sweetening into love. His every waking moment seemed a dream of Daisy Dobbs. The best and worst of it was, there was no escape. They worked together behind the counter part of each day; sometimes he could smell her and his knees gave way. He forgot his wife, he forgot his life entirely for want of Daisy. There was no cure but to have her and hope that once would suffice, but she kept declining his over-tures.

"I just want to be friends," he would say piteously.

"All right, all right," she had said at last in a weak moment. "Come over tonight and we'll talk. Talk," she repeated, "and bring something to drink, not beer."

"What's your choice" he had said, electric with gratitude.

"I don't care," she had said distractedly. "Anything. I feel like a night of it."

Jimbo gave up. His bottles were lost or filched— gone much rent money— and he looked clothed by Jackson Pollock in blood and mud. Cursing his folly, swearing to open his mouth no more, he set out for Daisy's house, where he had never been before, and left not a farewell glance for Sharlane, who stumbled back inside and col-lapsed on the couch with a towel of ice cubes over her face.

The crowd went its ways, the street grew quiet. Maria, returning from the library and a film about primitive tribes of Indonesia, came on the litter dropped from the line of cars— crushed cigarette packs, soda cans, fast food containers, flyers, pop-tops, orange peels, diapers.

Maria habitually picked up trash and carried it till she came to a garbage can. She could not fathom people who fouled the planet, and felt bound to clean up after them, but this was a disgruntling mess, just too much, even for her, and her hands, arms and under her elbows and chin were soon precariously overfull. Thus there was nothing she could do about the little dump of ashes, cigarette butts and matches but name it Nineveh as she reached the parking lot and stepped upon the carpet of unstable, many-faceted, roughly-trapezoidal chunks of green safety glass.

In the air, falling amidst her gatherings, she had a fleeting memory of some favorite beads she had lost in childhood— then thumped down on her bony hip, hurting her wrist and skinning an elbow. She scrambled up, amazed at having suffered no worse, and limped homeward empty-handed, fighting back tears.

Jimbo was gulping warm champagne on the rocks, enlarging his rueful tale, his voice full of chagrin. Daisy, having removed his torn jacket and soggy shoes and cleaned him up a bit, sat close on the couch, looking at him without a word and shaking her glossy curls vehemently each time he tried to apologize.

"That's the last thing I ever do," he promised.

"No, no, no, no," she soothed.

"Well," he laughed for the first time, "I sure am glad to see you," and suddenly finding her necessary breasts in his hands he shut his eyes and madly started kissing her face all over till her lips opened to his tongue her mouth's wet, full bloom.

Coughlan sat in a nadir at his desk, feeling what a fatuous wretch he was; saw the pathos of trying to make people happy.

The cumbersome mass of manuscript in the box under his desk oppressed him as it had not done in months, years, he could not tell how long. He could not stand the sight of it, could not bear to read any page, knew too well how prosaic it was, how painfully far from even a journeyman's shaping finish, how incomplete its ending, a mere, formal flourish, how ordinary a tome at best it might ever rise to be.

He pondered the stupendous, incomprehensible achievements of the masters, envied their inhuman genius and devotion, sighed, while the last light died from the sky and the room grew in brightness.

Something startled his attention. He turned to look through the narrow passageway lined with books into his other room. Someone was in there, he realized with a chill, yet it wasn't possible. How could anyone have got in? With an effort of will he turned back to his desk, but a prickle of fear made him quickly glance again. Someone was sitting in his favorite chair beneath the lamp— a huge, black-garbed man with bald pate, pants thigh-stretched to bursting, slim gleams of glasses above a massy beard.

Coughlan sat stumped, befuddled, frightened, recognizing the strange, almost-familiar figure, stymied to know then who it was that looked.

The vision lingered, imperceptibly faded. He struggled up, passed with trepidation into the other room. Everything was eerily as always, the coffee cups and bottles, the ashtrays overflowing with wooden matches and charred pipe tobacco, the toppled piles of books amongst which he wallowed nightly like a greedy monk. The light shone brightly on the empty chair.

He returned to his desk. No more pot for me, he vowed. On impulse, he bent against his paunch, strained forward, stretched a pudgy hand toward the ponderous box of paper, mentally assessing its heft, its twenty-one chapters with variant readings and notes.

He held his uncomfortable posture, wondering if he were now really to resume his labors, thereby at least escaping the bitter impotence of never finishing it, of living the horrors of not even trying to finish it before it passed beyond his psychic and moral grasp, worrying the worse pity of never knowing what it might have been polished and done, published or not, till finally, bludgeoned by the day's perplexities, he swallowed, swallowed again, and settled once more into staid reverie, promising his stars, I will, I will, soon, soon, I'll start to see what I can do.

Under a clear moon Sharlane was driving around the edge of Buzzard's Bay– Sagamore, Wareham, Bourne, the names meant nothing to her– driving and driving The Hulk's van, intending to leave it somewhere and go on, but as she rolled through each town there was no reason to stop. She had taken most of The Hulk's cash, and not three minutes after helping Frankie and Bill put their house back together, she had been on the road, amazed but proud of the numbness of pain, determined to take no more abuse, and only go with older men.

The Hulk lay on his back on the hard cell bunk in the white light with his eyes swollen shut. It was late, he was the sole inmate, the station was silent. His whole head felt immense, muffled, untouchably tender. All he could think to do was continue waiting impatiently for Sharlane to come bail him out. At moments he felt his old hauteur, but in the back of his mind an embryo of dread was forming, that she had somehow come to harm.

Jimbo was walking home in a daze. He passed the mud puddle with never a glance for his bottles; his feet crunched across the safety glass, but he gave no thought to these late incidentals– except for a weary, half-hearted effort to rehearse some alibi, to mollify his wife.

He realized his life had changed. He had been awakened from the deepest, sweetest of sleeps by a conscience-stricken, apprehensive Daisy, fully clothed, who gave him some coffee and told him about her fisherman in Alaska, gone to try his luck with the salmon, but due back soon. The champagne she had bought the day he left to celebrate his return. She didn't want Eddie to stay all night; she hadn't meant to get into sex with him. She was lonely and sympathy had overcome her; she liked him, of course, but just as a friend. "Friends," she said firmly, pushing him out the door, looking to see if her neighbors' lights were still on. "Friends."

On every corner a young man stood. "Good evening," said one as Eddie passed. "Do you fool around?" murmured the next. "King-keee!" assayed a third, admiring Eddie's battered, tattered look, but he hardly heard. Nearing home he walked more and more slowly, his whole being concentrated on Monday and the hour at work when he would– when he must– see Daisy again.

Maria was looking out her skylight at the moonlit bay, wishing she knew how to die. The pear tree and the purple Chinese money plant still bloomed in the semi-dark beside her door, but she couldn't care. She had tried to keep faith with the future, disbelieve in evil, and belong to the human family, but tonight she saw the futility of all things– of living and dying both.

She had a sudden, vivid memory of her husband, brazen, deceitful, vague, declaiming his favorite lines from The Battle of Maldon– *Thought shall be the harder, Heart the keener, Resolve must greaten as our strength fails.*

Strange creature! Blundering idealist and fool! She could hear his stentorian voice resounding through the sun-filled house of their years of tranquility together, she could see him in his underwear, shouting, "Agonies abate!"

In despair she fought to save her forgiveness of his desertion, not to lose at last her kind feelings for him. She reminded herself that even had he never, ever left her, he would still be long dead by now, and she here, exactly here, alone.

At four a.m. she tried the radio and got a news update, eerily clear from Cleveland. A murderer in the final stages of cancer, released from jail to die, had killed his wife and child. In Shaker Heights four high school girls had died in a drunken joyride. A Lebanese hotel had been blown up, no group as yet claiming credit. The only relief from an overwhelming sense of heedless folly was the final item, a one sentence report of a tsunami which had drowned three-thousand Bangladeshis, and seemed in its grandeur a kind of benediction.

Ashamed, she studied her reflection in the skylight– the deepening, darkening hollows under her eyes, her flesh-less nose-bone and ghostly, disheveled hair– and realized how near, yet how far, how long, how hard, the way might surely be.

At dawn she dozed at her desk over a new letter by Alpha Frend. "One hardly knows what to do," it begins. "I for one am writing to you..."

A DAY ON THE RIVER

Amassing trash for the seasonal pickup, moving on once more– though he himself is going nowhere– a bit the worse for wear no doubt, no longer young, idly sifting memorabilia that preserve little or no living sentiment, but don't yet quite warrant permanent disposal, thus might best be relegated to near oblivion of basement bins, no? Well... well... maybe. He wasn't always so indecisive or so nice in his distinctions. At least, not about trivia.

Among keepsakes, photos, postcards, trinkets, relics of romance, love aborted or worn out– he finds an unwritten, unsent letter dated thirty years ago with only the salutation: *"Dear Amanda, Do you remember our day on the river?"*

Harpoon to the heart. Sensed even at the time, struck far deeper than the others, stronger her barb's hold on him, grown by the year. Remiss not to have kept in touch with her, folly in retrospect. Touch indeed!

And here, after all this time, turns up to admonish him this blank envelope with only her name, Amanda Martin, for address, and his own wistful plaint.

Maybe there had been an earlier effort un-forwarded or unreturned, this merely would-have-been renewal of his vow to find her, a vow never relinquished in spirit, just never kept in fact, not for lack of allure, nor silence of unwelcome, but simply for lack of the least trace of her, of where she'd got to, who she'd become.

The yellowish, brittle envelope bears only faded ink, in a handwriting no longer his– slovenly his pen now from life at the computer. These days he can hardly recognize his own signature. Well, they are but seventy-five now, in their prime really, if one cared to visit the soul, see it that way, and him unencumbered for some while. Next thing to a recluse really.

And her? He feels a burgeoning excitement, the warmth of that muggy, mid-August afternoon flooding his chest, constricting his throat, that rank stink of the mud-bank in his nostrils, keen as youth itself.

Maybe their time has come round again. Or will. Why not? A forlorn hope, he knows. And yet? Why not a reunion– portentous word though to invoke an accidental hour together, a bit presumptuous perhaps. A second meeting of sorts maybe, a cup of coffee, a dinner, a film or play. A walk, a chance to reminisce. About what? That one kind gift of time declined, not taken, not seized, nor ever reclaimed?

What could she possibly remember of it? Of him? His stupid, staring solemnity! Who never else had a shy moment with women, not one, in all his life, neither before nor since. How strange!

They'd never even touched, much less kissed. He'd been too shy of her fond, grave demeanor, her eyes that seemed to hold him in complete cognizance and rapport. He'd kept from casual approach, even of toes treading water, had been at pains not to get near enough to have to draw back, timid dance! How bizarre really! One of a once.

He begins to rummage now in earnest. But nothing in boxes nor folders nor cubbies nor piled shelves nor musty attic remained of their one day in their found canoe, only that blank sheet of paper with its monumental question and the date penned months, maybe years, after his initial resolve to learn what had become of her– that impulse somehow always disrupted or foiled, in any event this one never acted on, never sent.

Persistent of hope, want, ache, if only just to lay eyes on her again, to see if she really was—or is– as he remembers her, always dulled or delayed into some dim futurity by how many others he could now neither name nor count, only know that her vivid image had materialized regularly through the veils of the passing years without particular cause, perhaps only remorse or disappointment or boredom with others, familiar stabs of regret fading into hopeless, practical helpless, irrelevance as life speeds on.

And what name did she go by now? Amanda Who? Amanda What? Now surely married. Twice, thrice, how guess or predict? Mother, grandmother. Sheer whorishness learned– which neither attracted nor repelled him, whoever, whatever she'd become, whatever life had made of her. He'd always accepted himself, her he would as well. For her he'd gladly be chaste, remain so, if he could just find and look upon her, read her face, imbibe her life, spirit and soul, the whole of her.

He realized he treasured her memory today more than ever— ever more by the minute it seemed, his one true love, who could never fail, or rather whom he himself had never failed, nor ever even tried nor wanted to try.

The dream of spirit more than flesh had simply never died in waking life, but still breathed unique among his realms of faint figments merged in anonymity. He knew it was childish, false, illusory, yet today he felt again the old, immutable longing for her, her above all others, above all prizes of success, less to caress, than just to tell her: I've always loved you, from the very first, our one and only day, our solitary hour together. Please, please, I beg of you to open your life to me, tell me everything you know, everything you ever did, everything that ever happened to you, for good or ill, everything I've missed.

With chill he wondered, was she suddenly dead? Could that be the psychic stem of this strange agitation? No, no, not that crude, that ghoulish trope! What could, what would she look like now? Who be? Oh, what life does to life! What doesn't it? Perhaps best not to see, never know, nor grieve. Who can stand the mirrored shards of failure, much less of age in women? He can. He could. Hers now would only stir him to unmet heights of tenderness.

He tried to think of those who might have known her, but only two came to mind, both dead. He could go back and look for her: he had no living family there, had not been back in many years, nor had she had been destined any more than him to remain in their native place, a small decayed landing twenty miles upriver from the rocky, harbor-busy coast, barely a stream really, between mud banks.

A chance meeting, remote acquaintances, spur of the moment, that old plank walk on stilts through the cat o' nine tails to that chained but unlocked, decrepit canoe in the vast expanse of mud that perhaps kept it safe from theft, next thing to derelict, battered, scaled with mud, but dry in the August flood of light.

They hadn't had bathing suits, what celestial luck, almost naked they lolled in the sluggish, shallow, tidal stream, might have embraced like Adam and Eve. But did they? They didn't. Why not? Because they loved each other. Or were already on the way. What other answer could there be? The paralytic shock of it, too soon even to kiss, too sudden, too risky, too intimate, too overwhelming. How foolish, how cowardly! Or naive!

Vaguely gossiping, praising the day, they had dog-paddled, him in his shyly tenting undershorts, her in flowered panties and spilling bra. The turbid, tidal flow carried them hardly ten yards inland in twenty minutes, both careful not to brush even fingertips, as if they might be lost forever to whatever lives they had already launched on, or owed, or planned.

Her breasts, oh, if only he could put his face in them now– pornographic darling– he's never thought of her this way, chaste his love till now, all un-indulged this excitation. Did she ever think of him? Mental wedding of one of course no wedding at all but only fantasy un-won. Where was she now?

But if they had made love it would now be done, he might never have loved her so again, but better perhaps, yes, better had they wallowed in the mud, better as the years went on, and children… and the bloody business of life itself, from which he had turned and turned. Well, he'd had his travels and his triumphs, surprising some who disdained him. Not that he cared.

They'd swum amid a kept-from-kiss, like a promise of future submission they hadn't wanted to presume on– how shy she was. No, not shy, only sad: he'd have left her as he'd left the others, or she him, though that he can't imagine—can't conceive of either now.

They could have debauched in sex on that stinking, low-tide, mud bank… children, the whole rigmarole, they'd be together now, if they had. Might, might, might really so have done.

But who had she become? Of her then only now the light of that day on her pale shoulders remains, the placid, stagnant river, the rich stench of decay, and now the rule of memory burning in his eyes too dry for tears.

He might have got up that next morning and gone looking for her. As he would be glad– it now seems– to give over all his past lives to traverse coasts, cities, seas and mountains the whole planet over to find her, his random freedom foregone, that rank, ripe smell they joked about their lasting redolence and compact.

But they had perforce unwitting swum back to the anchored canoe. They might simply have waited for the tide to turn and told their lives meanwhile. He now bitterly wished they had, if only to have had more time together, and him now some realer sense of her, but he'd had a dying bank-clerk father to say goodbye to and a distraught, elderly mother to abandon for a business meeting that would ultimately mean his making as a trader.

Up and up he climbed thereafter, came back only for two funerals and the sale of the house he would spend but two more nights in. He had never been a man of sentiment– curious his sole attachment to Amanda Martin. But then, this was different, not business at all, but the succulence of cunt, of tits and ass that he had devoted his leisure to, such leisure as he'd allowed himself, which cleared his head for calculations and instincts about the futures and personnel of companies in play.

The eve of that day for him had been straight back to the frenzies of Chicago, then New York, and the making of his fortune. He was a millionaire now, a minor millionaire. He did not care much for money– only for its making– nor possessions, nor even for sex any more, just women themselves, only the freedom to go where and do whatever he pleased. He had no morals, was curious, and liked to travel, kept to common ways, sought the pleasures of distinctive, independent women, seldom dined alone.

It had coarsened him, no doubt. A brief, childless marriage, and mistresses on three continents, and now nobody, nor anything more wanted, than consummate dinner company, nobody at all really, but only Amanda, whoever, whatever, wherever she was. He had everything he wanted but her– wanted to retire to her company, he mocked himself.

Impossible he knew, perfectly impossible. Next best thing though, to be set free, which meant finding her, and gaining his release from haunting fantasies of missed contentment, such as neither his nature nor style could truly covet, much less abide.

For a while, in his formative years, he had kept office so to speak in the bróthels of Europe, chiefly Amsterdam, Nice and Vienna, even for a while in Shanghai. He liked the women, squired them around, tried to please them, make friends of a sort, obliging, striving to rouse their ardent appetites, even as his flagged.

Then– he never knew why, it was mid-afternoon in a Spartan boudoir bare of all but bed, bidet and sink– with eyes of sheer hatred he never forgot, one tried to kill him with a hammer, and might have done, but for a shout in the street.

He glanced, deflected in mid-arc the swung steel head, but got a broken wrist.

She burst out crying and couldn't be assuaged nor understood, a tall, lean Yugoslav with little French, less English, newly immigrated. She wept in the taxi all the way to the hospital, burst out worse than ever when he emerged with a cast, still hoarsely sobbing wrenched free at the door, strode for a cab and disappeared without farewell.

Next day looking to apologize for whatever his original offence, he met her in the street. She burst into tears again, and couldn't be stopped. He kept pace with her longer strides. She couldn't escape, only wept the harder. Passing a bank he dashed in, got a thousand dollars in francs, ran after her and stuffed them in her bag.

She stopped, stared at his answering, gape-mouthed stare, then walked off whimpering. He let her go, but came back next day, and the next, mad to make love to her, but she was not to be found. Then he left town, never saw her again. He felt he'd learnt something, but what he couldn't ever quite say. He had never abused a woman but his own mother, and her only by abandonment.

As time went on he found himself seeking the perfect mate, who'd never wanted, never dreamt of one, never believed any such luck existed, even in fantasy. He had to laugh as more and more damsels bored him the moment he came, not that he didn't like them. He simply wanted nothing from them but their company. Not even sex, any more, though the act itself remained briefly diverting, especially if he pleased them.

A sense of comfort and calm seemed all he now desired, to find the right one to do little more than lie in the sun on weekends, now and then to roll over on top of each other.

He was jaded, he had to admit, a most undignified pass. He pondered unplumbed sodomy, but men left him cold. Thus he designed of aeronautical materials a dildo for women that with each thrust would palpate the clitoris, thinking, if nothing else, to make a fortune to pile upon his earlier bundles, perhaps in his later years to enter women's charitable fields at large.

For its maiden voyage, he chose his companion with care, a mature woman of high good humor and irresistible laughter. He laid in an industrial-size vat of lubricant, in the event of whole body engrossments.

After a grand dinner, a rare bottle of wine and an even more exquisite Spanish liqueur, they went home to his commodious bed, where, after some respectful, warming caresses set to, with his thighs lodged upon her comfy, comely shoulders, unique sensations for both, but once begun there was no moderating, much less quenching, her ardors, him entreating, "Thank you, Rest now, Calm now, Enough, Slow, Easy, Easy Does It, Please, Whoa, Cease, Now quit now, Desist, Ow, No more, Please, Oh, Oh, OWWW!" while she manacled him ever tighter, yodeling ecstasy beyond control or mercy, the outcome being baths of Epsom salts, patent schemes forgone.

Thereafter whenever they met in public they exchanged such irrepressible guffaws that subsequent speculations animated not a few, even became in some circles a sort of codified, social sport, one favored hypothesis being a prodigious tip on the market, that from prudence, perhaps even in hopes of a second, she kept from common knowledge by the unchanged, outward circumspection of her erstwhile, modest mode of subsistence.

Meanwhile, though all attempts to locate Amanda failed, he grew ever more determined to find her, whose image he now saw as the certain, only, magic key to the fulfillment of his life. He knew this for a doomed pursuit, sentimental, senile folly, yet he didn't know it, not quite, refused to succumb to mundane skepticism, and via indomitable desire convinced himself of the certainty of meeting her on some street somewhere some day, providing only that he keep faith with her.

He felt his heart rewarded with a kind of rationale of reason. He realized he'd never been in love before– not really– all along had gone from woman to woman for sheer neophilia, but here and now had somehow miraculously been granted a reprieve, one last chance at the real thing, if only he kept faith with Amanda, whoever, wherever, whatever she had become, that and that only in perfect dedication could answer for his existence, deification call it.

His Eremite's visage peered into unmet faces of aging women with such benign depth and profound inquiry that it seldom failed to evoke a concomitant response, if never yet the hoped-for, mutual cry of joy, and he had to remind himself that she might be most unlikely, coincidently, to match his adoration for her with one of her own for him, at least not at first glance.

And yet, and yet, how not? Life, real life was replete with symmetries, and once revealed to her, would she not feel her own life suddenly, finally complete? Nirvana might be come any day, any morrow. Such was his skeptic's first and only beatific conviction.

Nonetheless he began to fear, and rightly so, he felt, that unless he became worthy of her, she would never appear, or read him a-right if she did, and so strove both day and night to think only of her and to do only good with his dwindling assets, but as time went on his memory faded and she could not be visibly revived except as specter, limping and halt, pale and bent, bearing her mortality without complaint, still courageous, but blind, nearly blind, eyes on her feet lest they stray and tumble to a wretched heap in the street.

True love. What first? Bed of course at once, not for sex, but only to inspect the ruin of their nakedness, the towering grandeur of the grief of their love, the mighty mystery of its survival and triumph over the tribulations of time.

He knew she would not appear until he had earned her, to find, woo and win her he must deserve her. Still he did not despair, felt more and more on that airy verge, thinner and thinner, purer and purer, more and more confident, as he strove to make himself worthy, each night bedding himself with dreams of her, not always easy, sometimes even impossible to summon her yearning eyes, as if he'd somehow failed the day.

But how, how will he know her? Now so many he met, young and old alike, brimmed his heart to overflowing, a harmless dodderer with cane, in time two canes, stopping often to gaze in pleased delight at no one knew what or whom in particular.

A trifle sheepish, yet never without hope, he passed his dotage bench-sitting, chatting up every woman who came by, young or old, treating all who would accept to a glass of the finest of red wines, performing other services and helps as were useful, becoming a fixture at a certain shabby, many-windowed vintner's, and died unawares one brilliant dawn amid a dream of his long-sought perfect mate.

ADELMON'S DREAM

To John Street & Tom Lindsay

Handsome, ardent Adelmon had finally had his fill of women-kind. Not so much of what they were in their pristine, notional state, as of their predestined evolution into intimate, alien, ancient adversaries. As martinis are said to be, one not enough, two too many, three berserk or blotto– Adelmon reluctantly had to acknowledge– so, too, the female.

At age thirty-five, long undeceived by hopes of lasting ecstasies, let alone domestic tranquility, he hit upon an obvious if unthought-of stratagem, one naturally, unconsciously employed as surrogate by all men, and doubtless women, too, though he claimed no special insight into the secret hearts of that exasperating, undeniably superior sex.

He could not doubt he would have but little appetite for life without them. Resolute struggle to contain his hungers led him finally to cold turkey as his least dyspeptic dish, teetotaling its spice, facetiousness its face, absolute abstinence his sole hope of eluding lifelong subjugation– sex and possession, those twin bugaboos– henceforth proscribed, however humbling and humiliating such retreat must be.

Nor was it– he never doubted– likely to be an easy campaign, amid ever-tormenting titillation. He did not intend to become a recluse, or saint either: au contraire. He expected to be driven half-mad in his all-out pursuit of wholesome nirvana, but the rewards, yes, the rewards, the rewards– even the roads to rewards– the bare thought of them made him ache at his core.

At first his merciless antagonists hardly noticed a change in him– dimmed his acquisitive eye, double entendres passed him by like a deaf mute, palm strayed no more to plump buttock, nor traced willowy waist to spinal coccyx where cleft holds its humid allure, all commonplace, social embraces, all fleeting touch of lips proffered to sweet lips, all, all forsworn.

"Are you contagious?" said one to his shying away.

"Oh, no," said he. "I'm just giving it up."

"It?"

"Oh," he said stoically, "everything."

"My goodness!" said she, sashaying away, casting an inscrutable glance back over her glorious derriere. "How sad! Not to say improbable."

His bricklayer's livelihood kept him fit and well-muscled, and provided a simple, ample sufficiency, given his lack of lesser needs or ambitions. Women were his sole object. So it had been since his discovery of their all-engrossing otherness. No more a ludicrous appendage of volatile sensations that wrinkled by day, splayed at dawn, no longer uniquely mysterious– the penis, yes, the penis– had usage beyond the piss! Most wondrous usage! From which day forth he granted it primacy of place, in short, for all it could stand.

Man had, he learned, little enough rule of his member, but nearly none over women's flesh-hold, which soon became the deliberate quest, the study, the raison d'etre, of his whole being. Though winsome and shy, once enthralled, it grew willful and brazen as any beseeching phallus– mutual combustion he constantly strove to ignite.

Women were hardly immune to his boyish obeisance. Not few plied their wiles, and employed his ruddy-cheeked innocence as arm-piece, and thus he early learned how to suffer high hopes with forbearance. Amid the ruins of his many, eventual marriages, and the disillusion of countless mistresses by his endless infidelities– no matter the sincere vehemence of his vows to them and himself both– for a while he tried ladies of the night, an ill-starred resort.

None in the know– which overnight meant virtually all– coveted bed with one who flouted social punctilios with such indiscriminate abandon. Besides, ardors for cash begot neither heat nor commune nor peace of mind amid nether twinges and mental malaise. And soon he found himself anyway loath to favor one lest he offend another.

His saving regimen of total dispassion he suffered with steadfast commitment. He studied to master, strove forever to hold in mind, each woman he knew or met or spied in their every endearing aspect, mood, motion or mode, his nightly fantasies fired and informed by exact, infatuate observation. He came to know them as a shadow knows its fundament and source. His ever more well-stocked corral of oblivious darlings came tame to his wants, as gladsome fillies to apple or carrot.

The iron rule of his new ethic allowed neither amorous touch of them nor of himself, however he suffered, nor abject humpings of pillow or mattress. At first he tossed in lost sleep, rose haggard, worn and turgid, a bulging dam about to burst, but once wholeheartedly embarked upon the jelled seas of hopeless renunciation he could look forward to sleep in good season with bountiful dreams of beloveds by dawn fulfilled, and him well-rested and re-freshed.

Skirt bunched about her waist, moan-groaning, haughty Philo-mena, on her hands and knees in the grass, her wanton ass canted high, her back arched for an acrobatic kiss while Adelmon's quiff-slicked fingertips anointed her exquisite clit and nipples, his brim-ming cock sunk in her insatiably-seizing anus till it possessed his final spurt and dying drippage, at last he collapsed back on his haunches in solitary, all-prevailing beatitude.

The radiant smile she won next they met vanquished her imme-morial resolve never to succumb to his piteous pleas and risible ploys. She did indeed drive him near mad with teeming looks and subtle poses and turns as they strolled beneath the pollarded trees discoursing on the progress of global warming. Her fingers sought his as they paused to part, but his withdrew as if burnt. She smiled to think him more smitten than ever, approving his prudent, public restraint, looking forward to their next encounter, no less did he, she being now always and ever at his beck and call.

The god of dreams though did sometimes play the rogue, be-stowing un-meet moments. Adelmon's occasional, constrained fidgets he dismissed one day as poison ivy, the next as resurgent childhood hives from irresistible craving for raspberries so strong he had only to glimpse their rubiate succulence, to snatch at breath, tap toes, clap knees, flash acetylene eyes, mystifying, intriguing, fetching symptoms to those of his fond fascination, making him huff and blush for nightfall.

Husbands– honeymoons expired, wives in want of vigilant escort– observing Adelmon's sudden, supine servitude and deep enthrallment in the weaker sex's most inconsequential agitations and doings, lorded bemused amusement at his emergent eunuch's effeminate study of their dress and toilette, his doting subservience convenient foil for their own more important, masculine pastimes and devices.

Marital intimacies poured into Adelmon's avid ears, coddled him almost beyond sufferance, blandishing him with artful sights of deshabille or bath. His helpless enthrallment occasioned no puzzlement even under hubbies' noses, none marveled while his barely-contained ardors grew so intense he feared they must out themselves aloud, inciting his darlings to inflame them the more.

Men less aware of their own crude uses of fantasy– in truth distrusting and despising imagination itself– never questioned Adelmon's switched predilections, which they regarded as harmless, as indeed they were, unless he should croak of a stroke, and so end their hermit-like liberation.

"He wants to be a woman," said one husband.

"A fag manqué," quipped his buddy.

"He's the manliest man I ever knew," quoth a wife.

"What a laugh!" said the husband.

She guffawed so sincerely he glanced askance at her lowered gaze.

Another puzzled, "You have the ear of all these women: what's your secret?"

Adelmon shrugged up dolt-like palms, his, the only ear in question.

A plaintive wife asked why he absented himself from the tumid, opulent masked balls of mid-summer.

"I'm too old," said he with blithe note.

"Oh, come!" said she.

He answered only with doting, faint smile.

Their peripatetic flirtation quickened by the melancholy sight of a grand bank of bowed zinnias recently blazing with blooms a-flitter, a-glitter with magnificent monarch butterflies, the whole garden a crowded jostle of stippled, black, silver and reddish-orange wings, renowned Lepidoptera at feast on equally colorful stamens– goblets of nectar doubtless varied of tastes and highs– a mere month before had afforded Adelmon and Zarona many a delicious riff.

Now, with no warning, a stooped, old man stepped from an inconspicuous aperture in the vine-gnarled wall, without ado cut down the zinnias, each and every one exactly– it seemed– four inches from the ground, bundled them away in staggering armloads to a blackened compost sprawl, and without apparent notice of their presence, slipped from sight, leaving a desolate oblong of bare earth with stubs like four columns of ragged soldiers still a-march in perfect order.

"Not a one left," Zarona said sadly, turning about, and about.

Neither could he see a single, solitary wing of what had been hundreds, perhaps thousands of monarchs, with only increase, never diminishment, all summer long.

But then she clutched his arm tight against her in excited solace, "Look. Oh, look!"

A wraith-like, fantastic king of all kings floated above the garden, scarcely listing its stately wings in the breathless air, except to incline here, sail there, then waft once more around its old domain, as if reminiscing, yet unsure of what it was doing or why it was there, till finally it lofted away on a faint current, bound where?

There *was* nowhere, nothing ahead but a stupendous ponderosa pine tree forty yards out in the middle of an abandoned field, solitary and serene, its immense crown bristling with clutches of needles and cones.

In flight ten, then twenty feet up in the clear blue sky, the monarch looked to be lost, with no destination perforce in the emptiness of season but that monstrous pine in the withered, brown field where no speck of color remained.

Lone, lorn, frail, out of place and time, laggard thing, smaller and smaller with distance, seeming fool-hardy, sure to be blocked, if not ship-wrecked, in the ponderosa pine crown, abode of lithe squirrel and spry bird– why didn't it just simply sail on by? Or slip at ease between the sparse, barren branches below.

It did seem to hesitate, confused perhaps, perhaps at corporal strength's end, doomed, unless it veered, to be caught like a prize specimen in a prickly, sticky mesh of abrasive needles and scabrous cones.

Nonetheless–perverse, blind or hubristic by zig-jag and wobble, up it went, apparently hell-bent on the treacherous, green, grove-like crown high above the field.

Up it went, by fits and starts, sometimes more sideways than up, sometimes lost to sight as if reconnoitering possible paths through or snug dells to repose in, but then it reappeared, looped here, looped there, then stupidly, stubbornly, as if possessed or berserk, started up again, up, up and up, as if there were only the one direction, while they waited for it to turn back, sail around, or drop down, hug the ground beneath the bare, dead branches, roost awhile in the friendly field, nod to nostalgia, give due thanks for past felicities, mourn for all good things long in coming, then so strangely, so quickly wilted away.

But still it kept rising, rising, up, up, impossibly up, their suspense lost in apprehension as it rose by stages, climbing Everest's of air, then, apparently exhausted, but still called by the topmost boughs, it slowed, faltered, hung suspended, uncertain, a floating flash of color— perhaps ready at last to concede the necessary, the inevitable glide back down on wise wings to the prescribed altitude, whence, restored to due purpose, it would resume with steadfast spirit its time-hallowed flight to South America, there to perpetuate its kind, die in peace and harmony among all things rightful and real.

But— what's a monarch's way or will? — suddenly, to their anxious amazement, by a supreme effort of what looked to them exactly like conscious resolve— it flitted up, up and up like jumping, somehow jumping, jumping, jumping, it cleared the highest hump of spiring needles, and without pause of triumph, rest or farewell, gave one final, faint flit and was gone.

Adelmon cheered, Zarona clapped, like children they danced a whirl, then abashed, waited, mouths ajar, staring at the motionless tree-top, but the monarch never came back.

"Why? Oh, why did it do that?" Zarona wailed.

"Wanted to, I guess," said Adelmon. "Where do butterflies go to die?"

She looked at him and burst into tears.

In remorse he gathered her against him, his face bent to her fragrant hair— such a darling. He longed to clasp her bottom, well, her bare bottom, and he would, so he would, as soon as he was back in dream-land.

He felt their hearts thumping together, sighed and stepped away.

"Everything's so beautiful," she finally said.

"I know. I know," he said. And for the first time he felt he nearly did.

Adelmon— glad acolyte of women— adoring all, never thought to ask how they might view their unwitting roles in his nightly en-chantments. His aborning world, now he examined it, appeared at its simplest to be composed of three embodiments— *himself*, women *them*selves, and the nocturnal love-fests he fashioned for himself, but also— of course— now he thought of it— doubtless so did *they* entertain *their* idols, virginal perhaps in savior-faire, perhaps but perhaps not, pale compared to his own personally-conducted soirees, but nonetheless, out of sheer, familial sentiment, he hoped that his own incarnations now and then found generous admittance to their nocturnal ardors. Could such appropriations have consequence in the waking world?

These fantasies didn't exist in their own right, of course, neither his nor theirs, nor anyone else's, and yet they did, sort of, almost, he more and more had to accept. They were certainly in some sense real , if only contingent. But what did that *only* mean? *Merely?* A bit dismissive, that. And what degree of contingence?

Adelmon's dream-loves, in any case, began to proliferate beyond the known, give hints of incipient wills of their own— one, in a vacant moment, appeared without greetings, pushed him down on his back in bed, got turned round, knocking his jaw with a careless heel, squatted on his cock, bent and began sucking his toes, quite in spite of his distaste for the burlesque or perverse.

His tried and true darlings, his own fledgling offspring, so to speak, now were, apparently, becoming progenitors themselves of shadowy, shy sequelae, whose fleeting trajectories streaked through his absent moments, sometimes no more than eerie or mocking smiles, for or at whom he knew not.

Unbridled thought clouded, bumbled and tripped; raw conscience misgave. Was he demeaning them, degrading them, his beloveds? Would they, if they knew, begrudge his deliriums, of which, by his sole will and fabrication alone, they all partook with abandon, such as perhaps they had never experienced or even dreamt of, all common reticence ever more lost in licentiousness they might blush to witness even in others.

Was it a kind of subjugation? An invasion of privacy? Clandestine conquest? It was them, but not them. Whose imaginings were these, after all? They couldn't be copyrighted, nor even much recalled, as each more or less obliterated the last, at least at their summits of transport– he took no notes, too crass that seemed– but really he had become so lost to himself in so many silken embraces, he began to feel somehow... amorphous... ephemeral, solvent, a bit... visited.

The better he knew them, the more he marveled and adored, the more in dream he kissed and licked and nipped and caressed sweet fullness of hip and tit, suckled and slavered at swollen portals, succumbing only sadly, helpless, unmanned at last, by the all-vanquishing clasp of brute, oceanic sanctum, sighing, crying, wailing out his personal extinction in manifold arms, more than he could ever count or even remember, on his own bed alone at night moonlit or not.

The more gracious and receptive, the more ingratiating and brotherly his daylight demeanor, the more women adored him— how not?— while he bore with rare lapse of nonchalance the tantalizing joys of eye-fondling foreplay to early bedtimes and the night's true etudes.

Though new confidantes might be leery at first his repute and innate warmth soon secured them, called forth secrets and indiscretions, which met with gravitas rueful or exuberant, fed their affections— after all he wanted nothing from them but their confidence, their inner acquiescence— while he absorbed their very spirits, yet never a finger of his so much as brushed real palpability, though brushes of theirs were hardly rare, nor had he regrets, seeming sometimes almost absent, so that his most attentive intimates began to fear some wasting ailment, as he did now and then look a bit peaked, seeming to lack his former unfailing ebullience, which made them gather about protectively and pamper him with nutritious delicacies. His early evening yawn bespoke the onset of his day, for his idols' their end.

Meanwhile his puzzles bloomed and multiplied. What was real? Everything obviously. Inadvertent dreams and all, especially the mental, the equivocal— the physical to him was now obsolete except in dream. But why complicate? Yet how not?

Where's the reciprocation? he quizzed himself. What did he owe those he owed, if he owed anyone anything? But of course he owed, owed everything in fact. He ate, didn't he?

From the first Adelmon had possessed the delicacy– instinct, or perhaps trepidation– to exempt Zarona from the omnium-gatherum of his entranced loves. The night of the butterfly's flight he had conjured her with such vividness that he almost could not believe it was no figment, and quickly dismissed it un-kissed, with relief and pride both, lest she somehow feel defiled by him, abuser and thief of her chastity toward him, no friend.

That exception aside, Adelmon's devotions exalted him, and perfect complacence reigned in his harem, as one grandmother wryly styled it, perhaps, he surmised, deeming herself freed of his bondage by age– which a bit challenged him– while the more he imbibed her casual hegemony of experience, her shrug of contempt for convention, her dexterity with other people's children, the pleasures of rambles in the woods with her for lady slippers, her unapologetic hiked skirt and squat of nature, her frank regalement of former amours, her ingenious way with leftovers, himself having countless times enjoyed her dewy daughter in dreams, he now succumbed to the unplumbed novelty of the mother's flawless complexion, hoary mane and venerable manner, broke his oath of actual continence, blithely invited himself home with her for tea with intent to bed her before dinner, then escape by reason of previous engagement, but once within the confines of her modest abode, found himself the one possessed.

Pride-less, regressed to boyhood, he felt scarcely past puberty, her plaything, breathless and shy. "Now... just...a little... ah... *there,*" said she, his cheeks warmed, now one, now the other, by her abundant thighs, his tongue licking and lapping like a rapt cat at a splash of cream.

With a grunt she drew him up for a kiss, unerringly engorged his prick with no help of hand, and there kept him past midnight, her vaginal ripples and grips accompanying her musings upon all things under the sun, while he wallowed between troughs and near crests ever-withheld, till she finally with a certain imperial, if sleepy, benevolence, accepted his homage, causing him to resolve henceforth to dwell less upon anatomies, dive more deeply into eyes.

"What you want, dear boy," she decreed, "is a woman who comes when you tell her you love her."

He never got to spend the night. A lazy, late riser, she let him ache on her front stoop till mid-morning, then led him out with thermos of black coffee to wade in the wind-blown billows of yellow, maple leaves on their circular, woodsy trail to her trellised back door, charred toast with grape jelly, and leisurely, luxuriant resumption of bed.

Men sneered at the spectacle of one become an apron-strung muppet, but women it seemed steeped in warmth of communal consent.

This spell of grand tutelage felt like world's verge of all knowledge until one rainy noon, amid his preludial petting, he besought his usual admittance to her consummate vortex of delights—she was absently nestling and nuzzling him, one eye on the stupid clock.

"I'm sorry, my dear," she yawned. "No more till next year. With luck. My punctual, good hubby's due home in an hour. Once and I'm done for the day. He hates it when I have to fake it."

"You *are* a good soul," Adelmon allowed, ungrudging, this the first he'd heard of a spouse.

"Oh, god, yes, you wouldn't believe," said she, pulling on her voluminous under-drawers, which he nonetheless strove to impede.

As her fat, white ass finally slipped from sight she flipped a grand crescent of cheek at him, took her shopping bag, and vouchsafed him a farewell smile of shades he would be long construing, less with regret for Eros lost than impatient of latent implications yet coming, ever still coming into endless ken.

Alone and subdued, Adelmon suddenly pined for Zarona's unambiguous concord, why he knew not, only that it was time– past time– to return to cold turkey, lest his effort to dodge women's dominion slip forever beyond retrieval.

Strangely, as things sometimes fall out in real life, Zarona later that day sought him out, though grave of visage. "I think..." she said. "You'd better go see Mary Lee."

"I?" said Adelmon. "Who is she? Why should I?"

Zarona looked back at him sharply, then more gravely yet. "You don't know?"

"I don't," said Adelmon with stoic promptitude.

"Oh, Addy," she said, her first use ever of that brevity.

He drew breath of indulgence, gazed at her.

"You're the love of her life."

"I?" Adelmon scoffed. "I have no idea who *she* is."

"Well, apparently you once spent a night with her."

"No doubt," said Adelmon a bit uncomfortably. "Among not few."

"She knows that. She's been bearing this torch apparently for ages now– not few, by any gauge."

"Based on what?" demanded Adelmon, brewing umbrage.

"Hope, I suppose."

"Well...," said Adelmon. "I still have no idea who she is."

"She said she could never believe you didn't love her after such a night, which I suppose to you meant nothing at all. She never after met your equal, nor ever would settle for other or less— and anyway couldn't conceive you wouldn't some day come for her."

"She *must* have been a child," Adelmon murmured.

Zarona looked at him steadily. "She's dying. I told her I would bring you."

"Dear god!" said Adelmon.

"Who invokes God more than the atheist?" She held out her hand, which he affected not to notice.

Heads down, they walked very slowly together in the beautiful fall. "How old *is* she?" Adelmon wondered.

"Your age, I guess," said Zarona.

"Dear god!" he muttered, suppressing an urge to cite as curative model his magisterial grandmother.

They came to a house, knocked, were let in. Zarona vanished. He entered the sunny sick-room, where a white specter lay, hardly more than a bare skull with skeletal fingers outside the turned-down sheet like double quotation marks.

"Someone to see you," a quiet voice said.

Two eyes opened blind, wandered, wondered, widened at last in slow recognition, dry lips seemed minutely to part. Adelmon's memory failed or fled, or perhaps mere wastage of time had obliterated all of whatever had been— their hour or night, the time, place, the circumstances— nothing remained.

Hopeless and hollow, he lifted her nearest hand, kissed it and his tears rained down upon it, to his vast astonishment and gratitude. He felt he had never been so thankful for anything in his life.

"I'm sorry, sorry, so sorry..." he murmured.

"No, no, no," he heard.

He stayed, holding her hand, till her eyes slowly closed. He stayed on while they stayed closed, then stayed for a minute, then another and another and another minute more, at last sighed and tiptoed away.

In a dawn fit of futility and failure he went back at nine in the morning, to be told at the door that she'd died in the night.

He tried to feel relieved, but it was only to balm himself, not her, who knew aught of her real relief. A chill touched him, knowledge of inevitable change. He was no longer young, knew fantasies for debasement, day-dreamed no more, neither as pastime nor vagrance.

Nonetheless a kind of vestigial angst of desire occasionally plagued him. With light, half-conscious fingertips he grazed for comfort available earlobes, elbows, shoulders as he went among his dream loves as if to dispense perfunctory blessings scarcely felt, then withdrew into retrospects, no less in thrall though now more in memoriam for times past.

Having crossed some irreversible border, he could no longer lust enough ever again to make physical love with anyone, walked in blind dream of fruitless beauty even as he wearied, and was weaned of it.

One day in nostalgic rebellion he recalled a slut he'd once admired for her raucous, unregenerate squalor, but had long since lost track of. Now in rash determination of perfect unfeeling he found and fucked her half the night through till he fell asleep upon her breast unspent, woke to find her still staring past him at the ceiling, shrugged off her surly, abject offers to resume, his $50 token in turn brusquely rebuffed.

Wizened and scrawny, she'd hardly limped from sight before shame drove him on the run after her. She fought like forty squalling cats, scratched his face while he madly kissed her from ear to ear and forehead to chin, crooning endearments, till she burst out giggling like a girl, he tucked his despised bill down the front of her panties, fond as never in all the years he'd used her for lack of another, she daubed four fingers beneath her redolent mons, glossed his lips, and departed with warmth of a lost and found again sister in arms.

Her clinging pungence, however, revived in him the old, rampant, faceless desire he had thought waned if not gone, that now threatened a second, less edifying, irreparable downfall. Dire need for pure freedom gave thought of one sure antidote, the scent of Zarona's panties, just them and nothing other or more, hers and no one else's, strange and stranger, for he had never dreamt, much less fantasized, the least live touch of her, had always considered it the bonded integrity of their chary relations never to dwell on her sweet parts, not even her delectable nipples, which she hardly hid.

Now he could not have wanted body and soul of any hundred immortal goddesses as much as he wept for a mere whiff of the essence of this one, most dear female's vaginal cleft.

So strange, so strong, so perverse and compelling its spell, so persistent and inescapable, so preoccupying and disruptive, day in, day out, that meeting her unexpectedly one day in shamefaced confusion of one unable to keep from her even a single secret, no matter how wanton or ignominious, untoward or simply preposterous, he simply blurted his need, as if it were merely a minor foible.

"Well..." she demurred a bit taken aback, saw his face go taut, locked eyes at his ghastly chagrin, reddened as much as him.

"I'm sorry," he muttered. "I've never... I don't know... Oh, please forgive...I must... I'm so..."

Forthwith, she slipped them off with such alacrity, such athletic agility, that he gasped, then held them apart from him by two fingertips like some pitiful talisman or writ, herculean yet forlorn, as if their possession could never answer anything in question even for one millisecond.

He longed to lift her gently as a blown-down robins' nest of blue eggs and carry her into the deepest, crag-cribbed, pine grove, feeling her soft fingers at his nape, but he only stood staring his incapacitation till in sad acquiescence she turned wordless away.

Why? Why? Why couldn't he? Because he loved her. What other answer could there possibly be?

Her panties he kept from his face, washed them, put them away in safe secrecy to return to her in some future he could not conceive nor foresee, though henceforth they glowed in his dreams like an impossibly distant planet yet to be discovered and named.

Haggard Adelmon, lacking impetus for further trials of the heart, thereafter kept to himself in troubled thought or drank like a mute among men once his work day was done, half-conscious clods they sometimes seemed, bosses or shunners or minions of women, their overweening condescension, resentment, belittlement, contempt, hate or fear, alternately damping and firing their need to come to grips with tits and ass, in triumph or submission, briefly or not, beyond which, now and then, a kind of child-like idealism seemed strangely to blaze.

Like one newborn, he observed that the ratio of terms for the female to the male sex organ was many, many to few– very few. The penis had but a paucity of qualities– vulnerability, elasticity, spouter's ceaseless, heedless want of viscous-slick receptacle– while the all-engrossing, ineffable, indomitable cunt lived beyond language itself, at least in the minds of men, whose resentful derision signaled their ultimate nullification. Who among thoughtful humans did not recognize the breadth of this tragic breach?

All History confirmed it. Men conquered and ruled, women gave birth, made homes, served life– irrefutable basics, demanding in plain sanity of earthly well-being only that men make way, make room for women. But how reform nature? Rectify History?

Overnight Adelmon found himself become perfectly impotent, his longing for women wholly undiminished, rather increasing, but of a different cast, one that somehow dwelt upon itself, yet gained no relief, one in which his prick seemed to drip not semen but tears.

A philosophical being from birth, Adelmon was prepared for some impasse of life early or late, though certainly not one so unlikely. He was puzzled, sad, aghast at its advent, saw pleasure depart, and then the reaper, grim truth, arose like a blank tombstone– to bear, he swore, no inscriptions but the one indisputable one: Men Are Strife, Women Peace.

But what to do meanwhile? Everything, of course. In dire despair he set out to heal the immemorial rift. Day and Night he put his whole mind's might to it, grew gaunt with books and thought, felt so feeble, finally so futile and defeated, he shied from women's eyes, went only among men, who saw him transformed into dreambound derelict one day gloomy, snappish preacher the next, one none could abide.

Be a woman, he exhorted himself, lived in deepening silence amid men's voices.

They won't be satisfied till they have a penis.

I don't mind. I just don't want theirs getting in the way of mine.

I don't like women so much as I love them.

Vice versa with me.

I'm an equal feeler. I love and hate them, correctly in my humble opinion.

But you've got to admit there are real differences.

Men can't bear children.

Shrink them intestines. Make room. Science can do anything.

Women soldiers?

Wrong temperament.

Oh, yeah?

Frankly, Adelmon, you've got to marry one to know the first thing about women, any woman. You've never tested nor tasted the real fires.

Adelmon, the un-humbled, bowed.

Women said, "We never see you any more".

I'm busy.

At what?

My desk.

What would you do at a desk? All day and all night?

I sit.

Oh, come, they repeated their now mocking riposte.

You'll see, he kept saying as he darkened with age, slowed in mobility, so seldom appeared no one attended, finally hardly heard his whispers, simply a nameless birdcall, still a bit reminiscent, familiar, fading, mysterious, dolorous, forlorn.

A silhouette one day in a blaze of August sun Adelmon realized with joy was Zarona coming toward him with radiance. "Oh, Ad," she cried, her first such address, ominous to his ear, "I'm so glad to see you. I have something to tell you, that I know will make you happy."

"Only you make me happy, Zee," he grumbled, but she didn't seem to take his meaning.

"I'm getting married," she said, and seemed to glow from within, then swallowed audibly at his quickly-dissembled consternation that devolved into excruciating silence between them. At parting he entered her arms for a first and last embrace. She whispered, "I'll always love you."

He felt his eyelashes flicker against her cheek, as she surely felt hers against his. He went down the sunny hillside into shadow and didn't look back.

After ghostly attendance at her nuptials, Adelmon fled the feast, and sat down to things in earnest, shied from chances even to glimpse her, barred her from mind, missed her all the more, finally found consolation only in the knowledge of her continued existence.

The crack in the universe so long ignored, then deplored, finally borne only with acrid repugnance, its remedy though obvious in theory still only fitfully, dimly conceivable, nonetheless demanded at last a day of response, of utterance: Adelmon sat down to write:

> A wiser, kinder, more harmonious and just, happier future awaits the human race if and when half the world's authority devolves upon women.

Nirvana will not follow overnight, but the way forward is plain, sensible, sane, essential, the only hope in fact.

Over time fair measures may right the essential wrong of history at its original root of impassable divide and inequality, of physical dominance and aggression in men, of vulnerability of heart and child-bearing in women.

Exclusive, ruinous male rule will inevitably be ended, violence outmoded, disdained, practical kindness and understanding preferred, widely advanced, eventually to prevail.

To accept as irremediable the human male's inbred, egotistical incapacity, presumption, and inveterate folly, is forever to perpetuate it, however uneven its reign.

Pessimism has myriad strongholds, powers, customs, all well-known, condoned, unquestioned. The rich and happy will always be with us. But triumphant injustice, stupidity, cruelty and failure are not forever ordained.

If it can be conceded that Humankind's wisest exemplars agree that Democracy is the most desirable state which can be aspired to, no matter how little or incompletely understood, then the foundation-stone of universal salvation has already been laid long ago, at Athens or elsewhere, perhaps earlier.

What sort of democracy is possible, real, ideal, or even decent, tolerable, fair or satisfactory? Where? When? How long, if any, did any ever last? Is America a Democracy?

The rich yell "Yea!" The poor's landside roars, "Nay!"

"Nothing's perfect," speaks Content and Discontent alike. "Idealism is hindrance, no?"

No. Not at all. Practical resolution lies at hand, invisible as obvious.

Pray tell.

The two sexes, Men and Women, can supply saving wholeness, blessed harmony, when equal in numerical strength, provided that all bodies of decision, of authority, of governance of any sort whatsoever, from the most trivial to the most august, are constituted of an even number of members, 2, 4, 6, 8, etc., no 1, 3, 5, etc.

But always Half Male, Half female—no exceptions.

Electoral deadlocks will occur by sex or by difference of opinion, but debates will be stripped of obsolescence, favoritism, time honored hierarchies, distrust, as well as ignorance of the differing natures and needs of both sexes. Pernicious oppositions will gradually fade and be shed.

Interests of male and female will balance, will end immemorial male dominance, with enlightened male help, which will grow, as the sexes commence to side with each other.

The nature of women will be freed to domesticate, civilize, humanize, liberate the rule that will ensue.

Love of precious offspring and their wise nurture and education will rise in public regard and demand, and promote solidarity and confident hope among adults.

Some may say that women are as bad as men, or worse. No matter. Men will curb them, as they will curb men, the twain will improve the twain, and a new kind of bonded polity of respect and endearment will come to benefit all, especially the young, ever empowering and binding future generations.

It needs no great foresight to see the advantages, nor does it guarantee that wisdom, kindness, harmony and happiness will prevail, but such dreams will stand in better stead of fulfillment in time if women's lights are no longer shut out nor dimmed.

Gun Clubs with half women officers? Yes, yes.

Adjustments, some obvious, some never imagined, will be required, none beyond human ingenuity, good will and resolve.

A male President reelected perforce would be followed by a female President, elected by all, but no men could run. Second terms accepted. Otherwise single heads must alternate sex by rote, no exceptions.

Gender will replace party, eliminate cabal or faction.

But how? How? is the immediate question— how can Congressional elections and other awkward contests be designed to anoint half men, half women in every separate body, counsel, parliament, club or group, whatsoever?

How persuade the sluggish populations, over how many generations or centuries? The benefits once understood can hardly be resisted by societies of sense and good will. The way will be long, hard, strife-torn.

But success will breed emulation and give assistance to the less advanced.

How outgrow divisive religions, while preserving their benevolent truths? How equalize electorates by sex?

All things by good will, common sense, determination, example, solidarity, pride of harmony, idealism, love.

All Presidential and like lone, supreme authorities limited by alternating terms of an electorate male and female, limited to one reelection, of both sexes acting in concert.

Such a system recognizes the paramount importance of absolute governing equality between the two sexes so profoundly different, yet inextricably bound in union for the betterment of all in all– for the benefit of each individual male and female.

Pursuit of kind, good governance, never neglecting justice and mercy, will build to ever higher plains of wholeness, such that all human sorrow is shared.

Theory, Adelmon saw at once, was easy. "The How's" multiplied toward despair. Clearly it would need commanding, planetary majorities of universal persuasion, beyond human conception of the present epoch, next thing to the miraculous– perhaps the miraculous itself.

Adelmon, a born realist, who tolerated no dreams– except, of course, visions of women– this day had a dream he could not seem to wake from, an immense, towering height too tall, too broad, too deep for the eye to encompass or fathom; horizon without limits, impossible in its infinite magnitude of people so tightly packed no limbs were visible, only heads, all eyes turned up,

He tried to see what the mountain was made of, how far or high or widely it extended, but eerily it seemed to be composed of all space, all time, wholly and solely of heads with upturned eyes– toward god? Toward malevolent meteor that would end everything? He could not tell. It was only a dream, a dream.

Adelmon cried out then, half in distress, half in derision, "Welcome Dream!"

Then he realized that it was no mountain nor sky, but only human heads upon heads upon heads, a bottomless mass, piled beyond the stars, all gazing where?– he had to turn from their eyes, each visage unique, too vivid, too particular, too imperious to countenance– the first act of cowardice of his entire life as he realized that every human being that ever lived was present, all beseeching him.

He looked away, down in shame, down and down through bottomless ages, numberless, beyond numbers, he could not distinguish sex or age, then began to see earlier visages, Neanderthals, apes, headless swimming things trying to crawl from the sea, brave bare land, all striving to feed themselves, then their offspring, all the way down to the invisible, autonomous specks adrift in the tides, unconcerned with mortality– thought, hope, love, sacrifice, prophecy yet to arise.

Then all vanished, all was as it was but a moment before, but for Adelmon's glimpse of tragic grandeur.

Little or nothing, he saw, could be done in a day, or a year, or perhaps in a century of centuries, and he sat down where he was and cried like a child till his eyes dried.

Shamed, sunk in weakness, he addressed the non-existent gods, "Then let it begin here, in the self-lauded Land of the Free and Home of the Brave, whence to spread by example from age to age and nation to nation, gathering, consolidating, always becoming an ever more closely-knit association of like-minded states bound to-gether, sworn to assist others on the road to true freedom, real com-mune, fast kinship, where understanding, love and esteem between the sexes would be the paramount touchstone and bulwark of all existence."

He blanched at the massive transfer of wealth and usage that would be required. How persuade the male half of the race to share its dominions of power without eons of strife?

The variety, anarchy and immemorial, entrenched wrongs of the world called him to lie down at once and die of despair.

The movement would need a name, he saw, a whole new no-menclature. From time to time he rested in such pleasant, inspira-tional speculations. And if ideal democracies all the same quarreled and failed? But they wouldn't, would they?

Here at the end of the end of Adelmon's rope of thoughts he gnashed his teeth, having not smiled in years. It was not that he was not happy, just not happy enough to smile.

He felt the weight of time and human fate. His eyes watered constantly, tears not of sorrow, nor of joy, but of something else, exactly what he strove, in his remaining centuries, to apprehend and grasp.

Time fled. He trod the beach— that is, he hobbled, his sun-burnt, skeletal frame mossed it seemed toward the ankles or scabbed. He tilted toward the right, and occasionally, wearily, dizzily thought: What the hell! Topple soon, topple late.

Still he took fascination in the labyrinthine, channeled sands, the illimitable sea wrack, the towering, almost-imperceptibly-but ever-changing, ever-suggestive cumulus semblances crossing the horizon above the bay, and in the mute passage of beautiful women, at whom he gazed with ever deepening wonder and veneration.

One summer day he did not recognize Zarona at first. She was back-to, getting clumsily out of her clothes. When she turned all he could see was her immense, taut belly. Nearby her six-year-old son Alton was digging in the sand for water.

Adelmon, amid his dotage, gaped in amazement. How could she or anyone get so hugely, so perfectly round? He had a moment of strange conviction that all these years she had been pursuing him for no other purpose than to demonstrate to him her grand belly, its geometric perfection, gigantic watermelon cloaked in a straining bathing suit.

He no longer needed to sniff, but only to adore her in the most ordinary, agonized, pathetic way. She had hardly changed, had nothing of the imp in her, and accepted his congratulations with complacence. He knelt beside her until he saw her husband coming along the beach, bent and kissed her belly. She helped him back to his feet and he went on with his slow walk, often stopping or stooping to peer at whatever took his eye.

That year he occupied himself with the problems of an electronic electorate, how to assure that men and women were separately registered. And how to equalize should one sex outnumber the other, as must always happen. Could it simply be ignored? The vistas of problems dizzied and defied. The complexities merely of the U.S. House of Representatives almost made him laugh, let alone New Delhi, Peking, and Reykjavik et al.

He laughed all the while, silently, at himself, at his illusions, at the absurd creature he had become. Even to reform one single state of the most meager polity was beyond him. He thought, I shall have lived in vain. Yet, what did I expect?

Still he went on writing and writing what he knew could not be finished nor matter, except in some distant future. Behind a wrinkling brow, blandished by his love of the sun, he fought off despondence, kept faith with his life's lone vision.

Zarona's babe, Eva, Adelmon in time came to dote upon, occasionally dandled. From the girl's birth, as time passed and he reached his ninth decade, he seemed to have achieved a kind of senile sweetness, pronouncing himself the happiest, luckiest of men, knowing at last in her light what love was, the one and only, but wholly adequate reason to be glad ever to have lived at all.

At death he dreamt of a flittering, blue butterfly climbing the sky, realized it was Zarona's panties. By what practical means the sexes could be united he was never able clearly to envision, only that it should and surely would become first, foremost and forever among human ambitions.

LAST DAYS

One grey afternoon in the last days of the Fo'c's'le, Zeke Nauls and Phenny Lake happened in at the same time to have a last drink. They got schooners of beer at the bar, paid their 90 cents apiece, bowed Alphonse-Gaston deferrals to each other, finally with a certain, forthright decisiveness, took separate ways around the long, narrow beam table that bisects the worn floor, rejoined, sat down together in the west window and gazed at the great linden in front of the library across the street.

Washashores both, he was a handsome, women-ought-to-be-thankful-he-was-ever-born, shaggy-haired blond, and had been around. She too had been around, at least as long as him, and had known her ups and downs. The grey was on them both, with weathered lines at eye and mouth.

"Not exactly a happy occasion," he said.

Two reporters had just left. All week long, once the word was out, a ceaseless stream of stunned habitués had dropped in during the day to reminisce and mourn. The dour, infarcted owner, anxious to dispose of his business concerns, amazed by the furor, dismayed by the disgruntled post-mortems, looked ill at ease in his own domain, though the price of the property had increased by 1,500% in the 29 years since he bought it.

He had opened The Fo'c's'le as a fishermen's saloon in 1956, buying out the New Deal Tavern, established in 1934, upon repeal of Prohibition. Women were admitted in 1960, ending the last

Men's-Only on the Cape. On December 3rd, 1985, the Fo'c's'le would become Conrad's, owned by Gold Coast Properties, Inc., a group of gay businessmen.

"I can't even imagine it," Phenny said.

With morbid ennui Zeke ticked off, "Food not booze, pastel walls, gilt mirrors, clipper ship pictures instead of Portuguese fishing gear, little red curtains across the windows, separate little tables, no common benches, no life..."

"Wait till the Hell's Angels roar in for the next Blessing of the Fleet." Phenny sighed. "I guess I'd rather not have to see their faces. They always filled the place."

Zeke gave a glum snort. "Hey! Lotta people losing their living room."

"Their office," Phenny said. "Howard Mitchum. John Bennett."

"We oughta sit right here," he said, "and get bent."

She laughed, looked at him, laughed again.

"We really should," he said. "Last chance."

"I'm game," she said. "It's my day off."

He felt suddenly elated by anticipation of a proper wake. "I spent the best years of my life looking at that tree," he said.

"If you sat here long enough you saw everything," she agreed.

"Fact," he said, stretching his arms along the window-ledge, tilting his face back to catch a weak ray of sun just as Wally McPhee came out of Dodie's Pizza next door, went past without glancing in.

Zeke said with mild derision, "You had a little fling with him once, as I recall."

"Oh, yes. Several. We went round and round." She watched him out of sight with inscrutable eyes, then laughed. "Well, here's one of yours."

Amy Blue sailed by on a bicycle.

"Not half bad," he said with a nod. "And there's another of mine."

Straight toward them on Freeman Street came Sandy Dill with her perpetually skeptical expression. She saw them in the window and lifted her chin as she turned along Commercial Street under the linden.

"You never!" Phenny said. "I don't believe you."

He hacked a coughing laugh and eyed her. "You'd be surprised," he said. "I always got my share. In the old days. More than my share, actually."

"You always had a new one," she said.

"You were hardly a nun," he said.

"Oh, I was the original New York whore. Remember? That's what they used to call any woman who wasn't a townie."

"Lotta changes," he brooded.

"End of an era," she said, went to the bar and came back with refills. Her rather lewd breasts, of which she was girlishly proud, jiggled left and right in her favorite, faded jersey with its remnant of pale blue ribbon at the cleft.

"Another of mine, one-night of her was enough," he confided as Debby Gingrich and Ron Demaris came along by the four Doric columns of the Plain & Fancy, crossed Freeman Street, passed beneath the linden, looking preoccupied, as if immersed in diverse lives.

Phenny began to laugh irrepressibly.

"What's so funny?" Zeke said. "You don't believe me?"

She kept having fits of giggles, as if she were being tickled, and her tits jiggled exorbitantly.

"She's not such a dog," Zeke said, miffed.

"She's a peach," Phenny said, "if you ask me. I went with Ron for a while."

"Ron? I never knew that."

"Seventy-two or-three. We had a good time. Well. For awhile."

"I got some to my credit I wouldn't even want to admit to."

She began to laugh again, more intimately, looking at him from under her blue-shaded eyelids and dark lashes.

He felt challenged now, goaded to drawl with slow insinuation, "We ought to play a little truth game, have a little contest. Anyone who passes the linden, we have to say if we ever did them, even if it was only once, and we have to say what they were like. No lying. We have to swear to tell the truth. We'll start from scratch. Zero to zero."

"Which wins?" Phenny wondered. "Fewest or most?"

"Either way," he conceded. "Everybody wins."

"Wins what?"

"Whatever." And he jumped his eyebrows at her.

"In that case," she said, "we better have another beer." Gladly he rose and went to the bar.

Just then Stan and Bill passed by the linden, almost at the same moment, going in opposite directions, giving each other hardly a nod. Neither saw her in the window, nor was she sorry that old bedlam a trois was not to be exhumed.

Zeke came back with beers and shots of tequila, stretched out again and majestically craned his neck to see as far as he could in both directions along the empty street.

"Now," he said, "nobody'll come."

She sipped her tequila. "Long time since I've been on a binge."

"Getting old," he said.

Various passed, but offered no sport– Mrs. Meraunder with her crow-like gait and rouged cheeks; Johnny Ball muttering with dark menace, avenging old affronts with bursts of punches thrown at empty air; two gay waiters at last hilariously meting out some impossible patron's due desserts; and a large lesbian with a pert Pekinese on a long leash called Man Eater.

"There's no more straight people anyway," Zeke observed morosely.

"Doesn't bother me. What I mind are the rents."

"Lotta building nobody can afford to live in. I ran into Joe Costa back there in Portagee Heaven, he says, 'You come around a corner you been going around all your life and all of a sudden it's condo city. Overnight!'"

"Greed," Phenny said. "We always said it would happen. Buying up houses and raising the rents. You can't even find a pair of socks any more. Plenty of $400 sweaters though. Who can afford to live here?"

Zeke shrugged. "Drug dealers. High rollers. Do you remember Slim? Summer of '67 maybe."

Abigail Allain, wraithlike in white, floated unnoticed toward them on Freeman Street 'til, at the corner, she turned east. "Well," Zeke said, "I'm one up on you."

"She didn't go by the linden. You have to go all the way past on Commercial Street."

"Ohh. Kay. Scratch her. She wasn't so much anyway. Slim. Slim was this grizzled, old, black guy who showed up one day. All he had was a guitar and a hat and he did the talking blues up and down the street till the hat was full of money, and then he'd come in here and buy everybody drinks. A whole crowd of college kids followed him around with their guitars, trying to learn his tricks. "There's only one way," he'd say. 'Git black and go to jail.'

"He crashed a few nights where I was staying. He was like a corpse in the morning. We thought he was dead. He wouldn't even open his eyes till someone poured some whiskey in his mouth, then he'd reach for his guitar, and pretty soon he'd be tuning up at the kitchen table, whiskey in his coffee. He never ate, why they called him Slim, I guess."

"There were some real characters," Phenny said. "They'd all be sitting in here right now."

Time yawed in the silence, uneasy and sad, and both took an abstracted glance around the empty bar, had a hit of tequila.

A shadow of mirth like a cough forced Zeke's lips and depressed his chest. A hundred funny stories lit his eyes and he reached for a cigarette.

Phenny said, "I'll never forget the time Sonji was getting it on with this guy. She was being very cool, she'd drunk just enough. The toilet paper somehow got caught in her crack. She came strolling back from the Ladies trailing the whole roll."

Zeke flicked an ash off his boot and glanced out to see Dolph striding by the linden. "Moment of truth," he said.

"When he first came to town," Phenny confessed. "We'd get some oysters and drink some gin and then go for a swim. He was very ceremonious."

"Two to one!" Zeke ejaculated– prematurely it turned out– as Alycia and Louise coming from the east turned down Freeman Street, before the linden.

"No score for you!" Phenny crowed. "I'm shutting you out."

"Hey! I'm getting screwed. Where is everybody?"

"AA."

"Or dead. Or left town. Where'd they all go? They don't even come back any more."

"Burn at both ends, die young. That was the idea."

"It's called risk-taking now," Zeke said and coughed contempt.

Phenny hunched her shoulders and laughed with him. "Well, we survived. But if I ever lose my cheap rental..."

They looked out at the bleak street. "Maybe we should have a blackberry brandy," he said. "For the stomach."

"Then we should go out back and have a little smoke. For the head."

"I don't have any," Zeke said.

"I don't either."

"What happened to your little silver joint-carrier? You were never without."

"Somebody stole it. Right off my bureau. They liked it, so they took it. I don't even smoke any more."

"Lotta changes," Zeke said. "I never had a straight day from one year to the next. Get up in the morning, have a little toke. I can't count the times I almost stepped off a scaffold."

"Really!" Phenny said. "Once you went out the door you never knew where the day would go. And the acid. Ooh! And the mescaline! I don't know how anything ever got done."

"Some people went a little *too* far. Never did get back."

"There was a party at the Kibbutz. Very flashy people from New York. They had some liquid pot. About $200 a drop. You smoked it in a pipe that plugged into a wall socket. I looked around. Wally Jones was wiggling in his chair like a baby, Jimmy D was raving at himself in the mirror. I was the only woman there. I realized everyone was absolutely crazed, like everyone had turned into a monster..."

"Yeah," Zeke said. "Those were the days when you went home and pushed your wife out a window. If you still had one. How'd you wind up down here anyway?"

"I got on the wrong bus."

Zeke laughed. "Providencetown. I went as far as I could go. I knew it was the end of the line for me."

"You know what's weird?" she said. "The way townies can date you. You'll be sitting on the meat-rack and some old Portagee will say, 'How long you been here, Dear?' And while you're trying to figure it out, he'll say, 'About twenty-four years, right?' And you realize he's exactly right. They always know. How do they do that?"

Eddie Evenshire rolled slowly by in his pickup truck with two dogs on the seat beside him and two more in back. He had a cigar stub behind one ear and sawdust in his hair. He gave them a heads-up and revved his engine.

"Two to nothing," Phenny said and drained her tequila.

"No kidding. I can't see you with him."

"Oh, he broke my heart. Years ago."

"Him? I didn't know you had a heart."

"Oh, yes. At least I started out with one."

"So? How was he?"

"Lasted about a month. In like a lion. Out like a... Well. To tell you the truth I'm not all that fond of dogs."

Dimble and Mary strode by in step, elbows linked, both in black watch caps and hooded, blue sweatshirts, exactly the same height.

"No score," said Zeke. "You can't tell me."

"I wouldn't try. I always like to see them. They go back to the year One."

"Siamese twins. Zilch for anybody else. No consideration at all."

Mike Moon came over with the wastebasket, emptied their ashtray, stood for a moment, looking out the window. "End of an Era," he said.

Phenny followed him back to the bar and returned with two shots of blackberry brandy, just in time to catch Lionel passing the linden. "Three to nothing," she said. "Mr. Vanity, pulls in his belly in bed."

"One to three," said Zeke, rather dour as Zona Greer went by looking like a Bronte. "She's got a clit like a parrot's beak."

"Ohhh!" Said Phenny, wincing.

"That was the worst day the town ever had."

"What day?"

"The day the Patricia Marie went down. October 24th, 1976."

"Oh, God!"

"I was following Zona down the street trying to catch a casual bump, and I met Teresa coming the other way. She says, 'I can see you haven't heard, I don't want to be the one to tell you.' She was grim, I figured another one of her kids was dead.

"Then along comes Willis in his crazy phase, ranting at everybody. You could see people getting off the sidewalk. He yelled at me, "I'm glad to see *you're* still enjoying all *your* five senses."

"Oh, Lord!" Phenny said.

"Yeah. All hands, all seven. Big freak wave and straight to the bottom. Stove the pilot-house to pieces. And everybody related to everybody in town."

Phenny said, "I was sitting in here with Dickie Oldenquist about two nights before. For years afterwards I would dream this wall of water, I could hear him yell."

"A queer sea, they call that, a rogue sea, a sneaker. Wind and weird tides combined. No moon. There was a boat from Sandwich right behind. One minute she was on their radar, the next she was gone.

"The Sandwich boat heard a voice crying in the wind but they couldn't find him. Zona and I walked down to the wharf. People were gathered out on the end, looking out over Long Point. Some of them had been there since word got around. Nobody was giving up."

"Who was the captain of the Patricia Marie?" Phenny said.

"King. William King. Billy King," Zeke said. "I ran into Phil Souza right after the Inquiry. They had a huge deck-load of scallops. He said, 'Lots of boats do it. You got to take what you can get. You try a thing a thousand times and it works for you, and then...' He just shrugged."

"They had a Playboy bunny on the bow," Phenny remembered. "Bright red!"

"That was how I got started with Zona. She didn't want to be alone that night."

"Yeah," Phenny said. "It felt like the sun would never shine again. You couldn't move. People just sat around and stared."

Heavy, slow-walking, the widow of one of the lost fishermen went by. They gazed in wan silence after her.

"Yeah," Phenny said at last, "that was the worst. Well, I drink to them."

They clinked little glasses. "And the Captain Bill," said Jeke.

They clinked again.

"And the Victory II, last May 1ˢᵗ. Fourteen men in all. No survivors."

They touched glasses carefully, inaudibly.

"They'd all be sitting in here right now," Phenny said.

"Sully lived next door to me on Whorf's Court," Zeke said. "I looked out my window that morning. It was still dark. There was a new fall of snow on the ground. His two shipmates came to get him, he always overslept. They were tramping back down the street together. Sully was pulling his jacket on, his shirt was out, his boots were unlaced, you know how bushy-headed he always was, let alone when he'd just got hauled out of bed. They were ribbing him. It was beautiful the way they went around the corner laughing. Arm-in-arm. And that was the last of the Capt. Bill, those tracks in the snow."

"Everybody loved Sully," Phenny said. "He looked like a bear, but he was one of the gentlest men there ever was."

"Not to forget," Zeke said, hefting his empty mug, "the gale of 1841, when fifty-seven Truro men went down."

"I can't even imagine."

"You go down to the wharf. You look at those old boats... I never had the balls for that."

"The best day in our time..." Phenny said.

Zeke rose, collecting the empties. "I *shall* return," he said, went to the bar, brought back more beer and blackberry brandy.

"That was the day!" Phenny said, "the day the town got the benches back at the Public Hearing that got called after the Selectmen voted to take the meat-rack away."

"I was there. Who wasn't? They wanted to get rid of The Undesirables. Not only the trash under the benches, but the trash on top of the benches, too."

The Undesirables," Phenny said and laughed. "That was us."

"The riff raff," Zeke said, looking at the linden. "Well, it took a while..."

"July of '71," she said. "What was going on then?"

"Vietnam."

"Oh, yeah! Everybody hated everybody. Oooh, the police dogs, and the rowdy crowds, everybody zonked, kids with sleeping bags everywhere."

"Buncha beatniks," Zeke said and coughed a grin. "One of the Selectmen says, 'The benches are like an obscene circus. Things go on there at night too terrible to be publicly discussed. Let the women leave and I'll tell the men.'"

"You never saw such a reaction in your life," Phenny said, "when people woke up and found those benches were gone. There were petitions all over town. Frankie and Lynda Kane started that."

"Everybody sat on those benches," Zeke said. "Long-hairs, locals, young, old, rich, poor..."

"I was proud of the town that day. Just ordinary people– mostly women– stood up and said, 'I'm So and So of Such and Such Street. I favor return of the benches.'

"They said, 'My mother sits there, there ought to be more benches, not less.' That was the one issue the town ever agreed on."

"And then," Zeke said, "when the Selectmen voted to put the benches back a big cheer went up and everybody poured out of Town Hall yelling, 'We won, we won!'"

"Amen! Hey! I'm getting a buzz on. Yeah. Tourists. More tourists was supposed to be the answer to everything."

"Yeah," Zeke said. "More dishwashing and chamber-maid-ing for the fishermen's kids. Oops!" he said, glancing out to see Esther Mason coming along. "I'm going to the head. What's she doing back in town?"

"She never left," Phenny said. "Where've you been? Well, three to two, I guess."

Zeke bent inwards, as low as he could get, like Duck & Cover in grade school. "She became a real twat," he said direly. "Followed me down the street, yelling, 'I don't want to be the 74th or -5th on your list.'"

"Wish I'd seen that."

Wary but undismayed, he straightened up and watched her out of sight. "Remember Rocky Sachanadani, the Indian? Had a sari shop named Pier 69 where Dodi's is now? He enjoyed life, had a big heart. Every Indian Independence Day he gave a bash here. July 18th. Drinks on the house. No limit. People drank till they puked."

"Sunday afternoons were the best," Phenny said. "It was like one big living room with the sun coming in. Bare feet. Kids on the floor, dogs under the table. The all-time high of mellow."

"What about all the people that were going to leave money in their wills to have their funerals here?" Zeke wondered.

"Remember one year when everybody was broke," Phenny said, "Kimball Tardiff painted a sign on the window with snow on the letters—

A MERRY GRIMNESS
FROM THE REGULARS

"The priest tried to get it washed off. Like it was a sacrilege," Zeke said.

"Town of one street. You can't avoid anything or anybody."

"Long as I've sat here I never saw anyone from my hometown go by. Or anyone I ever knew from anywhere else."

"That's another good thing about this town," Phenny said. "Snipped that old life right off. Like you were new-born."

"I never did want to get stuck in a necktie. Like my old man."

"Yeah! When I moved down here it was like being able to breathe. I mean, I had a whole closet-full of clothes. And jewelry and nylons too— you wouldn't believe. Not to mention money. Well. That was nice at least, but all I spent it on was crap."

She glanced out at the empty street. "You learned how to survive. I wonder how many jobs I had, how many addresses. I never expected to be here this long though. What'd we miss? Do you ever regret?"

"Are you kidding? Good riddance. There was more going on here than anywhere. Nobody'd believe."

"You'd had to be here, I guess," she mused. "I used to wonder. It was like there was no time here. And now all of a sudden there's nothing but."

"Fuck time. Remember the missiles? Way, way back. A rumor went round there were secret missile sites in town. People were paranoid. This is the smallest place in the world."

"AND the largest," Phenny said. "I still find houses I never knew existed. It's like a labyrinth you never get to the end of."

"I don't know," Zeke said doubtfully. "Remember Dune Shack Charlie? He had the great dune shack. Other people dug out. He just added another story on. Crazy castle, all those windows."

"He wasn't too fond of people. He used to shoot at the sight-seeing plane."

"It was bugging his birds. He had about forty boxes on poles for the swallows. He kept records for twenty years, he had a whole bird world out there."

"When he died the National Seashore bulldozed his shack."

"Should have bulldozed them," Zeke said. "There aren't any more people like that. They're all gone now. Harry Kemp! Phat Francis! Manny Zora! Frenchie!"

"All sorts of outrageous characters. They all got on just fine. But the minute they left town they got locked up. The real world couldn't handle them."

"Lazlo was sitting at the bar one night, he looks over at me, he says, 'What this town needs is 5,000 shrinks.'"

"He made an art of obnoxiousness. I actually saw him make people cover up their ears and scream."

"He could've used a session with Will Silva. Remember when he heaved some guy through one window, went out the door, picked him up and heaved him back in through the other? And didn't even get flagged."

"And Tony Costa who tried to kick the ceiling."

"Did he ever?"

"I don't know. The one time I saw he hit the floor so hard I thought he was dead."

Freddy Rukkles drove by in his battered Saab. "There goes my nemesis," Phenny said. "Ego the size of the universe. He broke a diaphragm of mine, and that was only the beginning."

"So?" Zeke said. "Tell."

"Well." She shrugged, sipped her brandy. "I went to the doctor to get a new one, and he found a tumor. He said I had to have surgery. I was a naive kid, what did I know? He gave me a whole hysterectomy, scooped me out like a cantaloupe."

Zeke stared, half-comprehending.

"Yeah," she said, her voice going up, eyes out the window. "He said it was his decision to make, and he made it. I never really got to figure out if I wanted a kid."

Zeke had a twenty-two-year-old son in Oregon, but he wasn't sure exactly where, nor where the mother was, nor his first wife either, with whom he'd lasted about six weeks. He felt the sudden mystery of things, their huge insubstantiality.

"Four to two," he said and shook his head, mock-doleful. "I'm not trying to pad the score, but did we ever?"

"You'd remember," she said sweetly, and laughed her sensual, complicitous laugh.

What he remembered were the times she had eluded him. But there had always been others. Others and others and others. Now it occurred to him that they were two of a kind.

"You probably had more," she allowed. "I'm sure."

"No, women do better."

"Gay men do best. They don't care."

"I had a bunch of dogs," he said, modest.

"You were lucky m'dear."

"Wasn't luck. I worked at it."

"I never tried," she said.

"Women have it easy. You just sit back and pick your prick."

She smiled. "Whose round? Must be mine."

She went to the bar and stayed a while talking to Moon. Zeke eyed her cocked hips and round belly, filled with a sense of well-being, of growing higher and clearer by the moment, his thoughts adeptly linked, his mood elegiac and ebullient both. She was certainly the best; he must have been half aware all along, all these years, but how right, how perfect to have it brought home to him here today. And a strange apprehension seized him, that this was a last chance. He could feel his old life ebbing away. Everything belonged either to the past or the future, and the next moment might decide.

She came back with two schooners, no booze. "You didn't want any more brandy, did you?"

"Whatever you say," he said, deep in her aura of comfort. He drank and gazed at the linden perhaps for the last time from this window. "Are you with anybody these days?"

"Oh, I gave up all that. I'm the Long Ranger. And I think I might be saving that silver bullet for myself."

This went by him rather fast for all its implications, but still it had a certain tone, and a little limbo gaped.

"Maybe we missed something," he said cautiously.

She flashed him a sympathetic glance, dropped her eyes, after a moment gave her mug a quarter turn, took a sip, put her hands on her hips and looked past him at the street.

"It's too late, I know," he said.

"It's not too late."

"We could."

"We could."

"You get tired of being alone."

"I'm just getting used to it."

He felt bereaved suddenly by her impossible promise. In these things his intuition seldom erred, but as always he made his fateful pitch: "We could have a go. Nothing ventured, nothing gained. We might be just right for each other."

"We might," she said, sharp with reserve.

"So, why not?"

"You might have AIDS."

"I don't have AIDS."

"You might."

"Come on. I don't have AIDS."

"I don't know. You look to me like someone who might have AIDS."

"Come on. Don't do this to me. I never could stand your sense of humor. You know I don't have AIDS."

"You never know," she said, and gave him a teasing, all-forgiving smile.

"Not that it matters," he said shortly as Jasmine Wells went by, her cheeks aglow with the onset of winter, "but she was the worst dog I ever had. You can't tell a book by its cover."

Phenny sat on- one, two, three deliberate breaths more, her hands on the table– then pushed herself up decisively, and stood, looking down at him. "I hate to break up the party, but I just remembered something I promised myself not to do any more."

"Which is what?"

"Play games."

He coughed his disappointment, felt for a cigarette. "What'll we have left?"

"The Old Colony," she said. "The O.C."

He nodded, coughing– all pain to look at her.

"And the weather. That never changes," she said, giving him a last, remote glance, then smiled her old warmth, twiddled her fingers at him, and went east.

He watched her go, then stayed on, dull with loss, considering a move to the bar and patient wait for whoever might come; but eventually, after finishing both beers, he gave up the ghost of hope, rose on numb legs and prickling feet, stepped outside and slowly, ceremonially made a full circle in the middle of the street.

The linden was rattling a few, desiccated leaves at the snow crystals in the low cloud that now obscured the top of the Pilgrim Monument.

Seeing no one in any direction, he lighted his last cigarette, waved the match out, flicked it, and walked awkwardly west, not quite a straight line, temples pulsating, exhausted, amazed to realize that it was still only mid-afternoon, depressed to think how different things would surely be without the Fo'c's'le.

Made in the USA
Coppell, TX
04 August 2021

59955970R00184